Also by Jocelyn Kelley

The Nethercott Tales

Lost in Shadow

The Ladies of St. Jude's Abbey Series

A Knight Like No Other
One Knight Stands
A Moonlit Knight
My Lady Knight

D1304482

Praise for the Novels of Jocelyn Kelley

Lost in Shadow

"[A] fine tale of love among the spirited."
—The Best Reviews

"Kelley proves that she can easily cross genres. . . . Readers are treated to ghostly tasks, drama, and romance all wrapped up in a fascinating murder mystery! Fabulous!" —Huntress Book Reviews

"With wit, paranormal elements, and a keen feel for the era, Kelley builds the ideal amount of suspense and sexual tension to hook you on the series."
—*Romantic Times*

The Ladies of St. Jude's Abbey Series

My Lady Knight

"[A]n action-packed, fast-paced suspenseful romance featuring some sexy and sensual love scenes, but most of all showcasing an intelligent heroine."
—Romance Readers at Heart

"Jocelyn Kelley has outdone herself. . . . [An] extremely well-done story that will linger in your thoughts long after you turn the last page . . . 5 STARS!" —Huntress Book Reviews

"[A]n amazing medieval tale . . . Jocelyn Kelley will surely be an automatic-buy author for me."
—Romance Reviews Today

A Moonlit Knight

"Delightful . . . fabulous." —*Midwest Book Review*

continued . . .

"Whether you love history, historical romances, or simply high drama, this book is made just for you!"
—Huntress Book Reviews

One Knight Stands

"A splendid read."—Virginia Henley

"I'm hooked on this series! Exhilarating . . . an action-packed tale of honor, courage, and spirit that never strays from its wonderful romance." —Susan Grant

"The beauty of the Ladies of St. Jude's Abbey series blooms sweeter with each new novel. [Kelley] delivers a story of well-paced action, richly detailed in period lore, and caps it off with a hero worth fighting for." —*Booklist*

A Knight Like No Other

"A wondrous tale of love and honor set among one of the most troubling times of the past."
—Huntress Book Reviews

"Kelley brings new excitement to medieval romance with a powerful swordswoman heroine, a stubborn knightly hero, and a nonstop adventure that draws them together in a passion like no other."
—Mary Jo Putney

"Historical romance at its best!" —May McGoldrick

"Jocelyn Kelley is an engaging storyteller with extraordinary skill. . . . Lively and entertaining!"
—Margaret Evans Porter

Kindred Spirits

Jocelyn Kelley

A SIGNET ECLIPSE BOOK

SIGNET ECLIPSE
Published by New American Library, a division of
Penguin Group (USA) Inc., 375 Hudson Street,
New York, New York 10014, USA
Penguin Group (Canada), 90 Eglinton Avenue East, Suite 700, Toronto,
Ontario M4P 2Y3, Canada (a division of Pearson Penguin Canada Inc.)
Penguin Books Ltd., 80 Strand, London WC2R 0RL, England
Penguin Ireland, 25 St. Stephen's Green, Dublin 2,
Ireland (a division of Penguin Books Ltd.)
Penguin Group (Australia), 250 Camberwell Road, Camberwell, Victoria 3124,
Australia (a division of Pearson Australia Group Pty. Ltd.)
Penguin Books India Pvt. Ltd., 11 Community Centre, Panchsheel Park,
New Delhi - 110 017, India
Penguin Group (NZ), 67 Apollo Drive, Rosedale, North Shore 0632,
New Zealand (a division of Pearson New Zealand Ltd.)
Penguin Books (South Africa) (Pty.) Ltd., 24 Sturdee Avenue,
Rosebank, Johannesburg 2196, South Africa

Penguin Books Ltd., Registered Offices:
80 Strand, London WC2R 0RL, England

First published by Signet Eclipse, an imprint of New American Library,
a division of Penguin Group (USA) Inc.

First Printing, March 2008
10 9 8 7 6 5 4 3 2 1

For Sharon Schulze.
Thanks for letting me pick your husband's brain
about fires, and thanks for all the great lunches!

and

For Jan and Duncan Allsopp.
Thanks for your hospitality at Rawcliffe House
Farm. Hope you don't mind that I changed
your house into a castle. . . .

Chapter 1

China Nethercott did not guess, as she drove along the country lane, that she was being stalked.

Why should she? After all, she had driven three times in the past three days over this same road from Cropton to Nethercott Castle, her family's home at the edge of the North Yorkshire Moors. On those previous trips, her younger sister, Sian, had been with her. This afternoon, Sian had decided to remain at Mrs. Stone's house in Cropton and finish the quilt that the ladies had been sewing for the harvest festival that would be held in a month.

China did not enjoy sewing or the gossip that drifted north from York or inland from Whitby. She preferred being outside, wandering through the fields around the castle or going for a drive across the wind-blown moors. Each season brought a new vista, and she exulted in the changes.

She sighed. Since she and her younger sister had returned from London, she had had little chance to drive across the moors. She had tried to settle back into her old routine of overseeing the household, but found herself chafing at responsibilities she once accepted without complaint. She tried not to think that she had been content with her life then because she had not known any better.

Now she could not help wishing her days contained something more exciting than decisions about which foods to order and how she could best serve the local community. She knew many women envied her position as chatelaine of Nethercott Castle, but she wanted more.

More what? She was not sure.

But she also knew how important it had been to work on the quilts that would help raise money for a new roof for the ancient church in Lastingham. The parishioners were accustomed to discovering pools of water on the floor and in the eight-hundred-year-old crypt beneath it. The new bell that had been installed several years ago sounded lovely when it rang with the other two, echoing across the valley and against the moors, but she could not help worrying that they would tumble through the leaking roof.

China looked through a break in the trees edging the narrow dirt lane. With the road following high Rawcliffe, she had a splendid view of the valley below. The fields were awash with August sunshine, but the light held little heat. The month had been unseasonably cold, more like March than summer. Most of the farmers along the moors kept sheep, unlike in the south, where farmers struggled to bring crops to harvest. Word had reached Yorkshire that even the hardiest plants were failing because warm weather seemed to have forgotten to come. Nobody could remember such a cold summer.

Suddenly her horse neighed and tugged the cart

violently to the right. China groaned as the reins jerked on her arm, straining her shoulder.

"What is wrong with you, Bayberry?" she asked. The horse was usually placid, but now he whinnied again more frantically. Again the cart pulled to the right.

The woods closed in around the road, tall and thin trees set in sparse undergrowth. A rustling sound came from her left. She looked, hoping to espy some roe deer in the shadows. The day became strangely still. There was no breeze. Birdsong had vanished. Even the distant baaing of sheep was gone. It was as if she alone were alive.

She chided herself for her stray thoughts, knowing it would be silly to let her imagination trick her. She had spent most of her life trying to avoid that. There were enough rumors about the Nethercott family's peculiar ways. She did not want to add to them.

China then noticed something sticking out of the hedgerow on her left. Sunlight flashed off metal. Something long and metal. A gun!

Her first instinct was to slap the reins and set the horse to a run. Instead, she drew back on the reins, halting Bayberry before the horse could panic.

There had been rumors about a thief stopping carriages along the deserted roads of the moors, but those attacks had taken place on moonless nights. Had the highwayman grown bolder? Or—she gulped at the thought—more desperate?

She must not panic. It might be one of her neighbors hunting. And Squire Haywood, the local magistrate, had asked the men in the local parishes to help find the highwayman. Nobody had seen a hint of the robber, save for his victims. He obviously knew the moors well, which meant he must be a local resident. That was a horrifying thought.

"Stay where you are!" came a shout. The voice was oddly accented, but the words were clear and emphasized with a motion of the weapon.

China realized the metal thing protruding from the hedgerow was not a gun. The end was made of metal, but the rest of it was a wooden shaft—a spear! Why was a highwayman using a *spear*?

The man stepped out from the concealing branches. He wore leggings that reached just below his knees and a long shirt with short sleeves. Both were a faded red. A cloak with a cowl draped over an armored waistcoat made of strips of metal lashed together in the front. More pieces of metal hung over his shoulders and halfway down his upper arm. His shoes were leather, and as he stepped closer, she could see they were studded on the bottom. On his head, he wore a helmet that had a broad piece of metal to protect the back of his neck. A short sword was set in a scabbard lashed to the armored waistcoat. In one hand he carried the spear, which must have been almost seven feet long; in the other, he held a scarlet shield that was rounded to offer him protection on three sides.

Sunlight glinted off the mail and spear, surrounding him with a cool glow. He wore a frown beneath his prominent nose. His eyes were pale blue and his dark hair beneath his helmet closely cropped.

China stared at him, shocked. She had seen drawings of such clothing in her father's books about ancient Roman legionnaires who once held the area as part of their vast empire. She wanted to ask him why he was dressed so, but if she angered him, he might drive that spear through her.

But why was a highwayman dressed as a Roman soldier?

"Get out," he ordered, holding the spear inches from the center of her chest.

She obeyed, whispering a soft apology to the horse before saying, "If you are planning on stealing the cart, please treat my horse with kindness. There is no need to lay on the whip."

"I have no interest in your horse or cart."

Drawing her reticule out of the cart, she opened it and emptied a few coins into her hand. She held them out to him.

"I have no need of your money."

"Then what do you want?" She took a step toward the rear of the cart as his gaze swept over her. The road was deserted. Was her only choice her honor or her life? "I must warn you that I can scream very loudly. If you lay a single hand on me—"

"We have no time to waste. Will you be silent?"

China nodded, surprised at her own prattling.

"What is your name?" he asked.

"China Nethercott."

"From the priory—I mean, from the castle?"

"Yes, Nethercott Castle. Not many people around here remember that it was a priory more than two hundred years ago." She hesitated, then asked, "Are you interested in many periods of history?"

"All of them."

"Excuse me?"

"I am interested in all the periods of Britannia's history since I was sent here with other Menapian and Belgics when Carausius proclaimed himself emperor of Britannia while Diocletian was emperor in Rome."

"Excuse me?" she repeated, not recognizing any of the names except Britannia and Rome. She was ready to condemn the man as deranged, but it was an epithet she did not use easily. Too many people had labeled her sweet father crazy when he had simply chosen to live his life in his own manner and raise his three daughters to question the world around them.

He paused so long in answering that she wondered if he had gone into some barely conscious state. If he were truly mad, he might be unsettled by her questioning his fantasy and have become frozen in thought. She had read about such cases. No one comprehended why such a reaction occurred, and it was extremely rare.

Then he replied, "We are wasting time when . . . All right. Let me see if I can explain this in terms you will comprehend," he said in a calm voice that suggested she was the witless one. "I came here with members of my clan from the area you now call the Low Countries. I served my emperors—both the one in Rome and the usurper who claimed to rule Britannia and western France—by training troops at what is now known as Cawthorne camp."

She knew that name. Beyond the trees, on the edge of a flat hilltop that dropped sharply into the valley, were the ruins of a Roman settlement. Her father had spent many pleasant afternoons digging among the earthwork ruins, always excited whenever he found an artifact, even if only a pottery shard.

"But that camp has been abandoned for almost fifteen hundred years," she said.

"I realize that." He grimaced and shook his head.

"Why is it always the same? Why must all of you pester me with the doubts, the questions, the attempts to pretend you believe me, even though you think I am insane?"

"Are you asking me to answer those questions?"

"No!" He drew in a deep breath, letting it sift out past his clenched teeth. Glancing over his shoulder, he squared his shoulders. "I was talking to myself. Let us get this under way. *Tempus omnia revelat.*"

"Time reveals everything?" she asked, unsure because his odd accent was even more pronounced in Latin than in English.

"You know Latin."

"Yes, my father taught my sisters and I so we could read his books and discuss them with him."

His eyebrows shot up, and then he smiled. "It is about time that women were educated!"

That smile altered everything about him. Though his spear was still aimed at her heart, she could hope—for the first time—that he had no intention of driving it through her.

"I agree," she said carefully.

"And you are educated enough that you cannot believe that a Roman centurion stands before you."

"It is unlikely."

His smile broadened, creasing his deeply tanned cheeks. "It would be unlikely if I were still alive. However, more than a century before the camp in the trees was allowed to return to its natural state, I died here."

"Died? Are you saying you are a spirit?" She silenced the pulse of excitement bubbling up inside her at the idea of speaking with a ghost. If the man were truly mad, she reminded herself, he might imagine himself to be a ghost. That would explain his costume and antiquated weapons.

"You do not believe me."

"Your tale is extraordinary."

"Let me prove it to you. As I said, we do not have time to waste, so let us do this quickly." He raised his spear and set the base on the ground beside him. "Try to touch me."

"I would be foolish to come *closer* to you, sir."

"A prudent woman, I see." Setting his spear on the ground beside him, he drew out his sword. He placed it atop the spear. "Is that better?"

China glanced from the weapons to his entreating expression. He wanted her to believe him. No, it was more than that. He *needed* her to believe him. Or were her own yearnings reflected on his face? Her father had spent most of his life trying to prove ghosts existed, hoping to prove Nethercott Castle was, indeed, haunted. Since his death slightly over a year ago, this was—assuming she was not speaking with a deranged man—the second ghost to appear to her family. Her younger sister, Jade, had encountered one within the walls of Nethercott Castle in the spring. Now this man was averring that he was a ghost. . . .

Stretching out her hand, she took a half step toward him. There was an easy test to determine if he told the truth.

"Don't be frightened," he said.

"Why not?" She slid her other foot forward. "You have those weapons, and I assume you are skilled with them."

"And you have my word that I will not use them against you."

China bit back her retort that trusting her life to

of each generation to follow. I cannot change what
has happened in the past, but I can hope with your
help to change what has not yet occurred."

"Who is your descendant?"

"His name is Lord Braddock."

Her eyes widened. "The marquess?"

"Do you know him?"

"I know *of* him. Everyone in North Riding knows
of him, because he was admitted to the Order of the
Bath for his bravery during the war with Napoleon."

"Did Napoleon fight for the American colonies?"

China laughed, shocked that she could while talking to a ghost. A ghost! She could not wait to tell
her sister about this encounter. Sian would be excited
that a second ghost had appeared to the Nethercott
sisters.

"That war was over a long time ago."

"A generation ago?"

She nodded, puzzled anew. "Yes."

"I see much has happened since I last spoke to
someone." He frowned. "Why did my descendant
fight in a war against Napoleon?"

"About ten years ago, Napoleon crowned himself
emperor of France and tried to conquer all of
Europe."

"Certainly not Rome!"

"Yes, even Rome for a few years, but the English
and their allies defeated him in a great battle last
year."

Quintus shook his head. "He defeated Rome?
What a great emperor he must have been." His chest
swelled beneath his metal waistcoat. "And my descendant was among those who defeated such an emperor. My blood truly must run in his veins, the

blood of an undaunted warrior." His pride vanished.
"And such a man will die on the fifth of September
by a vile murderer's hand if you do not find a way
to protect him."

"The fifth of September?"

"The day I uttered the curse, and the day it is
always wrought upon the eldest son of each generation. The fifth of September of their thirtieth year,
just as it was wrought upon me."

"Do you know who will try to kill him?"

"No. I have told you all I know. Sometimes the
eldest son goes slowly insane. Other times, like this
one, he is slain. I cannot see the future any more
clearly than you can."

"You know the date. Why don't you know who is
trying to kill him?"

"I do not know how to explain it exactly." He
regarded her steadily, as if to ensure that she would
believe him. "There are times when I am completely
here, as I am now. I can see the living and even, on
occasion, speak with them, as I am with you. The
rest of the time, it is as if I am lost in a mist. It comes
upon me without warning. There is a coolness about
it, but not the same icy chill as when death drove its
claws into me."

She shivered at his words and wrapped her arms
around herself. "It sounds horrendous."

"That moment when I went from living to dead
was horrible, but the mist is . . ." His gaze turned
inward, and she knew he was seeking a way to express what no words could accurately describe.
"Have you ever sunk into a cool pool on a summer
day? Gone to the very bottom and just drifted
there?"

She nodded.

"Then you know how the water is filled with colors you could not see while looking into the pool. The stones along the bottom appear different, and they send the water swirling in patterns. The water itself is filled with noises you never imagined. Sounds that are soft and distant, ones swallowed by the world above."

"And the mist is like that?"

"It is when it consumes me. As the mist thickens, colors fade and my senses are useless, save for touch. I *feel* the passage of time like the brush of a faint breeze along my skin. By the time I sense a moment, it is gone, replaced by another, which vanishes just as quickly." He sighed, and she wondered if he was recalling the woman he had hurt so many years ago. "Then the mist recedes. The colors and the sounds return to what I always considered normal. It is as if I am rising out of that pool. I discover the next generation's eldest son has been born and grown to manhood and is in his thirtieth year. I know his surname because I tried to save his father from death or madness and failed. Other than that, the only information I have is that the curse will be enacted on the fifth of September by someone who feels betrayed."

"Betrayed by your descendant?"

"Yes." Another sigh slipped past his lips, but then he squared his shoulders. "Soon after I come out of the mist, I must contact someone to help end the curse, because the greatest irony of the curse is that none of my descendants can see me. I never choose the person who will assist me. I simply know when that person passes near."

"And you think I am that person?"

"Yes."

China had more questions, but they had to alert Lord Braddock so he could take the proper precautions to keep himself alive. "Where is your descendant now? He may have a list of possible enemies who would wish him dead."

Quintus pointed toward the trees along the edge of the cliff. "He is in the ruins of the Cawthorne camp."

"All right. We can talk with him, if he is still there."

"He is there."

"How can you be certain?"

He bent to pick up his spear and sword. "Because he is *in* the ruins of the Cawthorne camp."

"What?"

"He was exploring, and I loosened a rock in the earthworks. More came down."

"You buried him alive?"

Quintus nodded.

"When?"

"I suspect it was long enough ago that if we do not hurry, he will be dead, too, and the curse will continue for another generation."

Chapter 2

The air was getting stale.

What an ignoble end for a man who had ridden to face Napoleon's misguided troops and survived battles and been lauded—however foolishly—as a hero! Coughing as breathing became even more difficult, Alexander Braddock swore vividly.

Deuce take it! How had the roof collapsed? He had been careful to check the rocks' stability before he entered the cavelike opening in the earthworks in the old Roman camp. He knew better than to go into an ancient structure without confirming that it was safe. Despite his precautions, the roof over the entrance had come crashing down while he dug in the earth only a few steps inside.

He had tried to move the rocks, but shifting them brought more cascading down, along with parts of the ceiling. He winced and cursed when another one bounced off his shoulder. One of the stones had struck his head in the initial rockslide. He had been knocked senseless . . . for how long? He had no idea, but he could not make another mistake. The next rock could kill him. He needed to examine the jumbled pile of boulders and dirt with care. Moving the wrong one could destroy the cave completely. Along with him and the artifacts he had found. He had not guessed he would risk his life for a few pins, some pottery shards and what appeared to be a medallion.

Thinking was not easy. It was not only the stale air. His head ached with a dull pulsing. If he moved, his eyes lost focus. Then the shadows within his prison began to move as if they had a life of their own.

Would someone take notice of his horse before it starved to death? He was several hundred yards off the road that ran from Cropton toward Pickering. While riding here he had not seen another human. His hopes that a deer would suddenly learn how to dig through stone proved that he was starting to lose his mind.

Or had he lost it already? In the instant before the rocks tumbled down, he had caught a motion out of the corner of his eye. He had thought someone was there, but when he glanced in that direction, the sun had glinted with eye-searing brightness. He had not had time for a second look because the stones fell between him and the gleam, extinguishing it.

And him?

At least if he died he could escape the madness that infected his family. He had watched for its signs from the time he was old enough to understand that other men did not act as his father did. There had been whispered tales told when the servants had no idea he was listening—or when they were too upset to care. Those stories had been of his father and his grandfather and his grandfather's sire. It was hinted that Braddock men went mad before they reached their thirtieth birthdays. His was only a few weeks away.

Alexander coughed again, unable to stop. Sitting against the back of the cave, he stared at the stone and earth piled in the opening. The ground beneath him was damp, and a stench filled his senses. The reek of death. It had been his companion too long, and the wet dirt brought back the hideous scents of freshly spilled blood and offal and suffering. The rot belonged to the ground that received the blood and the bodies, sucking both down into itself.

Once he would have gone to such oblivion with satisfaction, but he had survived. Survived the battlefield. Survived betrayal. Survived . . . only to die within the earth walls raised by men who had been dust for a millennium.

Deuce take it!

He would not allow his memories to taunt him. He had come to the moors to escape the adulation he received wherever he went beyond his home near Whitby and the North Sea. Would those who cheered him as a hero come to the realization, when his body was discovered under the earth, that he was as mortal as any other man?

He shifted, then froze as he was pelted by thick clods of dirt. Maybe, if he could survive until dawn, the sunlight would creep past the jumble of rocks and let him see a way to escape. The afternoon shadows made the stones appear to be a solid wall.

His head fell forward on his chest, and he winced as the motion sent pain thudding through his skull. By all that's blue, if he was going to die, he should

do so and get it over with. He was through trying
to play the hero. That might be his first sane idea
since he bought his commission.

Something clattered outside. Had his horse gotten
loose? Or was there someone out there? Slowly he
raised his head.

Light! There was light coming between the rocks.
He crawled toward the stones and tore at the debris.

"Be careful!" he heard someone call as rocks came
crashing down. A large one just missed his skull.
"Let me remove the rocks from the outside. I can see
what I am doing."

A woman's voice. *Perfect!* First he had allowed
himself to be trapped, and now he had to depend on
a woman to free him. If his rescuer had been a man,
there would have been a handshake, maybe a few
pints of ale at a nearby public house, and everything
would have been even. A woman would expect a
more complex display of gratitude. Perfume? No, too
personal. A box of tea? Perhaps. Certainly Norah
would have insisted on something far more valuable
for such a difficult task.

He shook the thoughts from his head. He would
not be buying any gift to express his gratitude if he
did not escape this tomb. And a woman alone could
not remove the boulders that had locked together to
close off the space.

"Get help!" he called. His voice was weak, a
scratchy whisper that resonated in his head.

"I can do this." Her words sounded as if they were
being squeezed past gritted teeth as well as through
the narrow breaks in the rocks.

"You will hurt yourself!"

"Let me be the judge of that."

"Miss—"

"Cut line!" she snarled back.

Alexander was doubly shocked. He had not expected to hear Town cant so far from London. Not only was he being rescued by a woman, but an obstinate one. However, he was in no situation to be choosy. He had to be grateful that—for whatever reason—she had come to the ruins of the Roman camp.

He heard more rocks being pushed aside. When she cried out in pain, he asked, "Are you hurt?"

"Yes!"

"Did you drop a rock on your foot?"

There was a moment of silence, and he wondered if he had offended her to the point that she had taken her leave. Then he heard, "Two of the stones shifted and pinched my thumb between them." He was astonished to hear a hint of amusement in her voice as she added, "Do not fret on my behalf. It is not broken, but I daresay it will be colorful."

Two stones dislodged in front of Alexander, bouncing toward him, and he heard others scraping as they fought to hold their place. He had the fanciful thought that the rocks were an army trying to keep their enemy from driving a wedge through them to break their defenses.

He did not want to think of battle. The noise. The smells. The horrible vistas. The futility. He had also come to the moors to leave behind those memories, but they dogged him like a hound with a breast-high scent of the fox.

"Get back!" the woman called. "I am going to try to push some of the stones inward."

He crawled awkwardly away from the entrance, a long-legged crab with a battered skull.

"Are you away?" Her voice echoed oddly through the space now that he was crouched against the rear wall.

"Yes," he shouted back.

There was a moment of silence; then one of the rocks popped out and rolled toward him. The others collapsed to scatter across the floor. He tensed, watching to see if the ceiling would fall in around him.

"What are you waiting for?" the woman yelled. "Get out while you can."

It was the best advice he had received since told to keep his wits about him on the battlefield. Scrambling up and over the remaining stones, he grasped two handfuls of grass and hauled himself out. The shoulders of his coat were grabbed and tugged. He pushed his feet against the stones, trying to propel himself along the ground.

Just as his boots cleared the opening, a crash came from behind him. He rolled onto his back and up to sit. A cloud of dust struck his face. He coughed as he waved it away.

"It is fortunate that you stopped arguing with me," came the woman's voice from close by.

Alexander glanced to his left. His rescuer sat on a stone that was too large for her to have moved herself, her elbows propped on her knees as she struggled to catch her breath. A straw bonnet concealed her face, but strands of rich auburn tumbled down her back. A simple gown of light gray was ripped and covered with dirt. Her gloves were torn and stained with blood.

"It appears you are correct," he said, wondering if

he had the strength to lift himself to his feet. She looked at him, and words vanished from his mind as if he had never known a single one.

Her features were charming—slender nose, pale pink cheeks over the high arch of her cheekbones, a chin that suggested she was always as stubborn as she had been while rescuing him. Then he was caught by her eyes. They were the same pale shade as her gown, with hints of green and blue within them. He wondered if the colors grew stronger with her emotions. Now they were dull with fatigue, like an opal that had lost the fire in its heart.

With effort, he pulled his gaze away from hers to scan the area. Stones had been tossed in every direction. He counted two score. He had not guessed she had moved so many. The only sign of the hole where he had been was the cloud of dust and the collapsed wall.

"You were lucky," the woman said.

"Bad luck, you should say. After all, that wall stood for centuries, and I was fortunate enough to arrive just in time for it to collapse."

"Are you hurt?"

"No." He set himself on his feet to prove it, but wobbled so hard that he sat back against the wall.

Rushing to his side, she knelt beside him and tipped his aching head slightly to the right.

"Leave off!" he ordered.

"Hush! You do not have the sense God gave a goose. You have been injured quite badly, so at least stop squawking like one."

"Geese do not squawk."

"All the more reason you should not either."

He scowled, wincing as she touched the focus of the pain radiating across his skull. "I shall endeavor to be silent."

When he was about to add more, he heard her draw in a quick breath. He asked how bad the injury was. Waves of agony thudded inside his head like a storm tide upon the beach, rising, falling, pulling him one way and then another as they threatened to turn the solid earth beneath him into sand.

She removed her bonnet. Tearing off the ribbon stitched to the straw, she wound it gently around his head. "Where were you bound after your stop here?"

"To Pickering."

"That is too far to go when you are injured. Come with me to Nethercott Castle. There your wound can be cleaned and stitched closed."

"It is not that bad."

"No?" She waved her hand at him. "Get up."

Why couldn't he have been rescued by a man? This was mortifying.

"I would prefer to sit a moment longer," he said.

"Wise of you. My cart is on the other side of the wall, so you do not have to walk far."

"My horse . . ."

"Is fine, too."

"Who are you?" He was being brusque, but his manners would return once his head was no longer throbbing. When his eyes focused better. When every thought was not caught in the mire clogging his brain.

"I am China Nethercott." She smiled gently.

He could not pull his gaze from that lovely face. There was a shyness about her tilted lips that contrasted with her sharp orders when she had been trying to extract him from the cave.

With care, he lifted her right hand and looked at her swelling thumb. She had been correct when she said it soon would bruise.

"I am—"

"Alexander Braddock," she interrupted as she drew her hand back from his. The fire had returned to her opalescent eyes, a cool, restrained flame.

"How do you know my name?" he asked, curious what it would take to make the fire in her eyes flare out of control.

"I was told your name when I learned you were imprisoned beneath the earth here."

Someone had discovered he was imprisoned in the wall and then left? He fisted his hands, furious. Pain shot up his arms, and he looked down to discover drying blood on his torn fingers. He ignored them as he asked, "How did you learn that?"

Rising, she picked up her bonnet and set it on her head. A sudden puff of wind almost tossed it from her hair, but she pressed one hand against it as she turned away and called, "Quintus Valerius! Come and see! Lord Braddock still lives."

"Quintus Valerius?" Somehow he managed to get to his feet again. He was determined he would not topple over. "Is this some sort of hoax, Miss Nethercott? We are standing in the ruins of an old Roman camp, so you call your friend by a Roman name?"

"He is not my friend." She was no longer facing him, but he noticed how her shoulders had stiffened.

He was curious what she saw that disquieted her. The open area, more than three hundred yards long and half as wide, was edged by earthen wall. Grass and briars clogged the inner area, which was why he had been examining the wall. At the far end of the camp, the hill dropped steeply into the valley. Beyond it the moor rose long and broad, like the shoulder of a resting giant whose head was lost in the distance. White specks were sheep, grazing amidst the gorse and heather.

All looked as it should, so what was Miss Nethercott staring at? He blinked rapidly when rays of the sun seemed to cluster at a spot about two paces in front of her. The rays appeared to be moving in some sort of pattern. He blinked again. Harder. He hoped his eyesight was not permanently damaged.

"Maybe you and Quintus Valerius should speak privately, my lord." She edged to one side. "If you wish, I will wait by the cart."

"Speak? To whom?"

"Quintus Valerius." She looked at him, bafflement widening her astonishing eyes. "Can't you see him? He is standing right here."

"He? Of whom do you speak, Miss Nethercott?"

She pointed to the spot where the sunlight seemed to be congealing. "Right there. What do you see?"

"Some flickers of light." He blinked several times, then looked away as the reddish light became too intense. "I assume they are caused by the blows to my head by the falling rocks." His eyes narrowed as he frowned at her. "Why? What do *you* see?"

China exchanged a dismayed glance with Quintus. The centurion's anxiety gouged lines into his face. The sun glittered off the metal on his armor and the straps on his shield. She could not look directly at where the tip of his spear seemed to be on fire.

"He cannot see me. I always hope one of them will, but it is always the same," Quintus said with resignation.

"That is ludicrous."

"Yes, it is," said Lord Braddock from behind her. "Why are you talking to no one?"

She looked at him again. His anger was imposing and intimidating, but she would not let it daunt her more than she already was by his stern good looks. He was not handsome in the style of the dandies in London, even though his navy coat had been well made and his buckskin breeches and scuffed boots were of the latest fashion. There was a sense of raw danger about the planes of his face, as if he had endured so many potent emotions that his expression had not yet decided how to sculpt his features. An aura of power surrounded him. His pale blue eyes were ringed by a darker blue, almost the color of his coat. She was fascinated because she had never seen eyes like them, except . . . She glanced over her shoulder at the ghost. Quintus Valerius had the same colors in his eyes.

"Lord Braddock," she said in her primmest tone, "simply because you cannot see Quintus Valerius is no reason to assume that he does not exist."

"You *see* someone?"

"I see some*thing*." She took a deep breath. Her father had been ridiculed for his belief in ghosts. She understood the doubt, because she had harbored her own when her sister Jade claimed that she had seen the phantom of a murdered man in the spring. "You must understand the truth. Quintus Valerius was a centurion during the third century. Now he is a ghost."

"You are jesting." His mouth tightened. "Miss Nethercott, I should warn you that after nearly being buried alive, I am in no mood for jokes."

"I am quite aware of that," she returned in the same sharp tone. Holding up her hands, she scowled at him. "May I remind you that you are not the only one who has endured an injury this afternoon?"

"Did a rock fall on your head, too? That is the only reason I can fathom that you would believe you are seeing a ghost."

"Why? A rock fell on your head, and you do not see a ghost." She folded her arms in front of her. "I must ask if you need help climbing over the wall to reach my cart."

"I am quite capable of moving from here to there." He took a single step and fell to one knee.

"Is that so?" She was tempted to tell him right then why Quintus Valerius had sought her out, but Lord Braddock was being too mule-headed already. She should have more patience with him, because he had been buried alive. But she was so unsettled herself.

She had not only seen a ghost; she had talked to one and promised to save the life of one of England's bravest. One of the men who had flung the threat of invasion back onto the Continent and then squashed Napoleon's dreams like a child jumping on an ant. Gleefully and eagerly. Major Alexander Braddock was a decorated hero, a man to whom every Briton owed a debt of gratitude.

"Let me help," she said, bending and drawing his arm over her shoulder.

"I can manage on my own."

"I have seen how well you do on your own." Muscles strained as she helped him to stand—both hers and his. He must be hurt more than she had guessed. "We will go slowly."

She went on in a steady cadence as she steered him up the earthen wall. More than once she feared her knees would buckle beneath her, but she was able to keep him moving forward.

"Do you need to rest?" she asked when they reached the top.

"No." His word came out in a pant. "Do you?"

"Yes." She guessed he would be willing to take a pause if she did.

She guessed wrong. "All right. Stay here as long as you want. I will meet you at the cart."

Before he could lift his arm away, she clasped her hand on his wrist, holding it close to her. She scowled. "You may be the most intolerable man I have ever met."

"Why? Because I am honest with you?"

Her gaze locked with his. "Because you have not once been honest with yourself about your injuries since I dragged you out of that hole!"

"Miss Nethercott?"

"What?"

"You ask me to be honest. It is with the greatest sincerity that I say you have amazing eyes."

Instead of responding to his brazen comment, China said, "Very well. We must go down the hill as slowly as we came up. If you lose your balance you could fall and hurt yourself worse."

As she had on the way up, she counted to match their paces while they went down. She risked a glance back, but Quintus Valerius had vanished. Would he remain nearby, or had he returned to wherever ghosts went when they were not visible? So many questions raced through her head as she walked with caution down the hill, trying to keep Lord Braddock from falling on his face.

Was the ghost aware of where the attack would occur? The centurion was obviously well familiar with weapons. Did he have some suspicion of what would be used to attempt to slay Lord Braddock?

And why hadn't she thought of these questions when she had a chance to speak with Quintus Valerius?

"Careful, there," China said for what must have been the dozenth time. She would not have had to repeat it if Lord Braddock went down the hill at a pace he could control. "That is the way. One foot, then the other. Try not to slide on the slippery grass. That is the way. Careful, there." Number thirteen. "Just a few more steps and we will be on level ground again. You are doing well. Careful, there." Number fourteen.

She grimaced. Being a prattle-box did not come naturally to her. Sian could talk to anyone about anything, so her younger sister probably could have devised many different things to say instead of repeating the same warnings over and over.

But her sister was not there. China had to do her best with the situation that had been handed to her—at spearpoint!—by a ghost. So she kept up the steady stream of cautions until they reached the bottom of the hill.

"Just a little bit farther," she continued, unable to halt her mouth, which seemed to have developed a need to keep spewing out the obvious. "Nethercott Castle is less than a league away. Once we are there, you can rest. Do you have a favorite food, my lord? If it is possible, I will have it prepared for you to-night. That will help ease your pain. If—"

He pulled away and grasped the side of the cart. "You talk too much."

"I am concerned for your well-being, my lord. You might be grateful for that."

"Grateful?"

At the venom in his voice, she recoiled. Then she squared her shoulders and looked him in the eyes. Wasting time arguing would not get him the attention he required. "I rescued you, my lord. In return I am due some gratitude."

"Like a knight errant rescued by the lady who deigns to come down from her tower to save *him* from the fire-breathing dragon?"

"How badly was your head struck?"

"Maybe you expect a kiss, as that lady would from her knight."

His cocksure smile vexed her, and she retorted, "I would suggest you do not try such a thing. Then I would have to slap your face, and if I knock you off your feet, I shall only have to help you set yourself back on them again."

"I appreciate your consideration for my sorry state."

"It would be sorrier if you tried to kiss me."

"A threat, Miss Nethercott?"

She walked around to the other side of the cart and climbed in. Looking back at him, she said, "A vow, Lord Braddock."

Chapter 3

China's hands shook on the reins as she turned the cart on the uneven forest path. She had half expected Lord Braddock to demand to drive. Instead he sagged against the seat and leaned his head back, proving how weak he truly must be in spite of his determination to match her step for step over the earthworks.

"It is not far to Nethercott Castle," she said quietly. "Once we are there, your injuries will be tended to with more skill than I possess."

"You have done well enough." Lord Braddock spoke no louder than a whisper. "I do not wish to be coddled." He swore when the wagon bounced into a chuckhole.

She had to admire his pride, but it would do him no good. His skin had a gray pallor that worried her. His startlingly blue eyes were closed, and she saw bloody marks on his hands. Her bonnet ribbons around his head should have looked ridiculous, but his strength of will refused to be ignored.

He gave another low groan. Lord Braddock was

already hurt and could be murdered if Quintus Valerius's prophecy came true. Someone wished to kill the marquess, and he would be unable to defend himself in this state. She had to devise a way—and she had no idea how—to persuade him to remain at Nethercott Castle instead of traveling to Pickering. Those few miles could be fatal for him.

China touched Lord Braddock's arm gently. "Do not fall asleep, my lord. It is said to be dangerous to sleep right after an injury to one's skull."

"I am not sleeping," he mumbled.

"You almost are."

"Almost is not the same as actually doing so."

She usually despised a brangle, but she must keep him awake. If arguing was the only way to do so, she would. "You might find it easier to resist the siren song of sleep if you did not keep your eyes shut."

He opened one eye, then the other and, with a moan, pushed himself up to sit straighter. "Do all the natives of this section of the shire wag their tongues like you do?"

China kept her face serene so he could not guess how she yearned to tell him to stop insulting her and that she would gladly be quiet if he would just stay awake. "Isn't it beautiful?"

"What?"

She pointed toward the western sky. "The sunset. We have had such amazing sunsets this summer. The reds are more brilliant, and other shades seem to be blended in as if there is a rainbow at the end of each day."

"Pardon me for my lack of interest, Miss Nethercott, but the only thing that would be beautiful to me right now would be a foaming glass of ale or a nicely cooled glass of wine."

"Shall I stop the cart and let you wallow in a puddle until you drink your fill?"

"You have a tart tongue."

"When we arrive at Nethercott Castle, I shall see that you have a bottle of the finest wine in our cellar."

He swore.

She waited for him to apologize for such low language, but he did not. That he had been lauded as a great hero was no reason for her to think he possessed a sense of civility higher than that of the lowest man under his command.

"I would be quiet, Miss Nethercott," he added, "if you would be equally silent."

"I would be quiet, Lord Braddock, if you would keep your eyes open and refrain from falling asleep." She slowed the horse as the road dropped into a sharp curve toward the valley where Nethercott Castle stood.

"There is no danger of that when you are prattling."

"I said I would be—"

Suddenly the horse reared and neighed. As she fought to control him, someone jumped out of the nearby bushes.

"Stand and deliver!" shouted a man—the highwayman!—pointing a pistol at them. His black cape was spread behind him like a dark cloud.

She brought the carriage to a halt, even though she was tempted again—just for a second—to try to drive past him. She could feel the horse shivering through the reins. Or was it her?

Fighting back her fear, she dropped her voice to a whisper. "Do not say or do anything out of hand, my lord. The rumors of this highwayman suggest he is not easily frightened. If he discovers your identity, he may panic."

"Panic?" he asked as quietly.

"You *are* a proven military hero."

His mouth twisted.

The highwayman came closer, his pistol not wavering. Beneath his cloak he wore a dark greatcoat stained with mud. His cloak's hood concealed his face. As he neared, China swallowed her gasp, for he wore fabric around his face, leaving only his eyes and lips visible.

She watched as the thief's gaze flicked from her to Lord Braddock. She felt the marquess shift beside her. She hoped he would not try to be a hero now, when his reflexes were so slow.

The highwayman snickered. "I see I am not the only one who binds cloth about my head." His voice had no hint of education, but she did not hear the heavy accent that could make a Yorkshire farmer's words almost unintelligible.

Lord Braddock did not reply, and she remained as silent. The wrong move, the wrong word, even the wrong expression could be the very thing to convince the highwayman to fire the pistol.

"Ah, I see it is the lady's ribbon." The highwayman chuckled. "A favor for your bravery?"

China did not dare to allow the gasp swirling in her throat to escape. Did the highwayman recognize

Lord Braddock? His description had been in the local newspaper after his return from London, where he had been honored by the Prince Regent.

Lord Braddock still said nothing. She was relieved that he did not react to the taunt, even though his eyes sparked with rage. He must have learned to control his emotions on the battlefield. Or had he dashed wildly into battle, surviving only because men fell back in disbelief at his savagery?

As the silence grew heavier, the highwayman's lips became a rigid line. He put one hand on the cart's dash and aimed his pistol at a spot just to China's left. A slight motion either way would point the gun at the marquess's heart or hers.

"Your purse, sir." His mouth tilted in a smile, straining the black fabric wrapped around his head.

Beside her, the marquess tensed. His eyes burned with fury, but there was something more in them. Something with an intensity that frightened her even more than the highwayman did.

"I will have your purse, sir."

"You are welcome to it." Lord Braddock drew it from beneath his coat and tossed it at the highwayman's feet.

The highwayman faltered as he glanced at the purse, then at the two of them in the cart. He scowled at Lord Braddock as he asked, "Miss, will you do the honors?"

"Pardon me?" China answered, startled.

"If you would alight and pick up the purse the gentleman has dropped . . ."

Lord Braddock started to protest, but she interrupted him by saying, "If you step away, I will do as you ask."

China thought the marquess might halt her. He simply slid along the seat so he remained close to her as the highwayman backed away. When she stepped from the cart, she kept her gaze on the thief. He was not watching her. His eyes were focused on Lord Braddock.

She edged toward the leather purse. Picking it up, she was astonished when it made a clinking that did not sound like coins. She hid her reaction as she held it out to the highwayman.

"In my pocket, miss." His superior tone had returned.

Behind her, Lord Braddock swore before saying, "Do not go closer to him."

"You injure me, sir." The highwayman's eyes narrowed as he thumbed the grip of the gun.

"Take my purse and leave."

The highwayman laughed wildly. "I get what I ask for, sir. You and the young lady should not forget that." With another chortle, he said, "My pocket, miss, if you would be so kind."

China was torn between fury and fright as she inched toward the thief. Now would have been a good time for Quintus Valerius to appear and scare the highwayman away. Assuming the highwayman could see him . . . She stretched out her hand holding the purse and dropped the bag into the big pocket of his greatcoat.

He caught her hand before she could back away. The cart creaked behind her, and the highwayman said, "Sir, I would remain where I am if I were you."

"You are not me," snarled Lord Braddock.

"No." The highwayman bent over her hand, but his gaze and his pistol remained aimed on the cart.

His lips gave her fingers the lightest caress before standing again.

She heard his sigh of satisfaction. Disgust reeled through her, and she clasped her hands behind her as she inched toward the cart.

The highwayman's laugh was triumphant. "I have what I came for. Farewell . . . until our next meeting." He ran up the steep bank and vanished amidst the trees, leaving behind the echo of his horrid laugh.

China grasped the side of the cart. In the wake of the highwayman's disappearance, her knees were unsteady.

"Are you all right?" asked the marquess.

She raised her eyes to see anxiety and rage in his. "I am fine. What was in your purse?"

He glanced at the hilltop, then bent toward her. "Pottery shards. The highwayman will find they buy nothing."

"We should not linger here. Once he opens it, he will be furious." She pulled herself onto the seat. Her legs seemed to have the consistency of custard.

"I guess it is true that God watches over fools." Lord Braddock's voice was not as strong as it had been when the highwayman stood by the cart.

"Fool? Who?"

"You! He could have killed you when you walked right over to him and let him take your hand. He could have dragged you into the wood with him."

"He did not kill me." She raised her chin as she slapped the reins to send the horse along the road again. "And why would I be so foolish as to disagree with a man aiming a gun at us? I thought the wisest thing to do was obey." She tried to submerge the shudder as she recalled the highwayman's lips on her hand.

"Do you always take the wisest course, Miss Nethercott?"

"I try to." Knowing that she needed to take advantage of the opportunity that he had given her with his question, she added, "That is why I promised Quintus Valerius—"

"Not that silly tale again."

"It is not silly. It is true." She drew in the reins to slow the horse as the cart turned the last corner before they reached Nethercott Castle. "Quintus Valerius asked me to make a vow to protect you."

"To protect me?" His laugh was a faint echo of his previous ones. "Forgive me, Miss Nethercott, but why would a ghost ask you—a person I had not met before this afternoon—to protect me?"

"Because I am the one who sees him. He told me about the curse that afflicts your family."

"Nonsense," he mumbled. "It is all nonsense."

"Maybe, but I promised to protect you from the person intending to murder you on the fifth of September."

She waited for him to retort. When he did not, she glanced toward him.

His head was leaning at a drunken angle, and his eyes were closed. His hands fell like deadweights to his sides. He was senseless. When she saw blood trickling from under the makeshift bandage, she slapped the reins on the horse, determined to get to Nethercott Castle before the ghost's prophecy was proved wrong by Lord Braddock dying as the new month dawned.

Chapter 4

Alexander opened his eyes, and his arm curved around a slender waist. "Kiss me," he whispered in a state that was not quite sleep and not truly wakefulness.

"I beg your pardon?"

"Kiss me. Wake me with a kiss."

"You are no Sleeping Beauty, my lord." Miss Nethercott's address broke the spell.

He blinked several times, trying to stop his surroundings from spinning. He attempted to focus on what appeared to be the rough roof of a barn. Voices came from several different directions.

"Lord Braddock, if you please," said Miss Nethercott as her face came back into view.

Deuce take it! She kept finding ways to get her lips enticingly close to his. Her arm slid beneath his shoulders as she drew his own arm up around her. He smiled. If that was what she wanted . . .

He moved to kiss her.

And missed.

He heard muffled laughter. She chided whoever

had laughed, but he could not doubt the amusement in her voice.

He intended to stand and show them that he was not a buffoon. He tried to push his feet against the cart, but they refused to work any better than his eyes.

"I will need your help, Henley," Miss Nethercott said as she kept her arm around him so he did not slide farther off the seat.

"Right away, Miss China."

Turning his aching body, Alexander saw a gangly man in deep gray livery with a head of bright red hair. Or was it on his head? Maybe there was something scarlet behind him. It looked to be something rectangular and almost four feet tall. He blinked. The scarlet square was gone.

"Henley," Miss Nethercott said, "if you would take Lord Braddock's other arm, we should be able to ease him out of the cart."

Henley choked before asking, "What happened?"

"He was injured at the old Roman camp. Would you please help me get him inside?"

"Yes, Miss China."

Henley pulled Alexander's arm over his shoulder, drawing him away from Miss Nethercott. If Alexander had half his wits about him, he would have protested, because he liked having her soft curves pressed to him. If he had *all* his wits, he would know better than to be so close to a bewitching woman.

He paid no attention to his surroundings as he was guided along a dirt path and through a door. He did hear Miss Nethercott say something about sending men to trail the highwayman who had halted them.

The shouts of anticipation at capturing the cur battered his skull.

Slowly, with Henley's help, he climbed a set of winding stairs to a broad passage. He was relieved when the footman steered him through a nearby doorway. Even though he did not want to admit the truth, not even to himself, he doubted he could have gone any farther.

"Right into bed," Miss Nethercott said from behind him.

She did have a skill for saying provocative things. He wanted to tell her that, but the words would not form on his tongue.

"His boots and clothes are filthy, Miss China," Henley protested. "If you would like me to remove them . . ."

"Just his boots for now." There was a catch in her voice that suggested she was not indifferent to him.

Alexander smiled, then winced as the motion sent anguish across his skull. He collapsed on the bed like a stringless marionette. Hands grabbed his right leg, and he grimaced as his boot was yanked off. His leg fell with a heavy thump against the side of the bed after his other boot was removed. He had not needed someone to help him undress since his first Season, when he had enjoyed too much of Bacchus's juice.

Hands pulled him across the bed. Pillows came up to surround him, but on the left side of his head, it was as if he were lying on serrated knives. The pain returned, so strong that he gasped. He thought he heard Miss Nethercott say something. The words vanished into the void opening up to consume every thought.

* * *

"Fascinating." Sian Nethercott smiled at her older sister as China finished telling her afternoon's adventures. "No wonder you sent the message for me to return posthaste."

"I may need your assistance in persuading Lord Braddock to remain here until the fifth of next month." She leaned back in the comfortable chair in the solar. The tall windows were arched, the top third of the glass colored with depictions of the moors through the seasons. Rain ran down the uneven glass now, and a fire flickered on the hearth.

As in every room in the house, books were scattered on top of every flat surface. Chinese pottery and artifacts were interspersed with them. One of her father's dreams had been to sail to the Far East. Even though the dream had never been fulfilled, he had surrounded himself with imported art and ceramics.

China preferred her sister's art. Sian's sketches were stacked with care on a shelf opposite the hearth. Sian always planned to frame more of her work, but the pile grew larger each year because she was too busy finding new views to sketch.

Little in the room had been changed since their ancestors first raised Nethercott Castle from the ruins of an abbey. Stuffed heads of animals peered down from over the hearth. China had promised herself to have them removed, but had not spoken with the housekeeper about that.

"The fifth of September is about a week and a half from now," said Sian.

"A long time."

Her sister's smile broadened. "I was about to say it was not a long time."

"That is because you have not met Lord Braddock yet. He is a stubborn man."

"And a handsome one, I hear." She gave her gentle laugh. "Every female in the house is atwitter with his . . . What did Mrs. Mathers call it? Oh, yes. Disheveled elegance."

China hid her surprise that the housekeeper was gossiping about a guest.

"Aha!" crowed Sian.

"What are you 'ahaing' about?"

"Look at you! You are aglow thinking of Lord Braddock. 'Tis not like you, China. You are usually reserved with sharing your emotions, even with me. As if you do not think what you are feeling is quite proper."

"You are being absurd."

"Am I? Are you having improper thoughts about the handsomely disheveled Lord Braddock?"

China frowned. "I will not dignify such a ridiculous question with an answer."

"Which means yes." Sian's musical laugh filled the room. "Trying to dissemble with me is futile. I know you too well, and there is a sparkle in your eye I have not seen in a long time. You look different from when you left the quilting party."

"Different?"

"More alive."

"Are you sure you are not seeing things?"

"Seeing things as you are?" asked Sian. Leaning forward, she went on. "Tell me more about this ghost."

"I have told you all I know." She was relieved that her sister had changed the subject. "He was a Roman legionnaire, and the marquess is his descendant and may be in danger from an assassin. I know nothing more than that so far."

"How Father would have enjoyed this puzzle!"

China sighed. "Yes, he would have. Jade was hopeful that her run-in with a ghost would enable us to prove to the world that Father was right when he said ghosts were abroad in Yorkshire." Her eyes widened. "If Lord Braddock comes to believe that a ghost truly has a hand in saving his life, he surely would state that publicly. Who would fail to believe a decorated war hero?"

"It would certainly confirm Father's theories, especially to those who denounced him and his ideas."

As soon as Sian left the room, the grayness of the evening seemed to drape itself over China again. She rose and went to the windows. Staring out at the garden, which looked as if it were about to give up all attempts to grow, she sighed. Thinking of Lord Braddock telling everyone about the *real* ghosts of Nethercott Castle would have been much simpler if he could see Quintus Valerius. The marquess thought that she was half-mad. She wished her sister Jade were here. Somehow Jade had convinced others to believe in the ghost that she had first seen in the hallway outside their father's book-room.

Or, to be more truthful, she had persuaded her sisters, who were ready to hear those tidings.

But now China had an even greater task: She must persuade the marquess to believe in ghosts before he became one himself.

Agony.
Unbelievable agony.
How long had it been since the pain smashing

against his head had sent him spiraling into an unending world of agony?

Since . . .

No answer formed in Alexander's jumbled mind as he raised his head. Only more pain. Slowly he released the breath he had not realized he was holding while he struggled to escape the serrated torment. It centered on the left side of his head. Its heat enveloped him.

A blur met his eyes as he opened them. He was no longer outside. No wind across his face.

When he had gone to the Roman camp, the wind had died to the stillness that seemed to come only on the hottest summer or chilliest winter afternoons. Was he still in the camp? No. He remembered being helped into a house, but little else.

Something moved in the shadows. Rolling onto his stomach, he reached for his weapons, his gun, his saber, his pistol . . . whatever was closest at hand. He found only soft bedding.

Something moved.

By the window.

He stared at the motion, holding his breath. A single sound might betray where he lay. The faint light from the window was eclipsed for a moment by a shape. He blinked rapidly as the silhouette took the form of both man and beast.

He was seeing things. He must be. There could not be some otherworldly form standing between him and the starlight.

But there was certainly something moving by the window. He needed to be prepared to defend himself. He would not lie on his belly, waiting for it to come closer.

With care, he edged up to sit. He was not on a bed, but on the floor next to one. Had he fallen out? A coverlet hung inches from his face, and richly embroidered curtains hung from a wooden canopy eight feet above his head. He realized what had been moving by the window: the reflection of light from the hearth to his left. A fire burned there, leaping merrily in tune to music only it could sense.

Relieved that nobody had seen him overreact to shadows, Alexander looked in the other direction. A trio of windows bowed out from the wall. Diamond mullions crisscrossed the glass. A table and a pair of chairs were set into the bow. An upholstered chair and a smaller table had been placed next to a single window that reached high toward a ceiling laced with thick rafters. Framed pictures hung on the walls, but he could not discern what any portrayed. Two odd masks, painted in brilliant shades of red, yellow and green, hung near a door. Ribbons streamed down from them, and he wondered if anyone had actually worn the grotesque faces. On the stand by the bed and atop the chest set at its foot were stacks of books.

Nethercott Castle.

The words appeared out of Alexander's misty mind. He was at the home of Miss China Nethercott.

Then her image appeared in his head as if she stood in front of him.

He turned, startled to discover she truly was standing before him.

"What are you doing out of bed?" Miss Nethercott asked with a stern frown.

"I cannot tell you."

"You should be in bed."

"I agree. Every time I move my head, it aches worse." He sounded petulant, but he did not care. He had not expected her to walk into a room where he was supposed to be abed without the courtesy of a knock.

Or had she knocked? The clangor in his skull might have drowned out other sounds.

Going around to the far side of the bed, she picked up a pair of pillows. She plumped them before coming back to put her hands under his arms. He was about to tell her that he could stand quite well on his own and did not need her help, but he discovered he did . . . again. He was relieved when she assisted him to his feet and onto the bed.

"At least stay in bed," she said, "until we can be sure the wound on your head will not start bleeding again."

He was no longer shocked when she was able, without any strain, to push him back toward the plumped pillows. That he was so weak warned him that his injury was more serious than he had guessed. The pulsating anguish near his left ear told him that the center of the pain was there, but he tried to ignore it as he watched Miss Nethercott go to the larger table. She poured something in a cup and brought it back to him.

His memory had not betrayed him, because Miss Nethercott was an appealing woman. Not beautiful, as the women in London were when they painted on their face powders and donned fancy gowns. Rather, she was lovely. A sprinkling of freckles across her nose suggested she possessed an impish spirit he had not witnessed. Her red hair was no longer a wild mass of waves falling about her face. That, he decided, was a pity. Then he noticed that a single strand had escaped from her chignon to slide along her neck and drape over the skin revealed modestly above her gown's neckline. Slowly his eyes rose to meet hers.

Miss Nethercott held out a cup to him. "Do you think you can hold this?"

"What is it?"

"Chamomile tea. Tepid tea, because I did not want you to scald yourself."

His nose wrinkled.

"It will ease your aching head. I assume you do have an aching head, after I saw where at least one rock tried to break a hole in your skull."

He decided the best answer was silence. He held out his hands, which had an embarrassing tremor. She cautiously placed the cup in his hands, her fingers steadying his until he could manage the slight weight. Sipping the warm but strong tea, he sighed and relaxed into the nest of pillows. He winced, but reached up to touch the stiffness around his forehead.

Miss Nethercott caught his hand. "Do not touch the bandage."

"I do not need you telling me what to do with my head."

"You need *someone* when you are as helpless as a babe."

"Not quite that helpless, I trust."

She smiled and shook her head. "No, not quite that helpless, but most babes are not in danger of being murdered in a few short days."

"Murdered?" Before she could respond, he answered his own question. "Oh, that ludicrous story about your ghost and his dire forecast of my future. For an otherwise reasonable woman, Miss Nethercott, you have the oddest attachment to that tale."

She sat in the chair by the bow window, and he admired how the firelight added a thousand shades of color to her hair. "Lord Braddock, you have the oddest attachment to calling the person who saved your life a liar."

Alexander stared in astonishment. She was plainspoken, but she was—he had to own—completely right. She *had* saved his life. Twice. All she asked in return was for him to heed her warnings so his life would not be extinguished.

He should apologize, but some kernel of pride halted him. If he did, he would be admitting that he believed her silly story.

"What time is it?" he asked in lieu of an apology.

"Two hours after sunset."

"I spent the whole day in bed?"

"You *should* have spent the whole day in bed recovering." She crossed her arms haughtily. "No more getting up and trying to walk around when it is quite clear you need to rest. Where did you think you were going?"

"I have no idea. I woke on the floor."

"Do you often roll out of bed?"

"No."

"Do you walk in your sleep?"

"I trust you are curious about all the things I do at night."

"At this moment, what you do at night is not my concern. Keeping you alive and well is."

He started to scowl, but halted when the motion

pulled against the bandage's taut line. An oath rang through his head, reverberating into pain.

"You need to rest here until you feel better," she said.

"I can—"

"If you can get out of bed, then we can discuss it."

He recognized the challenge in her voice. *Deuce take it!* He owed her for saving his life, but he did not intend to spend a minute more of it listening to her orders.

But a single push against the mattress warned him that standing alone would be impossible. She had known that. As he would have known if he were not being so beef-headed.

He collapsed against the pillows with a groan. "I need to send a message to my friend in Pickering. The vicar at St. Peter and St. Paul Church."

"Reverend Ponsonby?"

"Yes. He was expecting me to arrive yesterday."

"I will have a message sent in the morning to let him know that you are here and safe. If you want to add more—"

"That should be enough. How long will it take to arrive? I hate to have him worry any longer."

"We are more than two leagues from Pickering, so the message will reach him tomorrow before tea."

"Two leagues north?"

"Yes." She smiled gently as she stood. "But you should not be worrying about continuing your travels on those rough roads now."

Her words brought forth another memory. "The highwayman! Has he been found?"

"No."

He heard the underlying frustration in her voice. How long had that beast been preying on the countryside? Could finding the highwayman and bringing him to justice be the way to repay Miss Nethercott? He almost laughed. That was an idea worthy of the acclaimed hero Alexander Braddock, not the man he truly was.

As if he had spoken aloud, she said, "Do not worry about that thief now. You should concentrate on getting better. Why don't you rest and give your head a chance to heal?"

He could not argue with that good advice. He closed his eyes, intending to open them again and thank her, but he sank down into sleep once more.

Later, he told himself, no longer caring when later came.

Chapter 5

The misting rain hung in the air. No drops fell. It was simply there, a shimmering curtain of silver that muted the colors of everything. China was accustomed to such weather in the early spring, but it was August.

She glanced toward the hints of trees along the ridge. Rawcliffe was the wrong name. Maybe it had once been a sheer precipice, but the wood had tamed it. She had clambered up it many times during her childhood. She was startled that she could not recall the last time she had wandered among the trees. Long before she took on the duties of running the household.

Behind her, the house was being consumed by the fog. She could see one wing of the three stories of stone, but the crenelations at the top were invisible. Here and there a gargoyle face peeked through the fog.

The garden was suffering from the lack of summer warmth. Few flowers bloomed, and the blossoms that had looked weak on unsteady stalks. The kitchen garden was doing only a bit better.

China wandered away from the stables and other outbuildings. The house vanished into the low white cloud as she walked to where—on a sunny day—she could see the very tops of the trees by the Roman camp.

Suddenly the silvery mist seemed to glow, as if the rain had become tiny scintillating embers. Fog congealed into light. She took several steps back, blinking as the brilliance burned her eyes. Only her sister's descriptions of how a ghost gathered light from the visible world kept her from fleeing to the house.

Then the light dimmed, and the centurion's ghost stood before her. The plates on his chest armor reflected the light, and the metal on his shield and weapons glistened with more than the rain.

"*Ave*, China Nethercott," the ghost said, raising his spear in a salute.

"*Ave* to you, Quintus Valerius." She moved forward so she did not have to shout, but paused when a chill struck her like a fierce wind. It was coming from him.

"You should call me Quintus." He grinned, for the first time not looking like a well-trained warrior. "That is what my friends called me."

"As you wish, Quintus." The idea of being friends with a ghost was unsettling, but no more disturbing than anything that had happened since she first encountered him.

"How does my descendant fare?"

She smiled, warmed by his concern for Alexander. "I expect he will be able to get out of bed by day's end. If you wish to see for yourself, you are welcome to go inside."

Quintus glanced at the shadowy house. "I am not sure if I should do that."

"Who is to tell you what you can and cannot do? Your commanders are long dead." When she saw his face lengthen in sorrow, she hurried to add, "Forgive me, Quintus. That was thoughtless."

"But the truth." He leaned his tall shield on the top of his foot and rested one elbow on it.

"Tell me more about the curse."

"There are constraints, though I cannot say who dictates them. You see, I cannot always decide when I will appear and how long I can stay."

China considered this for a moment before asking the question she truly wanted answered. "How did you die?"

Quintus looked to the sky, and she knew he was thinking back to the day he took his final breath. "By sword," he finally said, touching his heart. "Here. That may be why so many of my descendants have met their ends the same way."

"What happened to the others?"

"Most died by sword. For others, the death seemed an accident, being trampled by livestock, falling off a city wall. Several met their ends more slowly, their minds destroyed by madness by the fifth of September."

"And if Lord Braddock succeeds in surviving that day with his mind intact?"

"The curse is broken, and his son would never have to withstand it." A smile warmed his rough face. "When the mist would draw me back into it, I would never have to return again."

"It seems simple enough."

"No one has succeeded in fifteen hundred years.

The life of each generation's firstborn son has been extinguished like lamplight." He hesitated, running his hands along the top of his shield. "You should know one other thing."

"What?"

Quintus cleared his throat and avoided her gaze before murmuring, "Those who tried to help have perished as well."

She stared at him in disbelief. "Why didn't you mention that before?"

"I did not think you would go with me to free my descendant, and he would have died in the collapsed wall."

"But you should have told me!" Her mind was blank with shock.

"You must be cautious. Those who died did so because they failed to identify the murderer until it was too late."

China wrapped her arms around herself, but the cold was within her. She liked to think that she would have gone to Lord Braddock's rescue no matter the consequences. Yet, if she had known the truth of how her fate was now tied in with his . . .

She sighed. They were all pawns, and the game would be played on the fifth of September. The only way to win was to find a way to stay alive past that day.

"Do you have any other questions?" Quintus asked.

She felt unable to form a thought. "No, not now. Perhaps later."

"Ask them, and I will answer as much as I can. Until then, you must do what you can to prepare. I suggest you make sure Lord Braddock is hale, so he can defend himself."

"As I told you before, you are more than welcome to visit Lord Braddock's bedchamber today to assure yourself that he is recovering."

"I am in your debt, China."

"Then repay it by finding a way that Lord Braddock can see you."

"I cannot do that. You must make him believe."

"How can I? He has said several times that he does not believe in ghosts."

"You misunderstand me, China. You must make him believe, not in ghosts and death, but in life. He must remember how precious life is, so he will help you save his." He vanished, leaving only the mist gleaming in his wake.

And a sudden downpour.

Paying no attention to the rain falling like tears along her cheeks, China stared at the place where Quintus had been. Make Lord Braddock believe in *life*? How was she supposed to do that?

"What is *that*?" asked a woman who was entering Alexander's room. Her caramel blond hair was pulled back demurely. She carried a tray, and her gaze was focused at the far side of the room, where light danced.

"Sunshine reflecting off something." He tried to stifle a yawn, determined not to be tricked by a flash of light again. How could he be tired? He had slept yesterday away, and until late this morning.

"But there is no sunshine."

He glanced from the woman to the light on the

opposite wall. She was right. It was raining harder now than it had been moments ago. What *was* that light? It had a movement within it, like rippling water mirroring the sunshine. As if something had disturbed it. As if it were—

"A phantom!" breathed the woman.

Alexander swore silently. He had heard enough about ghosts from China Nethercott. Hearing more from her household would try his already strained patience.

"Who are you?" he asked coolly.

"Sian Nethercott, China's younger sister." She struggled to smile, but her gaze kept flicking toward the wall, where the faint light was fading. "China is busy, so I thought I would bring your midday meal." She leaned forward to set the tray over his legs. "Do not be overwhelmed by the amount of food. Cook thought to give you a variety so you could choose what you want to eat." She backed away, her smile wavering as she looked past him again.

"Thank you, Miss Nethercott," he said as he regarded the feast. He could select toast and jam or a poached egg or meat and hearty bread or some sort of fish or what smelled like mushroom soup. Each dish gave off a tempting aroma, reminding him that it had been more than a day since his last meal.

"If you need anything, ring the bell on the tray." She turned toward the door, but gave one more look at the wall, which now appeared no different from the others.

"May I ask one thing before you go?"

She paused. "Certainly."

"Is your sister prone to fancies of imagination?"

"China?" She laughed. "No, not China. She is so

sensible that many wonder how she can possibly be one of the eccentric Nethercotts."

"Oh? Your family has a reputation for being unconventional?"

"My father was interested in many topics, my lord. Some were commonplace. Others were not, but he pursued them with equal fervor. Some people did not understand that." She seemed to think that explained the matter.

"I see," he said, although he did not. Further questions would be ill-mannered.

Alexander was famished, but he found his eyes moving again and again toward the wall where the irregular circle of light had been. It reminded him— even though he did not want to be reminded—of the light he had seen in the Roman camp when Miss Nethercott spoke of the ghost.

Deuce take it! What was happening in this isolated house on the edge of the moor? Moving the tray with care, he swung his legs to the edge of the bed. Or he tried to. The covers seemed to weigh as much as a pair of cannons. He struggled until he was sitting with his bare legs dangling over the side like a child. He had not noticed before that his boots and breeches were missing. He wondered who had undressed him. It would be a pity if it had been the elder Miss Nethercott. He would want to recall her disrobing him.

The door opened, and China entered, her hands behind her back. Her eyes widened. "What are you doing up again?"

"I am only partially so, if you will take note. I thought it wiser not to go much farther until I knew where my clothes were."

"Being cleaned and mended. They should be returned to you within the hour. Are you finished with your meal? I can take your tray, if you are."

He wished he could appear as calm as she did in these odd circumstances. "I am weary of remaining in bed." He grinned. "Alone, that is."

"Save your roguish Town ways for someone who will enjoy them. With that injury to your head, I doubt you would be capable of much in bed beyond sleeping and healing."

"Try me."

China gasped as she saw twinkles of challenge and amusement in his eyes. She had not expected him to say something so out of hand. Had she misunderstood Quintus? Lord Braddock seemed to have a firm grasp on life's pleasures.

You must make him believe, not in ghosts and death, but in life. He must remember how precious life is, so he will help you save his.

The ghost's words had been clear, and so was the marquess's flirting.

"No, thank you." China hated using that prim voice, but it was a good reminder for him—and herself—that she was his hostess and nothing more. As well, she needed to think about how she would persuade him to remain at Nethercott Castle. Using seductive wiles—even if she had ones she could trust—would be imprudent. He might tire of the chase, or she might find herself forgetting it was only a game.

And now he was sitting in front of her with his legs bare, acting as if he often had discussions with women while in such undress. Perhaps he did, but she found herself glancing too often at the firm muscles below his shirt, which reached only to his mid-thigh.

She needed to do what she had come into his room to do. From behind her, she drew out what she had brought. "This walking stick was my father's. I thought you might need it until you are less dizzy and wobbly."

"I do not want to depend on a cane."

"It is not a cane. It is a walking stick. Many people who walk on the moors find walking sticks essential because the terrain is so uneven." She held out the stick that had been her father's favorite. It had been carved by a shepherd near Danby Beacon to the north, and the shaft was decorated with images of the birds on the moors. When the marquess did not take it, she leaned it against the foot of the bed. "You may use it or not, as you wish, Lord Braddock."

"Call me Alexander."

She had been about to turn away, but looked at him. He wanted her to call him by his given name? That would suggest an intimacy that she found disquieting. "Why?"

"I am your guest, dependent upon you. I should make it easier for you." The twinkle returned to his eyes. "And as my hostess, you should grant my requests."

"I should?"

"And you should allow me the privilege of addressing you as informally."

Her calm shattered abruptly when it became impossible for her to maintain it. "Very well, but would you *please* put something over your nakedness?"

"I was not sure if you had noticed."

"Of course I noticed."

Heat flashed up her face as he gave her a slow grin. Her words had suggested more than she intended.

"I would return beneath the covers . . . if I could." His teasing tone vanished, and she realized how much energy he had expended to appear more hale than he was.

" 'Tis silly for us to act uncomfortable in this situation," China said with sympathy. Going to the bed, she yanked the covers from beneath him.

He grabbed the bedpost. "Take care! And give me fair warning. You could have knocked me onto my nose."

"Must you always consider the worst that could happen? If you will swing your feet up, I shall pull the covers over you."

He slowly did as she had asked. It was agonizing to watch his slow, careful motions, but she did not offer to help. Even if he were not offended, the thought of touching his bare skin unsettled her in ways she had never imagined before. Now she could imagine all too well. The rough, male feel of his skin. His gaze sliding along her. The intense, coiled power unleashed in his eyes in the moment before he brought her mouth to his. She shook those too-tempting images away as she lifted the tray off the bed and drew the covers over him.

He swore.

"What is wrong?" she asked.

"There is something wrinkled under me."

"Smooth it away." How could she have fantasies about a man who was short-tempered about everything and everyone around him? "The walking stick is here if you need to get up to . . ."

"Handle any personal business?"

"Yes." She did not need a mirror to know her face was almost the color of her hair. It might have been easier to discuss such things if she had a brother. She started toward the door.

"China?" he called.

"Yes?" She did not look at him.

"Your sister believes you were telling the truth about seeing a ghost."

She forced her rooted feet to turn her to face him again. She feared she would see a taunting smile on his lips. Instead, he wore a baffled expression. As if he could not believe that he had halted her to discuss ghosts.

"Sian knows I am honest," she said.

"Has she seen the ghost, too?"

"No, but *she* believes me when I tell her what I have seen." She locked eyes with him. "Just as I believed my other sister when she told me that she had seen a ghost. You may have heard of the resolution of the questions around the death of Sir Mitchell Renshaw. Jade's participation in that came about because she heeded the words of a ghost that appeared right here in Nethercott Castle."

He did not answer for a long minute. He stared at her as if appraising her anew. "I am sure she believes that ghosts are around, and I am sure you believe that as well, but I cannot."

"I am not asking you to believe in ghosts. I am asking you to believe what I say about the fifth of September. Someone will try to kill you." She swallowed harshly. "And there is a good possibility I will die, too. I need you to believe that the danger is real."

"I am not sure I can do that either."

His cool, precise words stung more than she had expected. Furious, she retorted as she walked out, "Then you may have sealed our doom."

Chapter 6

Rain swirled along the uneven glass of the book-room's windows, creating shimmering crystal ropes. China's father had loved the cozy room with its three walls of shelves holding as many books as could be squeezed in. Vases filled the shelves over the door, so many that it was impossible to see all of the Asian designs. Her father had never been able to resist buying "just one more." On the other wall, long windows were set on both sides of the wide hearth.

China used the writing table for correspondence and making lists to share with the household. Now she was doing the latter, because Cook was waiting for instructions on what to prepare for the guests her sister had invited to Nethercott Castle. Sian had been eager to entertain since their return from Town two months ago.

With the to-do about Alexander, China had forgotten about the gathering. Only upon entering the book-room to find one of her father's books on the Roman settlements in Yorkshire had she seen the half-finished list.

She came to her feet and wandered to the window. During the best of times she despised planning such events. Now, when she could not stop thinking about Alexander and the curse, she had even less patience with such silly arrangements.

How was she to persuade him to believe in *life*? After repeating the conversation over and over in her mind, she knew she had not been mistaken about what Quintus had asked her to do.

You must make him believe, not in ghosts and death, but in life. He must remember how precious life is, so he will help you save his.

She understood the request, but she had no idea where to begin. She needed to do something to save his life and her own. If she—

"Am I intruding?"

China looked behind her, startled. She smiled when she saw Alexander standing in the doorway. The disheveled, half-dressed man she had last spoken to yesterday had regained a rakish elegance. His coat was clean and his breeches repaired. The bandage wrapped around his head was gone, leaving only a small white patch by his left ear. With his cravat jauntily tied and his black hair brushed back from his startlingly blue eyes, he appeared worthy of the title marquess.

"You look much better," she said, knowing it was an understatement. He looked so handsome that she was finding it difficult to do anything but stare.

He bowed his head. "I feel much better, and I walked here without falling on my face once." He held up the walking stick. "I owe you another apology, China, for aiming my frustration at you."

"There is no need for an apology." She put her

hand on his arm and guided him to the closest chair. Standing so close she could see that his hair was damp and a hint of soap clung in front of his right ear. She fought to keep her fingers from touching the thick bubbles.

And lost.

"What are you doing?" he asked, astonished.

"You had some soap on you. That is all." Her cheeks grew warm as she quickly lowered her hand and motioned toward a chair. "Why don't you sit? You must be exhausted. Mrs. Mathers mentioned that you have not slept well."

He sat and gave her a quizzical look. "Why would your housekeeper say that?"

"She wished me to know, as your hostess."

"No, that was not what I meant." His blue eyes narrowed. "*Why* did she say that? What gave her cause to believe I was not sleeping well?"

"She mentioned only that your covers were tossed in different directions." She gave him a quick smile she hoped would hide her abrupt disquiet with a very personal topic. "You know how housekeepers like to keep an eye on everyone."

"True." He released his breath in a slow sigh. "During my short stay at Braddock Court, I quickly learned that Mrs. Pollard was not a woman to cross. She rules the house and its staff with the efficiency of Napoleon ordering his generals." A faint smile tipped his lips. "And with the same stubborn refusal to acknowledge those who do not share her campaign against idle hands."

China sat in the chair facing him. The heat from the low-burning fire on the hearth nibbled at the dampness in the room, but could not banish it completely. "Was avoiding your housekeeper why you decided to come and visit the Roman camp?"

He laughed.

Astonished, she wondered if that had been the first true laugh she had heard from him. She liked the sound. It was as hearty and animated as the first spring breezes sweeping down off the moors.

And she could not keep from joining in. Her higher-pitched laugh balanced the rumble of his.

Like they belonged together.

Her laugh faded. She hardly knew the marquess, and what she had discovered about him vexed her. He was too much a military officer, giving orders and expecting anyone nearby to obey them. She had been tempted more than once to remind him that she was not a sergeant under his command. But he was making an effort to be charming on this rainy afternoon. She needed to remember her own manners.

"That may be the true reason," Alexander said with another chuckle, freeing her from her uneasy thoughts. "However, I have told my household that I was coming to look for the past while visiting the family of one of the men I served with on the Continent." He glanced out the window toward the hills leading up to the moors.

"Your past?" She could not help thinking of Quintus Valerius. Had Alexander been drawn here so his ancestor's ghost could warn of his possible murder?

"No, the past of the moors. There are many old sites known only to wandering sheep. I am curious to find as many as I can, perhaps even write a guidebook for other explorers."

"What were you looking for in the Roman camp?"

"Artifacts." He ran his fingers along a book on the table next to his chair. "But, to own the truth, that camp is new compared to what else I hope to see while I am here."

"Ancient stones and burial sites?"

"You know about them?"

"I was born and grew up here. My parents were blessed with great curiosity, a trait that my sisters and I have inherited. While other daughters were taught needlework, we learned about prehistoric sites on the moors."

"Will you show some of them to me?"

She smiled. "Of course. I will be glad to show you some of the older places and introduce you to Reverend Wilder. He knows of even more interesting places than I do. But we could start with the stone cross on the forest road to Levisham, once the fifth of September is past."

"Forget about that. I will not be kept from seeing what brought me to the moors."

"Alexander, you must be careful until then. You are risking my life as well as yours."

"You cannot expect me to believe that some old story about a forgotten curse in my family could mean your death too."

"Whether or not you believe it, that is the truth. If you could see Quintus, you would understand."

"The problem is, I cannot see him." He sighed. "However, I will do nothing to risk your life. Yet, if the stone cross is close to Nethercott Castle, we should be safe."

She suspected he would go in search of the stone cross by himself if she did not acquiesce. Again, she wished Quintus had given someone else the duty of persuading this stubborn man to heed good sense. She was failing.

Glancing at the window, she said, "If the rain stops before sunset, we could drive to it. I am surprised you have not seen it before. Your estate is along the shore north of Whitby, so certainly you have traveled across the moors before this."

He leaned back and looked out the window as well. "I never visited this area before I inherited the title. From the time my father was a child, my grandfather and he were at daggers drawn with each other. I went to Braddock Court the first time a few months ago."

"How sad that you never knew your grandfather." She thought of the curse. Had the harsh words that drove Alexander's father from his home been the curse of that generation?

"My father did not believe so." His tone warned that he had no further interest in discussing the topic.

"It is a shame that you gave what you found at the camp to the highwayman."

"I gave him shards." He reached under his coat. "I did not give him this." He drew out something wrapped in a handkerchief.

As he began to unwrap it, she leaned forward, eager to see what he had hidden from the thief. A sooty shadow appeared through the fabric. When he lifted away the last layer, she saw a black item the approximate size and shape of a shilling.

"What is it?" Rising, she looked at the black circle on his left palm. As he tilted his hand so the smooth surface caught light from the hearth, she gasped. "There is a man and a woman on it." She traced the faces with her fingertip. "Is it jet?"

"I think so."

"Such artistry. I doubt anything made in Whitby now could compare with this piece." Straightening, she went to a shelf and drew down a book. "If you are interested in the Roman occupation of Britain, you might find this book interesting."

"What is it?"

"Mr. Hutton's *The History of the Roman Wall.* Almost twenty years ago, he walked the length of Hadrian's Wall from Newcastle to the Irish Sea. I found it very interesting to read."

"You seem to have many interests."

"My father called me incurably curious."

He smiled. "I would say that was a compliment."

"I took it as such."

"If I may, I will take this book to my chamber to read later."

"Please do. You are welcome to borrow any book while you are here."

Setting the piece of carved jet on the arm of the chair, he came to his feet with care and used the walking stick when he swayed. He glanced at her, and she returned his gaze without comment. Did he think she was going to treat him differently because he was weakened by the wound? She had learned he did not wish to be coddled.

Wandering along the bookshelves, he said, "It would take me several years to read all of these." He turned. "Have you?"

"Read them all?" She shook her head. "Not yet. I daresay the only one who ever did was my father."

"He had eclectic taste."

"Too eclectic, in some people's opinions."

"And in yours?"

"He was the most interesting man I have ever met, and nobody else's opinion could ever change that."

Putting the book on a nearby table, he came toward her. "There is so much sorrow in your voice, China."

"It has been more than a year since he died, but . . ."

"I understand. There are many times when I wish I could show my father something amazing that I have found, or ask his advice on some aspect of the family's estate." He glanced at the jet piece he had set on the chair.

"What I wish for most is the chance to speak with my father again." Her breath caught. She had not intended to say that. Her sister Jade had tried to arrange that, something she had not told China until after her last encounter with the ghost of Sir Mitchell Renshaw, but nothing had come of it. Why were they holding on to such hopes?

"I understand," he said again, closing the distance between them. "I was . . . away when my father died."

She heard the slight hesitation, but did not press him to explain. Like hers, his grief remained a raw wound.

"I am sorry," she whispered as he halted in front of her.

"As I am. I am sorry for my poor behavior since we met." His hand curved along her cheek. "China, I owe you my life. I should have thanked you before now."

She struggled to get words past the clog in her throat as a thousand excited breaths fought to escape at once. His skin against her face was coarse, but deliciously warm. "You would have done the same for me if our roles were reversed."

Lifting her right hand, he tilted it so the scratches left from digging him out of the collapsed wall were visible. "I regret that my foolishness caused you pain."

"There was nothing foolish about what you did."

"I should have checked the security of those stones more closely before I entered the wall. I must have let my anticipation of what I might find blind me to the unsteady state of the wall around the opening."

"If you say you checked it," she whispered, "I am sure you did everything humanly possible." She did not speak Quintus's name or mention his warning again. When they stood in soft shadows, surrounded by the dusty smell of the books she loved, she wanted no one else to encroach.

A smile tipped one side of his mouth. "Maybe so, but the roof collapsing showed me how mistaken I was."

"A mistake? *You* are admitting to making a mistake?"

"This one time. Actually these two times."

"Two?"

"I should not have dressed you down when you tried to help me."

"You truly did take quite a knock to your head." She grinned, daring to hope he was beginning to heed her warnings at last. "I can think of no other reason you would be acknowledging your mistakes now."

"I can." He cupped her elbow. "I am being as candid with you as I would be with one of my tie-mates. I know I have been beastly to you, China."

"Alexander . . . " She forgot what she was going to say as his fingers traced an aimless path along her arm.

"Yes?"

"This is nonsense."

"What nonsense is there in correcting a mistake? If one cannot learn from one's errors and rectify them, what is the purpose of recognizing those errors in the first place?"

"You *are* talking nonsense."

"Maybe. Maybe not." Stroking her cheek with the back of his hand, he said, "Humor me."

"I would if you would do something humorous."

"You are dangerous with words, China."

"A woman is not allowed to learn to defend her honor with sword or dueling pistol, so it behooves her to hone other ways."

"I would as soon face a saber than your rapier wit."

She rolled her eyes. "If you have a point, will you get to it?"

"You sound annoyed."

"I am."

He seemed honestly nonplussed. "With me?"

"There is no one else here, and I assure you that I am not annoyed with myself."

"Why are you bothered by me?"

Bothered! That was a far better description than annoyed, for being near him disrupted her calm.

"I think it would be better if we changed the subject."

"Most certainly." He stepped back, amazing her because she had not thought he would retreat. When he picked up her hand, he bowed over it. "Miss Nethercott."

She was about to ask him why he had returned to addressing her so formally, but the brush of his thumb against her palm sent a shiver up her arm. His gaze caught hers, and he did not release it as he cupped her hand in both of his. Slowly, he raised it toward his mouth. His breath warmed her trembling fingers, and she held her own breath, waiting for his kiss on her hand. Instead, he tugged her to him, releasing her hand and sweeping his arm around her waist.

She opened her mouth to order him to release her, but his slanted across it. Shock became yearning, and annoyance became delight before she could draw another breath. There was nothing hurried or furious or dominating in this kiss. It urged her to soften in his arms. His tongue caressed her bottom lip, tantalizing her, before it boldly drove into her mouth. In shock, she gasped. That sound mixed with his laugh before his lips swept along her neck. She knew she was a fool to let him touch her like this, but she could not push him away. She wanted to savor these unfamiliar sensations, to sink into them, to become lost in them . . . with him.

As his mouth moved to her ear, she could not restrain the quiver that shot along her. She grabbed his lapels and turned her head so her mouth was on his. His arms folded her against his chest. His heartbeat accelerated like a runaway wagon on a steep road. Hers was going even faster, her pulse pounding in her ears while their mouths moved like dancers through the pattern of a frenetic reel. Her hands swept up his back, and she delighted in how the strong muscles reacted to her touch.

"Oh . . . I am sorry." The voice came from beyond Alexander.

Sian's voice.

China stiffened and pulled back, staring at him because she needed a moment before she looked at her sister. He gave her a roguish grin, and she almost smiled back. She caught herself. She had let him seduce her into his arms with his beguiling words and sparkling eyes. She would be wise to pay no attention to either from this point forward.

Chapter 7

"I . . . I . . . I am sorry, but I needed to speak with you, China," Sian said from the doorway. "I did not mean to interrupt . . . anything."

China turned to face her sister, glad to discover she did not need to worry about seeing Sian's dismay or curiosity. Sian was looking directly at Alexander, who was leaning his elbow with apparent nonchalance on a bookshelf.

"Come in," China said.

"Miss Nethercott," Alexander added with a bow. "As you can see, the food you brought has done its job of getting me back on my feet."

"I am pleased to see that." She glanced at China, then said, "Our guests are here."

China wanted to hug her sister, who was acting as if nothing were out of the ordinary. Instead, as she crossed the room, she said, "Please excuse us, Alexander, while we greet our callers. You are welcome to stay here and read. If you need help returning to your room, anyone will be glad to assist you."

"Actually I would appreciate your assistance."

"But my guests—"

"I would enjoy meeting your guests, if you do not mind. I do not know many people in Yorkshire."

"Certainly you may join us," China said, wishing she felt as sincere as she sounded. She hoped she could maintain the façade while walking with him and her sister through the house.

Again she did not need to worry. Sian kept Alexander busy, asking about his impressions of the Roman camp and Nethercott Castle. China wished she could put people at ease as readily as her sister did. It had always been simpler to stay in the background, allowing her garrulous sisters to take the lead. Now Jade was no longer living in Nethercott Castle, and Sian might not be much longer. Sir Henry Cranler had been paying a lot of attention to her in recent months, whether at church or at the market in Pickering. Had Sian heard the rumors that Sir Henry was ready to ask for her hand?

It was silly to listen to rumors. They had less substance than milk froth.

China was so deep in her thoughts that she almost collided with Alexander. He put out one hand to steady her, and she recoiled from the craving searing through her. It was too powerful to endure for more than a second.

His mouth grew taut, and she realized she had offended him. She tried to tell herself it would be for the best to have a wall raised between them. When he lured her into his arms and sprinkled amazing kisses across her face, she forgot her vow to Quintus.

"I am sorry," she said, even though he would not realize what she actually meant.

"As I am. I did not mean to startle you." His blue

eyes seemed to see right into her, and she could not help wondering if he perceived the truth.

"Hurry!" Sian laughed as she motioned for them to follow her down the stairs to the ground floor. "The carriage was coming toward the gate when Webster came to alert me."

"A footman," China added quietly as her sister almost ran down the stairs.

"I assumed as much." Alexander leaned his hand on the oak banister while he descended each riser with care. "Your sister never hides anything she thinks or feels, does she?"

"No. I think she is that way because she is an artist. When she sketches, she puts all of herself into each drawing. She confronts life the same way."

"An enviable way to be."

"Yes."

He paused at the bottom of the stairs, his hand resting on the thick oak newel post. "If you envy her, then why are you the opposite? You hide your thoughts."

"It is not easy to be honest with someone who thinks you are being irrational."

His dark brows shot up; then he laughed. "Or could it be that you choose your words and use them as weapons whenever you have the opportunity?"

"If so, you have offered me many."

Smiling, he offered his arm. "I have to say, China, that I am going to enjoy letting my hard head heal in the company of two such intriguing sisters."

China could not halt her own smile as she put her hand on his arm. With slow, steady steps, they walked across the octagonal foyer toward the grand front door.

It was seldom used because the double oak panels weighed as much as a workhorse. The windows on either side were almost as tall as the doors, but only half the width. Arched at the top, they were decorated with glass images of the house itself, installed at the request of her great-grandfather. Blue and gold urns, as tall as Alexander, flanked the doors. They were set on short mahogany tables carved with dragons and flowers. Of all the ceramics her father had collected, this pair of urns and tables were China's favorites.

Alexander had no trouble going down the trio of shallow steps outside the door and into the courtyard. On the road leading from the gate came the sounds of hoofbeats and wheels splashing through puddles, announcing the arrival of Sian's guests.

Alexander whistled as he looked around the courtyard, then chuckled. "It is a castle! With a crenelated wall and gargoyles hanging from the roof. I thought the name was an affectation."

"It is. Mostly. The castle never had to defend this valley. It is far too new for that."

"Can you walk the parapets?"

"Yes. When you are steadier on your feet, I would be glad to show you how to get up there."

"With a musty old castle like this, it is no wonder you believe in ghosts. What other stories do you have of spectral sightings?"

"Before now, only the one seen by Jade."

"You are jesting. Every old house has ghostly groans and phantom visitors."

"Not here." She gestured toward the carriage entering the courtyard through an arched gate. "And these guests are the living, breathing sort."

The carriage came to a jerky stop, and China glanced at the coachman on the box. Oddly, he was handling the reins with a single hand, a dangerous grip. The carriage door opened, and a man she easily recognized stepped out.

Lord Turnbull was as tall as Alexander and strikingly handsome. Dark hair, dark eyes, a well-muscled form. The greatest problem, in China's estimation, was that he *knew* he was strikingly handsome.

She hid her exasperation. When Sian had spoken of extending an invitation to their neighbors, China had assumed her sister meant the vicar and the families who lived on the farms leading up to the moor. Or maybe Sir Henry and his spinster sister, Deborah. She had not imagined that Sian would ask bothersome Lord Turnbull to call from his estate in nearby Bransdale. Sian must have forgotten how the viscount had tried to court China several years ago.

China had not.

Every memory of that intolerable spring was imprinted in her memory. No matter where she had gone, even into some of the wildest parts of the moors, he had always found her, pressing his suit and paying her compliments. She had begun to understand how it felt to be a pheasant or roe deer, stalked by the hunter.

Forcing a smile, she reminded herself that it would be easier now that the viscount was betrothed to Lady Viola Upton, who had come to stay with her maiden aunt in York last year. Why would any man pay attention to China when he had such a beauty for his own?

As if on cue, Lady Viola Upton emerged from the carriage. She was as beautiful as Lord Turnbull was handsome, dressed like the pattern-card of elegance in a gown of pristine white. As always. Her bonnet with its dyed feathers was set perfectly on her blond hair. As always. She glanced down her nose and around as if she had found herself transported into the basest neighborhood in some backward country. As always.

And, as always, China found herself vexed by that arrogant attitude.

"A bit fancy for the country, don't you think?" murmured Alexander.

China glanced at him in astonishment. She had expected him to consider Lady Viola a bright and elegant spot in daisyville.

He winked at her, and she struggled not to laugh. Just when she thought she understood one part of the puzzle that was Lord Braddock, he surprised her anew.

She schooled her face into a polite smile as she stepped forward to greet Lord Turnbull and his fiancée, but paused when a second woman alighted from the carriage. Miss Lauraine Upton was her cousin's companion. She had been burdened with a father who had gambled away the family's estate shortly after she was born. He had died in a duel during which, it was whispered, he allowed himself to be shot, because he could not face the creditors he had yet to pay. Without title or money, Miss Upton had no choice but to accept the arrangement of serving her cousin, staying in the background, saying little. She was almost the same age as Lady Viola, but had few hopes of ever marrying. China wondered how anyone could be grateful for such a dreary life.

"Welcome to Nethercott Castle," China said as she

walked across the courtyard. "I hope you had an uneventful trip from York."

"It was," Lady Viola said with a sniff, "until that odious highwayman tried to halt us."

"Tried?"

"I gave the order not to stop for anything. I had to think of the ladies' safety." Lord Turnbull stepped forward and lifted China's hand to his lips. He was about to kiss it when his betrothed cleared her throat quietly. Like a chastised child, he released China's fingers. "I daresay the ball did no more than graze our coachee."

"What?" Looking up at the box, she saw bloodstains on the driver's sleeve. No wonder he had been holding the reins with a single hand. "Sian, have Mrs. Mathers bring supplies to tend to him at once."

When her sister did not reply, China glanced over her shoulder to see Sian rushing into the house. Her sister would waste no time finding the housekeeper.

China turned back to her guests, ready to make introductions, but Lord Turnbull said, "Braddock, I did not expect to see you here." His smile reached no farther than his lips, for his dark eyes were as cold as stones in midwinter.

"You know Lord Turnbull?" China asked, smiling at Alexander. "Did you serve together in the army?"

"No." Alexander added nothing more.

Her smile faded, and an uncomfortable silence thickened. Only Mrs. Mathers hurrying out of the house broke it.

China nodded when the housekeeper gave her a quick smile to let her know that the coachee was not badly injured. She guided her guests toward the house. 'Twas not a good beginning to a visit that might stretch out as long as a fortnight. Her eyes widened at the thought. The dreaded day when Alexander's life could be taken was within that fortnight. Should she reveal the truth to Lord Turnbull and ask for his help? Before she divulged a single word, she needed to know the cause of the antipathy between him and Alexander.

As soon as they stood in the octagonal foyer, the viscount said, "Allow me to introduce my betrothed, Lady Viola Upton. Lord Braddock."

China tensed, but Alexander acted as if he had not heard the venom in Lord Turnbull's voice. Taking Lady Viola's hand, he bowed over it. "It is always a pleasure to make the acquaintance of a lovely woman."

"Thank you," Lady Viola said with a girlish titter. That sound vanished when she added, "This is my cousin, Miss Lauraine Upton."

"We are happy to have you here with us at Nethercott Castle," China said, hoping the other woman would look up from her contemplation of the tips of her shoes, but Miss Upton did not. "You have had a long journey from York. I assume you would like to rest before dinner."

"Rest?" asked Lady Viola with another birdlike laugh. "We did not come here to rest. We came here to hear more about the ghost."

"Ghost?" China flinched. Surely they could not have heard of Quintus.

"The ghost that your sister Jade saw here is the talk of York. Isn't it, my dear?" She slipped her arm through Lord Turnbull's and smiled eagerly. "Everyone is agog over the idea that your father's bizarre work might yet be proven fruitful."

"I would not call ghosts fruitful," murmured Alexander, so low that China doubted the lady heard him. "Better to describe them as dead on the vine."

China gave him the fearsome scowl that usually had a dampening effect on her sisters, but her frown brought only a smile from him as he turned to greet Miss Upton.

When China looked at her sister, Sian was wearing a shocked expression as she listened with what was—for her—an unusual air of quiet. Later, out of earshot of their guests, China must ask Sian what possessed her to ask Lord Turnbull and his companions to visit Nethercott Castle.

"So you had an encounter with the highwayman?" asked Alexander in a deceptively calm voice as they walked out of the foyer.

He acted as if he were about to set a trap for Lord Turnbull. She could not imagine why.

"I think that is obvious." The viscount's voice was tight with emotion. Fury? Anxiety over his coachman? Irritation with Alexander? She could not be certain which it might be.

"Where was the attack?"

"On the other side of Rawcliffe, about a half league from here."

"So far?"

"I just said—"

"I am not questioning your ability to judge distance," Alexander said in a tone that suggested the opposite. "I am surprised that the highwayman is journeying so far afield."

"Such low creatures do not announce where they plan to be." Lord Turnbull's smile grew cold. "It is not like a general deciding where he intends to have a battle. On the roads, one must always be alert, prepared for anything."

"It is good your coachman was."

Wondering why Alexander was baiting the viscount, China said to halt Lord Turnbull's reply, "Do come this way. I think you will enjoy the views of the moors from the upper floors."

As she turned to lead them toward the stairs, she faltered at a soft cry of dismay from Lady Viola. She looked over her shoulder to see the lady peering around herself.

"She is gone!" cried the lady.

"She?" asked China.

"Princess is gone."

Lord Turnbull hastily explained, "Princess is her dog."

"My dear Princess is more than just a dog. She is my dearest companion." Lady Viola seemed to take no note of how Miss Upton winced at the words. "Oh, my stars! Where is my dear Princess?" She suddenly burst into tears.

As the viscount and Miss Upton tried to comfort her, China started for the door.

Alexander put his hand on her arm and said, "Allow me."

At his gentle touch, she almost whispered that she would allow him just about anything.

He saved her from saying something foolish by adding, "I will look for her pup and get you a report on how the coachee fares."

"Thank you."

"Trust me when I say I am pleased for any excuse to excuse myself."

She waited for the hint of a smile that rushed

across his lips whenever he made a jest, but his face remained stern as he left.

China went to where her sister watched, wide-eyed, as Lord Turnbull attempted to soothe his betrothed. Putting her arm around her sister's shoulders, China gave Sian a weak smile.

"I am sorry," Sian whispered.

"For what?" she asked as softly.

"When she sent me a note asking if they could call to speak of what happened with Jade, I agreed without considering the consequences."

Giving her sister's shoulders a squeeze, China said, "I am sure this will be the worst of it."

"Stop feeding me fibs." A grin tugged at her lips.

China swallowed her laugh before offering her own assurances that the dog would be found. Lady Viola refused to believe what anyone said until, ten minutes later, Alexander returned with the dog on a makeshift leash.

With a cry, Lady Viola knelt and embraced the small brindled dog. It lapped her face and bounced about, catching its claws in her gown. She seemed indifferent to the snags. Standing, she said, "Lord Braddock, you have been the nation's hero, but today you are *mine*."

"I am only delivering your dog to you, my lady." His smile seemed strained, but his voice was as smooth and practiced as a courtier's. "The lads in the stable found her cowering in the carriage and were about to bring her to the house."

"But how kind of *you* to bring my precious Princess to me." She gave him a very warm smile.

"I am sure she would like to recover after her harrowing experience," Lord Turnbull said, moving closer to his fiancée. He glowered at Alexander, any pretense of congeniality gone.

Unsure whether he spoke of the lady or her dog, China hastened to say, "If you will come with me, you can relax in your rooms."

For a long moment, no one moved; then Alexander looked at her. "Lead the way, China, and we will follow like proper goslings."

China kept up an unusually steady prattle that allowed no one else to slip in a word. A single glance at her sister was enough to let Sian know that she needed help to keep the men's words from evolving into a brangle.

Sian took over the conversation as if it were the most natural thing. As her sister mixed comments about the rough roads rising to the moors with stories about the paintings they passed, China was impressed at how unforced each comment sounded.

As they reached the private chambers on the upper floors, Lady Viola said, "I had no idea that Nethercott Castle would be such a magnificent house." She faltered, then said, "Forgive me, Miss Nethercott. One cannot know what to expect on the edge of the moors. Such a wild place. I prefer being within the walls of York."

"You will find that few of the natives here have been eaten by beasts." China regretted her words as soon as they left her lips. A good hostess allowed her guests a certain latitude when they were exhausted.

She was very grateful to the castle's housekeeper during the next half hour as the guests were settled in their rooms. Mrs. Mathers insisted that each bed-chamber be aired at least once a month in case someone unexpectedly called and needed to stay overnight.

China was astonished how many servants were traveling with her guests. Lady Viola had, in addition to her cousin and her pet dog, a French maid named Yvette and four other servants. Lord Turnbull had brought his valet as well as a man whose principal task seemed to be to guard the viscount's chest of cigars. Two other servants could have belonged either to the lady or the viscount. China was unsure, but knew Mrs. Mathers would arrange for quarters for them near whomever they served. None of the chambers in Nethercott Castle offered attached rooms for so many attendants.

While the housekeeper was sorting out who was who, Sian was called away to answer a question about the evening meal, leaving China alone with Alexander by the stairs to the family's private rooms. Wondering if she should say anything about his lack of manners, she hesitated a moment too long.

He said quietly, "I would have appreciated being warned that someone like Turnbull is calling."

"Someone like Lord Turnbull? What do you mean by that?"

"Exactly what I said."

"Lord Turnbull is a respected member of a respected family, and he attended some lectures my father gave several years ago in York and Scarborough. He and Father continued corresponding— albeit infrequently, because the viscount was seldom at home because of his military duties—right up until the time of my father's death. When my father was bedridden, I read him the viscount's letters, and Lord Turnbull showed nothing but genuine interest in the topics Father studied."

"Not a surprise."

She fought to restrain her annoyance at his tone that suggested both the viscount and her father were addled. Ice slipped into her voice. "Is there something you believe I should know about him? If there is, speak it instead of making veiled accusations."

For a long moment, one that stretched until she could see the tension growing taut across his lips, he said nothing. Then, just as slowly, just as deliberately, just as coolly, he edged toward her. She was aware of how alone they were in the long expanse of hallway, but she did not surrender to the instinct to move back as he came closer.

He reached out as if to cup her chin. Jerking his hand away, he said gruffly, "I know much about him, China, that I would not punish your ears with telling. No matter what you think of me, I am a gentleman, and I will not intrude on another man's chance to atone for his mistakes. All I can tell you is that you would be wise to invite other guests to Nethercott Castle the next time you are bored."

"Bored? When have I had a chance to be bored? Not since I was waylaid by a ghost and then had to dig you out of that wall!"

"Ghosts! I have heard enough of them. Enjoy conversations with Lady Viola and her mute cousin, but do not include me."

"You are welcome to excuse yourself from whatever gatherings you wish."

He stared at her, and she knew her voice had been too sharp. But, for once, she did not rue speaking her mind. Not at all. Turning on her heel, she walked away before she could say something she *would* regret.

Chapter 8

The steps high in the north tower were so steep that they were more like a ladder than stairs. China gathered in her skirts and climbed, as she had so many times before. Oddly, she could not recall doing so since her father's death. There had been so many details to tend to in the wake of that tragedy. Household accounts and overseeing the servants and doing the tasks necessary to keep the castle and its farm running. Her sisters had been willing to help, but she had found herself taking on more and more of the duties, letting herself become lost in the minutiae so she did not have to think about her pain.

That had changed when she traveled with her sisters to London for the Season. She had left behind her duties and had started to come to terms with her sorrow. Upon their return to Nethercott Castle a fortnight ago, she had been pleased when Sian assumed some of the tasks. There remained enough work to keep China from dwelling on their loss. Still, now it was more the comfort of memories than the vicious prick of grief.

Balls of dust rolled about the floor as she emerged

through a trapdoor into the tower room, cradling her right hand. She had bumped her thumb on the climb. Opening the closest window, she let fresh air surge in and sent the dust racing across the rug over the stone floor. Instead of arrow slits, there were five windows along one side of the circular room. A tapestry hung on the bare stone behind her. The stitches had faded long before it was brought to the top of the tower to provide her and her sisters with a make-believe castle where they could pretend fairy tales came true. Once there had been child-size chairs and a table, but they had been removed. She wondered when.

This room had been her sanctuary. She had often come up to the room with a book and a skirt filled with a half dozen apples to spend an afternoon learning about some ancient civilization and their beliefs or to read one of the novels her father had adored, even though he would never own up to it.

She walked to the built-in bench that followed the curved wall beneath the windows. Opening the top, she heard a skittering sound. Mice, she guessed. She gave them time to scurry away before she reached in to lift out a pile of books. A few had been chewed on, but most looked the same as when she had stored them.

She closed the lid, sat and drew her feet up beneath her. Fresh air surrounded her, the breeze teasing her bare arms. The day had a touch of summer, not hot but with the warmth that heralded the turn of the season. Leaning the pile of books against a closed window, she lifted the topmost one. She opened the cover and smiled at the title page. The story of King Arthur, his knights and the ladies for whose honor they battled. She had first been enchanted by them when she was ten years old.

"That looks like something dear to you," said Alexander as he climbed the last few steps into the tower room.

China fought not to tense at his intrusion into her haven. Since their cold words an hour ago, she had struggled to regain control of her high emotions.

"My father gave this book to me." Her fingers brushed the cover. "It is Mr. Scott's *The Lady of the Lake*. I have been looking for it." She raised her gaze to meet his cool blue eyes. "How did you know about this room?"

"Sian told me that you might be here."

"Did she?" She would have to remind her sister that she came here to be alone.

"I can see why you like this tower room." He went to the center window, and she realized he was not carrying the walking stick. His steps were studied, but sure. "If that hill were not in the way, I swear I could see into the Roman camp."

"It actually is a bit to the right, and higher along the ridge than most people realize."

Turning, he smiled. "I assume our journey to see the stone marker on the way to Levisham has been postponed."

"Yes. I need to be here for Sian's guests."

"Here?" He crossed the room toward her. "What are you doing for your guests up here, China?"

"Allowing them to rest and recover from their journey."

"Recover their manners is more likely."

She shook her head. "You are thinking as if you were in London. The Nethercotts are known for their willingness to speak their minds, and our guests enjoy taking advantage of an atmosphere where they can be blunt."

"As long as they do not take advantage of their hostess."

"Words *you* should take to heart."

"Because I warned you to be cautious around Turnbull or because I enjoy doing this?" He tilted her mouth up beneath his for a swift kiss, lighting her senses like a hill beacon over the dark moors.

"Both." Her voice quavered, but at least she was able to get the word out.

"I see."

She looked away. Could he tell that she was only partially honest? His kisses were delightful and dangerous at the same time, tempting her to toss aside good sense to savor them again . . . and again . . . and again. . . .

"What is this place?" Alexander asked.

Amazed at the commonplace question, she glanced at him. A mistake, because powerful emotions were displayed across his face. Was he making an effort to check his feelings and do as he expected her other guests to do? To treat her as a respected hostess and nothing more? Her fingers tingled with the longing to grasp his lapels and bring his mouth down to hers.

But he was making an effort to treat her properly, and she needed to do the same with him.

"It was a childhood retreat for my sisters and me. When we outgrew the toys once stored in the tower, I came here to read."

"It looks as if you have not spent any time up here recently."

"I have not." She rubbed her hands together. "I

did not need to come here to be by myself when I felt alone."

"Alone? I thought your sister has been living with you."

She tried to smile and failed. "She has, but somehow I still felt alone."

Sitting on the bench, he glanced out a window. "Because there was someone missing from your family."

"Yes, and I have missed Father so much." She blinked to hold in the tears thickening in her eyes.

"I am so sorry, China." He held out his hand.

She put hers on it. When he brought her to sit beside him, she leaned her head on his shoulder. She needed his strong warmth beneath her cheek as she struggled with the tears that wanted to wash down her face.

"Thank you," she whispered. "I know I should—"

His voice was clipped. "You should what? Meet someone else's expectations? The canons of Society allow you less than a year to mourn a parent. Do you think grief stops because mourning is over? Such rules might give comfort to those with weak brains or offer an excuse for the ones who are making only a show of sorrow, but you deeply and sincerely miss your father."

"I really do." Tilting back her head so she could see his face, she whispered, "Your own father died not so long ago."

"Yes, and I will carry that grief as part of me for the rest of my life." He gave her a crooked smile. "Not that I think of it often, but it is a part of me, as all my other experiences are."

"You must have seen a lot of death on the Continent."

His smile vanished. "That is a part of war. I made sure it was not a part of *me*. What happens on the battlefield is unfortunate, but it is the way of war."

"How is that different—"

"China, it is no topic for your ears." He laughed humorlessly and stood. "Or for mine. I put it out of my mind with my return to England." He looked away and said quietly, "I would prefer to speak of something else."

She could see the logic in that. She had heard veterans of the wars in America discuss their service, but seldom did they speak of battle. More often, they recalled complaints with food and long marches.

"So why are your guests here to talk about ghosts when you tell me there are no ghost stories attached to the house?" Alexander asked.

She rose as she said, "Father often played host to a *conversazione* where topics were limited only by one's imagination."

"Including things that make sounds in the dark."

She opened her mouth to reply, but halted when a scuffed ball rolled across the floor from behind her to where he was standing. "Where did that come from?"

He picked it up. "You tell me. It is your house and your special room."

"There should not be any balls here. All the children's toys were put away years ago."

"One was obviously missed."

"Or . . ."

Shaking his head, he set the ball on the floor. "Do not confuse simple oversights with ghostly actions."

"I was not." She smiled. "*You* are the one looking for spectral explanations. I was about to say that Mrs.

Mathers's grandchildren live in Stape, the next village to the north, so they may have come up here to play. If so, I want to be certain their ball is returned to them."

"You have a very kind heart."

She looked up into his incredibly blue eyes. They were afire with the craving she knew so well because it ached inside her. In his arms, she could push aside thoughts of everything and everyone, living or dead.

With a choked, half-spoken word, China pulled away and moved to put space between them. She sensed Alexander's astonishment. How could she explain to him that—even if he did not believe—she must concentrate on the vow she had made to Quintus?

"Enough!" Alexander swung her into his embrace. "I have had enough of cat-and-mouse games."

"What games?"

"You and me. I came up here because I am not a man who likes to leave something unfinished." He pressed his lips to her right cheek.

"And what did you leave unfinished?" She fought not to melt into him.

He kissed her left cheek. "Do not play coy with me, China. I prefer when you speak plainly."

"But you *did* kiss me."

"I did." He teased the curve of her ear with his tongue. At her sharp intake of breath he laughed, the sound flowing against her ear like thunder, slow and building to a crescendo. "But I was not *finished* kissing you."

"I had no idea there was something like a finished kiss."

"There must be, because I am not finished with

wanting to kiss you." He brushed her lips lightly with his.

"And when will you be finished?"

"I am not sure." He kissed her, a swift touch that made her eager for more. No, not eager—desperate.

"Will you let me know when you are finished?" She was unsure how she could continue to form words with lips that wanted to be against his.

"You will be the first to know, but we are spending time talking when I have some work to do."

"Work?" She pulled back a half step and stared at him. "You consider *this* work?"

"If it is, I am one lucky man to have it as my job right now."

Her laugh softened beneath his lips before becoming a soft gasp when his fingers edged up from her waist to her breast. Every thought, every sensation centered on the gentle caress of his finger sweeping up along her. Not *every* sensation, for there was a whispered buzz deep within her. Another finger hooked in her sleeve, edging it down over her shoulder, and the sleeve fell down her arm. He cupped her breast in his rough palm. He thumbed its tip, and she moaned with a need she had never known until now.

When he drew her to the floor, he leaned over her. His eyes were no longer cool. They were afire as if with the heart of a flame, searing her with a craving for more. More of his kisses. More of his touch. More of his skin against hers.

He bent toward her and she closed her eyes, anticipating his mouth on hers. Instead, his tongue stroked her breast. She could not silence the soft cry of his name as she arched toward him, pleasure careening through her. Sifting her fingers up through his hair, taking care to avoid the area where he had been injured, she held him against her as he set her skin on fire with the flames that had shifted from his eyes to his tongue.

When he raised his head, she opened her eyes to see his smile. It was all she needed to know that he found as much delight in tasting her as she did in relishing his touch. Reaching between them, she took his hand and drew it to her other sleeve. At the same time, she slid her tongue into his mouth to sample its heat.

A loud crash shattered the pleasure. China sat up, tugging on her dress as she looked around the room in shock. "What happened?"

"The trapdoor slammed closed."

"How did that happen? There is not enough breeze to move it."

"It is your house. If you don't know, then how would I?"

"Must you always be so reasonable?" She laughed softly. "Now, those are words that yesterday I doubted I would ever say."

"I think I should listen only to your question and nothing more, if I want to keep doing this." He gave her a quick kiss before standing up and going to squat next to the trapdoor. Grasping the iron ring at one side of the door, he pulled up.

It did not move.

"Maybe I am weaker than I thought," he said with a half smile. He yanked on the ring again. The metal strained in the wood, which creaked a protest.

Without a word as she pulled her disheveled dress back into place, China edged over beside him and hooked her own hand in the ring. "On the count of three. One. Two. Three." She tugged. Pain whipped up through her arm and lodged in her shoulder.

But the door remained closed.

"Does it lock?" he asked.

"There is a bolt on the bottom side, but why would anyone close and lock it when we were up here? Surely whoever closed the door would have seen . . ." She glanced away, suddenly shy.

His finger on her cheek turned her face toward him. "If we had been seen, the door would not be locked now. Your servants would have sent a chaperone for you instead of locking us together up here. Do not fret about that."

"You are right." She sat on her heels. "So it seems we are stuck up here for now."

"You do not sound worried about that."

"Sian often comes to speak to me before dinner. Even if she does not, when we do not arrive for dinner she will have the house searched from top to bottom. You do not need to worry about missing a meal."

"You know quite well that was not what I meant."

She smiled. "I know."

"You are saucy today."

She draped her arms around his shoulders. "I am always that way when a handsome man is kissing me."

"Always?" He laughed as he put his forehead against hers so their eyes were wondrously close. "I suspect under that Miss Prunes exterior, you are quite the hoyden."

"Miss Prunes?"

"A prim woman. It seems you did not learn too much cant in Town."

"I learned enough to know I should call you a presumptuous pup for addressing me so!"

With a chuckle, he pulled her to him and pressed her down to the floor. "And I will call you incomparable, darling."

She was not sure whether to be shocked at the compliment or the endearment, but he gave her no time to speak as he claimed her mouth anew. Even knowing she should listen for the door to reopen, she quickly became lost in his easy seduction of her senses. His tongue parried with hers as he deepened the kiss until she no longer knew where her mouth began and his ended. It did not matter, for they were locked together in rapture.

He lifted his head away and smiled at her as she whispered, "Why did nobody tell me kisses could be like this?"

"It is something you have to discover for yourself. And I want to discover a lot more about you."

"A journey of discovery is best when shared." She ran her finger along his jaw, and shivers of exaltation rippled through her.

"You are learning quickly, darling." His mouth glided down her neck, then up again so he could whisper in her ear, "As for now . . ." He looked past her and cursed.

Shocked, China watched as he stood and walked away. She came to her knees to stare at a single gray tendril slipping through the cracks around the wooden door in the floor.

Smoke!

She jumped to her feet and shouted, "Fire!" Putting her hands on either side of the open window, she called again, "Fire! In the north tower!"

"Do you see anyone below?"

She leaned out as far as she dared, then came back in as she shook her head. "At this hour, the stablemen are having their evening meal in their quarters beyond the barns."

Smoke, thicker and blacker, seeped past the door. She rushed to open the other windows, then wondered if she had made things worse as more smoke pushed around the door.

"No!" Alexander called when she started to lower one. "The smoke is going to come up here anyhow. Leaving the windows open will give us fresh air. Stand back!"

He slammed his foot against the door. The wood did not budge. He tried again. Same result.

"Dammit!" he snarled as he kept kicking at the door. "Let us out! We will not let you cook us alive, too."

China stared, astonished, at the change in him. "Come away from the smoke! Come over by the window where you can breathe."

"You don't tell me what to do, Rexleigh! Shut up and help me. We must get out of here. I will be damned before I give the frogs the satisfaction of dying because of their dirty tricks."

"What are you talking about?"

He whirled to face her. His eyes were wild and his jaw clenched so tightly she was unsure how he could spit out, "I told you to stow your jabber, Rexleigh. One more word . . . " He began to cough as more smoke poured through the cracks.

She seized his arm and pulled him away from the smoke. The gentle strands had become a flood tide of choking smoke. He shook off her hand and pushed her aside. She hit the window bench, her knees folding to drop her down on it.

"No!" she cried as she jumped to her feet and grabbed his sleeve. "Get away from there! What is wrong with you?"

"I told you . . ." Again he jerked his arm away. When she clamped her hands on it, he raised his fist.

She gasped. Was he about to hit her? "Alexander, stop!"

His hand froze inches from her face. He looked from her to his fist and then back to her. "China?" he asked as if in disbelief. "What are *you* doing here?"

"Don't you know where we are? In Nethercott Castle. In the north tower." She clasped his fist that was still suspended close to her. Lowering it slowly, she watched the savage light fade from his eyes.

"Nethercott Castle?" he repeated. The fierce light faded from his eyes. With a moan, he pulled her close.

She eased back when they both began coughing. The dark smoke puffed into the room as if someone were below with a bellows.

Through the thickening cloud that reeked of something dreadful, Alexander groped toward the floor. He touched the iron ring. With a yelp, he jerked his fingers away. He pulled off his coat and wrapped the sleeve around his hand.

She gasped when she realized what he intended to do. "Don't try to open it! If the ring is that hot, the flames must be close."

Standing, he took her by the shoulders and steered

her away from the trapdoor. "Is there any other way out of here?"

She tried to answer, but her throat and lungs stung as more coughs erupted from her. She pressed her face to his shirt and breathed in the scent of him, an undeniable maleness. He stroked her back and hid his face in her hair.

"The windows," she managed to whisper, relieved that he seemed to be himself again. "Across the roof and down the gargoyles on the eaves. From there we should be able to reach the parapets."

"Is it possible?"

"We talked about trying it when we were children."

"But never did?"

"No."

He started to draw in a deep breath, but halted when he began to choke. Stepping away, he took her hand. "Show me which window."

The smoke flowed out of the windows, keeping her from seeing anything. Her eyes teared as she squinted against the thick smoke. China had been certain she knew the room so well that she could find her way around the small space with her eyes shut. She was wrong. She bumped into the window bench once, stepped back, and had difficulty finding it again. She turned several times before feeling it beneath her outstretched fingers, and ran them along its top until she passed the right window.

"This one. The roof is about five feet below us. We will have to hang from one of the gargoyles by our fingertips and feel our way down with our toes." She shuddered. "It rained earlier. The roof will be wet and slippery."

The smoke closed in around her. She began to

cough and cough, bending almost double. Her head filled with sounds. The flames burning through the door? She could not tell.

"All right, China. We must go. We cannot stay here any longer."

Or that was what she thought she heard Alexander say. Through the roaring in her ears and the coughs exploding out of both of them, she could not discern much but noise.

Then she heard another male voice say, "Wait. Help is below."

She forced her eyes open. Dimly through the black, stinking smoke, she could see the outline of a figure doused in light. Quintus!

"Where are you, China? We need to go now!" Alexander lifted her onto the window bench.

"Keep him from leaving," Quintus pleaded. "Madness and death await him outside."

"What about in here?" she asked.

"In here?" Alexander sounded perplexed, and she wished that he could see his ancestor. "China, we must go now! The fire is burning through the door. When it hits fresh air, it will explode through the whole space."

"Please," Quintus said, his fingers reaching out to her. He jerked them back when she shuddered with abrupt cold. "Please, China, keep him from going out there. I will explain more later. Heed me when I tell you that help is below."

Hoping she was not ensuring both of their deaths, China edged away from the window. "We don't have to go that way, Alexander. Help is on the way."

"Help?" His face, barely visible in Quintus's light, was streaked with smoke. "How do you know?"

Telling him that Quintus had revealed the truth would goad Alexander into climbing out the window. She hated to lie, but said, "I heard someone shouting up to us."

"Through the door?"

"Yes."

"Could you understand the words?" He struggled not to cough on each syllable.

"Enough to know they are coming to get us as soon as the fire is out."

"We might not have that long. The smoke . . ."

Quintus interjected, "It is almost out. Give them just a bit more time."

"Just a bit more time," she repeated, pulling Alexander as far from the door as possible.

Before he could protest, the door was slammed back against the wall. Sian called up. "Are you there?"

"Yes, and we are all right!" China shouted back, then ordered, "Alexander, you go first."

"And leave you here in the smoke?"

"This is no time for chivalry. Go first so you can help me."

He nodded, or she thought he did. Her eyes were blurred by the smoke. Lying on the floor, he dropped his feet into the hole and lowered himself down. She heard a half dozen voices trying to direct him as he dropped to the floor.

"Hurry, China! It is much easier to breathe down here," he shouted.

She glanced over her shoulder to where Quintus's light was barely visible through the smoke. His face was lined with fear, an expression she had not expected to see on a Roman centurion.

"Thank you," he said. "The day of greatest danger to him is on the fifth of September, but every day until then is filled with peril. You saved him today."

"Every day?" She choked as if she suffocated anew.

"Thank you," he repeated, his voice fading along with his light.

"China?" Alexander's shout suggested that if she did not hurry he was going to come back up and carry her down.

Pausing to pick up her copy of *The Lady of the Lake* and slip it into her smoke-stained bodice, she lowered her feet over the edge of the opening. Now was no time to think of modesty. Strong hands settled around her waist, and she released her grip on the upper floor. She started to gasp when they drew her down the length of Alexander's strong body, but the sound came out in more coughs.

He did not release her when her feet touched the floor. As he steadied her, he leaned on her as well. She realized why he did not want to show any weakness when she saw Lord Turnbull. Lady Viola was standing next to him, holding her dog's leash. Miss Upton was on the viscount's other side, her hand clenched on his arm. Squire Palmer Haywood stood to her left wringing his hands, his face as pale as a death mask.

Despite the fact that he was of medium height and build, quite average in looks and temperament, Palmer Haywood was a man who expected to be noticed. He always wore bright colors, today a scarlet waistcoat and saffron cloak. His family, unlike hers, had lived at the edge of the moors for only the past generation. Their wealth had come from repairing ships along the North Sea. Although there had been some whispers about the squire being invested with a title once the war was over, nothing had come of it.

"Squire?" she asked, taking a single lurching step toward him, then halting when her legs threatened to collapse.

"Miss Nethercott, I had not heard that you were up there!" He shook himself and squared his shoulders, then looked around wide-eyed at the others. "We thought only Lord Braddock was trapped in the tower. Are you hurt?"

Coughing, she waved away his words.

"I was here," the squire said, "because of the attack on Lord Turnbull's carriage. I wished to ascertain for myself what damage had been done to him and his party."

Hearing coughs behind her, she reeled to where Alexander was half bent over as his lungs tried to expel the smoke. Putting her hand on his back, she asked, "How are you doing?" She could feel how he strained to breathe. His breath rasped against her hair.

Before he could answer, Sian threw her arms around China and Alexander and began to sob. China untangled herself from the dual embrace. Alexander gave her the slightest nod and a hint of a smile before he began to cough again, for the reek was even more powerful here than above. He lurched a few steps along the hall to sit on a bench. That was enough for China to know he was doing as well as could be expected. After comforting her distraught sister, she looked around at the damage.

It was not as bad as she had feared. Water pooled in any low spot, and shards of porcelain were scattered along the hallway. Two chairs and a small table were upended, all three showing scorch marks to match the ones on the dark blue runner. Wall covering hung in tattered and charred shreds near a window where the rod holding the draperies was blackened and bare. Black wisps remained in the air, and she sneezed as the stench filled every breath.

With a soft cry, Lady Viola dragged her unwilling dog to where Alexander was sitting and began to pelt him with question after question. Was he all right? Wasn't he so wondrously brave to protect their hostess? Did he have any idea how frightened she had been by the whole experience? She did not give him a chance to answer a single one.

Beside China, her sister whispered, "Her fiancé must be the most patient man in the world."

"Why?"

"Lady Viola was about to crumple into tears when she discovered Lord Braddock was caught upstairs above the fire." Sian's mouth twisted in a wry smile. "I should not say this, but it seemed as if her anxiety had a single focus. Lord Turnbull was vexed. If Miss Upton had not calmed him, I have no idea what he might have done. He did not like his betrothed lamenting about another man, especially when the squire was a witness to it all."

Farley, the butler, cleared his throat, and China turned to him. "Yes?" she asked.

"I thought you would want to know that the fire is out, Miss China, and that it appears to have started by the window." He shook his head. "But how do draperies catch on fire all by themselves? There was nothing in the hallway that could have started it."

"Was there anyone burning something outside today?"

"They were changing horseshoes earlier, so it is possible that a spark could have come in and set the draperies alight."

"What is the odd smell?"

"It seems to be tar pitch."

"How would *that* get into the house?"

The butler shrugged as he wiped his hand across his blackened forehead, smearing the smoke residue. "All I can guess is that it could have been a spark from the blacksmith's work that came through the open window. An accident." His eyes, shifting quickly away, told her that he thought the possibility was slight.

So did she. The stable was on the far side of the house, and the wind had not been strong enough to send an ember over the roof and through the window. And she knew it had not been an accident.

In her mind, she heard Quintus's grim words: *The day of greatest danger to him is on the fifth of September, but every day until then is filled with peril.*

Who so wanted to slay Alexander that the murderer had been willing to kill her too? Today had warned her how determined the murderer was. She wondered if they would survive the next attempt.

Chapter 9

Someone was coughing. Hard.

China sent a servant for water and then hurried along the corridor. When she saw the cougher's bright saffron cloak, she knew it was Squire Haywood.

"Are you all right?" she asked as soon as she stood beside where he was bent double with his coughs.

He glanced up at her, and she saw tears along his cheeks. He wiped them away and choked out, "Smoke."

She took the glass the maid handed her and held it out to him. "Take a drink of water. It should help."

His hands shook so hard she lifted the glass to his lips. Some of the water spilled on his scarlet waistcoat and on the floor, but he managed to gulp down most of it between coughs.

Sending the maid for another glass, China took his arm and steered him to a nearby bench. He sat heavily and dashed away the last of the tears that rolled along his face.

"Embarrassing," he muttered.

"Don't be embarrassed. The smoke has left all of us much the worse for wear."

"You look lovely."

She smiled. "You are too kind, but smudges of smoke have never been attractive."

Coming to his feet, he held out a handkerchief. "You are welcome to this."

"It will take soap and water to get me clean." She put her hand on his arm. "But thank you."

"As you wish. You know I would do anything for you." Color flashed up his face. "I did not mean to suggest that I should wash . . . That is . . . I would never . . ."

China took pity on him and chuckled. "I did not misconstrue what you said. We have been friends for too many years for me to see anything but kindness in your words."

"Is that how you see us?" he said softly, clasping her hand.

She gently pulled her hand from his and was relieved when he released it. He had been eager for her company in the months before Father died, but had not called since then. She had heard that he was courting a widow living on the north edge of the moors. Either that had been only a rumor, or the situation had changed.

She quickly spoke of another subject. "Did you learn anything about what started the fire? When I examined the area, I did not see anything unusual, save the strange smell that Farley said could be tar pitch."

"An interesting opinion, even though I saw no sign of that. Whoever set the fire left no clues. A wise move, because burning a house is a felony, and the punishment is hanging. Maybe I will learn more after I question the witnesses."

"When you are finished, you are welcome to join us for dinner."

He shook his head. "Maybe some other time. Duties first."

"You know that Sian and I would enjoy your company."

"Yes." He took both hands this time and gazed deeply into her eyes. "I promise that as soon as I learn anything, I will let you know."

"Thank you." She tried to withdraw her hands again, and when he hesitated to release them, she feigned an attack of coughing, using both hands to cover her mouth.

He cleared his throat. "I should let you rest. Good day."

She nodded as she watched him walk away, his steps uneven. There were too many questions and no answers. Nobody had seen the fire start. Nobody could explain how the trapdoor had closed and locked. And why had Lady Viola been dismayed when China arranged for the butler to assist Alexander to his room? She acted as if Alexander were her betrothed rather than Lord Turnbull.

It was too bizarre to think about. China went to dress for dinner, wishing she had even one answer.

Her maid quickly supplied it. Bernice was a local girl, not a fancy French maid like the one Lady Viola had brought with her. Bernice's Yorkshire accent was almost as broad as she was, and her sole bad habit, beyond gossiping, was believing that the lads in the stable who flirted with her had good intentions. Dressed in a simple gray gown and a starched white apron, she was seldom without a smile.

But this evening was one of those times. She had not smiled once as she brushed China's hair. " 'Twas inevitable there would be trouble. Nay, I was not surprised to 'ear those screams."

"The fire was put out, and no one was hurt." The platitudes were easier to speak than were the fears still roiling within her. If nobody had noticed the flames and smoke . . . No, she did not want to think about creeping across the roof with Alexander.

"Truly 'tis unfortunate that 'is lordship 'as to be 'ere now."

China was tempted to agree, but she could not, especially with her maid, who loved to prattle about everything at Nethercott Castle. All she could ask was, "Which 'his lordship'?"

"Either one. 'Aving both 'ere at the same time is an invitation to trouble."

"Why?" China watched Bernice's face in the glass. Her maid, usually so eager to share chitchat, was hesitating, as if deciding what to say and how to say it.

"Lord Braddock and the Turnbull family are now enemies, Miss Nethercott."

"Enemies? Why?" She recalled the ice in Alexander's voice each time he spoke to the viscount. The sound vanished when he addressed anyone else.

"They say"—Bernice never explained who *they* were, and China had learned not to ask—"that Lord Braddock 'as 'ad scant dealings with the Turnbulls since Lord Turnbull's sister, Norah, broke 'er betrothal to 'im to become Lady Maurice Erwin."

China was astonished. Alexander was an enticing man. If he had kissed Lord Turnbull's sister even once as he had kissed her, why would Norah have ended their engagement?

Trying to keep her voice even, she asked, "Did *they* say why the betrothal was dissolved?"

"No, although they 'ave 'inted it was because she did not like 'im buyin' a commission to fight the French." Twinkles appeared in Bernice's brown eyes. "But I shall do my best to find out the truth, Miss China. 'E is quite the well-favored gentleman, isn't 'e? Not only that, but 'e 'as that grand title and the lands to match. I 'ave to say I am not the only one curious about why she would toss 'im aside for another simply because 'e wanted to be a 'ero."

"Bernice . . ." Even though she had been thinking quite the same herself, it was inappropriate for her maid to speak so.

"Forgive me, Miss China, but I thought ye should know, with yer havin' taken a likin' to 'im and all." Bernice clamped her lips closed, knowing she had said too much again.

China did not scold her. Every member of the staff was likely to be discussing the same topic. "No wonder there was so much tension when I welcomed Lord Turnbull and his companions this afternoon."

Bernice continued to brush China's hair. Her smooth rhythm never faltered, but her voice did as she answered, "If I 'ad known before, Miss Nethercott, I would 'ave alerted ye."

"I know you would have."

"Please don't tell anyone I told ye this. Mrs. Mathers would send me back to the scullery if she knew I was gossipin' about Lord Braddock and yer other guests."

"I shall not say anything." Reaching back, she grasped Bernice's hand. "I appreciate your being frank, but promise me that you will not speak of this among the staff. Promise me as well that if any member of the household tries to speak to you of the antipathy between any of the guests, you will pass along my request that the subject is off-limits."

"It shall not be easy to persuade them, Miss China."

She smiled. "I have seen you be very persuasive. I trust you to do what you can to halt the gossip before it reaches our guests' ears."

"But if I 'appen to 'ear someone speak of the reason . . ." She laughed as she finished pinning up China's hair in soft curls that fell around her ears.

China swallowed her sigh. Even with a pledge to prevent the guests from overhearing the whispers, Bernice could not keep from enjoying the gossip. And, China had to own, she was curious why any woman would give Alexander his congé.

Alexander sat on an overturned bucket and watched Naylor pick at the food on his plate. The coachman's right arm bulged with bandages beneath his bloodstained livery, but he had regained some of what Alexander assumed was his normal color.

"Jumped right out of the bushes, m'lord," Naylor grumbled as he pushed beans around on his plate. "I ne'er saw 'im until 'e was callin' for us to 'and over our valuables."

"Did you get a good look at him?"

"Not as good as I would 'ave liked to. I was whippin' up the 'orses, tryin' to go 'round 'im, so Lord Turnbull and the ladies would not be 'urt."

"You are a devoted servant, Naylor."

The man wore a weary smile. "Kind of ye to say that, m'lord, but if I 'ad been a bit more alert—"

"Bah! No one expects a man to keep his eyes on the road and still see both sides of it."

"Lord Turnbull 'as very strict standards."

Alexander was tempted to say what he thought of the hypocrisy of the viscount's having *strict* standards for others when Turnbull never established such high goals for himself. To speak so to the coachee would be rude. Such a turn of conversation would be uncomfortable for the man who suffered enough—not just from the ball wound to his arm, but from having to serve Turnbull.

"What can you tell me of the highwayman?" he asked.

"A black cloth covered 'is face, and 'e wore a cape that 'id the rest of 'im." He set the plate aside and picked up a tankard near his feet. He took a deep drink of the ale, wiping his mouth with his hand. "I ne'er saw 'is mount."

"Your description matches that of the man who halted Miss China and me a few days ago, but you encountered him almost a league from where we did. I wonder why he is wandering so far."

"The local magistrate might 'ave set a watch for 'im."

"When the fox has the dogs on its tail, it goes to earth. Why would a highwayman risk everything by being so far from his lair?"

Naylor started to shrug, then winced. "I don't 'ave any answer for ye, m'lord. 'Ave ye talked to the lads in the stable? They might know somethin'."

"That is a fine idea, Naylor." He stood with care,

staggering slightly. His head still felt as if it might float away, even as pain ground into his skull. He held out his own tankard, and the coachee took it with a grateful smile. "I think I will speak with them now."

Almost an hour later, Alexander's hope had faded. The lads knew tales of the highwayman, some of which might have been true. Most, such as the tale of the black-cloaked thief carrying off a full-grown cow on his shoulders, were not.

There must be answers. He needed to find them. Telling himself to forget the accursed highwayman, he went to look at a closer problem—the fire that could have killed both China and him.

In the corridor where the fire had begun, he examined the stained walls, the small puddles of water hidden in the corners, the charred table. He looked up when he heard footsteps and saw Mrs. Mathers. The housekeeper was a matronly woman whose hair and eyes were only a shade lighter than her gown. Around her eyes hints of creases suggested she smiled often, even though she was not smiling as she approached where he was squatting next to the charred table.

"I do not wish to hurry you, my lord," she said quietly.

"Am I going to be late for dinner, Mrs. Mathers?" He came to his feet and wiped soot from his hands.

"Miss China would be distressed if you were."

"She seems to appreciate everything running on schedule."

"She has enough to worry about."

He concealed his surprise at the housekeeper's answer. It was both a polite response and a scold, revealing how much the housekeeper concerned herself with the well-being of the Nethercott sisters.

That thought convinced him to be honest. "I am investigating where the fire started in hopes of being able to tell her more than we know now."

"She knows someone is anxious to see you dead."

"*You* know that?"

"As the housekeeper, I am privy to much, my lord," she replied, as if that answered his question.

"There seems to be nothing here to suggest what caused the fire," he said. "Other than that smell of tar."

"We found nothing out of the ordinary when we cleaned up the debris." She laced her fingers together in front of her. "Both Farley and I instructed everyone to keep their eyes open for anything unusual."

He nodded. "No one found anything?"

"All they found were some scraps of gritty fabric that had not burned completely, and shards of glass and ceramic from broken pieces. Two paintings were completely destroyed." She sighed. "One was Miss Sian's work. She is an accomplished artist, my lord, and it was a shame to have even one of her pictures ruined."

"I am sorry to hear that."

"And sorry, too, that there was nothing to point a finger at someone in this house for being behind the fire?"

"For the first time, you are misreading me, Mrs. Mathers. I have no reason to suspect anyone in this house of wanting to do it such damage."

"As well as damage to you and Miss China?"

He had to admire how forthright the housekeeper was. "Does she have any enemies?"

"None that I know of, but that does not mean much."

"I suspect it means a great deal." He smiled. "I am sure you keep a close eye on the Nethercott sisters."

Mrs. Mathers's smile became warmer. "It is one of the best parts of my position, my lord. I have known them since they were tiny babes, and after their mother died, I felt almost as if they were my own. I have watched them grow to lovely young women. I will not stand silent while someone threatens them."

"You do not believe China has any enemies?"

"She does not, but you do. She was warned about that by the phantom she saw up at the old camp."

He clenched his jaw so as not to spit out the oath that would scorch the housekeeper's ears as surely as the fire had the wall. He had hoped to find an ally with the housekeeper. Instead, she was now talking about ghosts.

"I know you do not believe, my lord," Mrs. Mathers continued, "but anyone who has lived their whole life near the moors, as I have, knows without question that there are more things occurring around them than can be explained by logic and science."

"But specters that come with warnings of impending tragedy? That is a far-fetched tale."

"Is it? Your own father, it is said, believed in ghosts."

"I never heard that."

"It is not spoken of any longer, but there were many whispers when he was not much more than your age. The rumors said that he was riding across the northern edge of the moors alone when he became lost. No one saw even a hint of him for almost a fortnight, and it was believed he had been set upon by bandits and killed for the coin in his purse. Then one day he returned to your family's house a changed man. It was shortly afterward that he left Yorkshire."

"He left because he and my grandfather had a battle-royal, and they parted ways, never to speak again. There was nothing supernatural about it."

Mrs. Mathers regarded him with pity. "If your father told you that, he was not being honest."

"He told me only that they quarreled. He never explained why."

The housekeeper arched a single eyebrow.

The motion irritated him. "That he did not wish to relive the argument does not mean there was anything out of the ordinary about why he left Braddock Court and never returned. Such brangles happen often between fathers and sons."

"Yes, they happen, but not for the reasons your father gave up his ancestral home." She glanced around the ravaged passage. "There were many rumors why he rushed away so soon upon returning home, but I found only one believable." She paused for him to ask her to explain. When he remained silent, she went on. "Your father saw something so accursed on the moors that he knew he must flee."

"Even if I were to assume that you are right, China does not seem frightened of what she believes to be a ghost. She has described it as a Roman soldier and even has a name for it. Quinlinus or . . ."

"Quintus," Mrs. Mathers said with quiet precision. "Quintus Valerius, a centurion."

"Around whom she feels comfortable, not terrified."

"Because that is how she sees the spirit that has

been wandering the moors for centuries. Even if the spirit was originally in the body of a Roman soldier, we cannot know how it manifested itself to your father. Whatever he saw changed his life, as seeing Quintus now will alter Miss China's and yours. One thing is certain: Whatever it is seeks an escape from its connection to Rawcliffe and the moors."

He scowled, wanting to refute her words. He wanted them not to make any sense. But they did.

As a child, he had tried to understand why his father refused to step foot outside during the full moon. His mother had insisted that Alexander be sent to a neighbor's home each month around the full moon, but he sneaked home one night. What he witnessed terrified him, and he had willingly stayed away each month after that. He had wanted to speak to his mother about what he had seen and heard, but did not want to add more to the burden she bore.

Odd, he had not thought of that night for years. Scanning the damaged corridor as if for the first time, he knew he must not let the past muddle his thoughts. He had been trained to look at facts, not superstition and supposition.

The facts were clear. Even if the fire had been an accident, someone had closed and locked the door. No matter. He would keep his eyes open, and he vowed to do everything he possibly could to protect China.

He bade the housekeeper a good evening and walked away as a smile inched along his lips. He knew exactly where to start. By staying close to China, he could offer her the best protection. Never had a dangerous task sounded so wonderful.

Chapter 10

The dining room was empty when China walked in a half hour after she had finished dressing. It was one of her least favorite rooms in the castle. The dark paneling and the crests set into the tall, narrow windows suggested the house was centuries older than it truly was. The floors were uneven, leaving the chairs to get caught on the edges of stones or to rock when one shifted. None of her father's collectibles were displayed here. He had disliked the dining chamber as much as China did. With no hearth, the room was often damp and cold, even during the hottest summers. If it had been the intention of the builders to make the room as uncomfortable as possible, they had succeeded.

Her gown of pale green silk whispered against the floor as she went to the long table in the middle of the room. Like everything else, it had been made to look ancient, even though it was less than a hundred years old.

China smiled. Her sister had outdone herself in arranging the evening's dinner in the wake of the fire. The windows had been cast open wide, allowing the rising wind to sweep away the stench of the smoke. The table was set with the family's favorite Flow Blue china and heirloom crystal. Silver platters glittered in the light from the candelabra placed at each end of the long mahogany table. On the sideboard of the same rich wood, more candles burned brightly.

Servants wandered in and out, finishing the preparations. The six place settings were close together at one end of the table to allow for easy conversation. For a moment, China was tempted to ask the servants to move them farther apart so they could avoid discussion of the afternoon's events.

"Don't be silly," she chided herself. A good hostess would make sure her guests had as many opportunities as needed to discuss it, even if she wished to stop thinking about how close she and Alexander had come to dying. "At least I shall not have to worry about keeping the conversation going."

"With yourself?" came Alexander's voice from the door behind her.

Turning, she wondered if she would ever become accustomed to the sight of him entering a room. He was not as classically handsome as Lord Turnbull, but there was something about him that drew her eyes as well as the eyes of every female servant in the room. Not even his slow steps or the walking stick lessened his aura of strength and tightly controlled passion.

"Am I early?" he asked when she did not reply. His waistcoat was a surprisingly bright green that matched the ribbons in her bodice and sleeves. In his casually brushed black hair, the small bandage was vivid. His blue gaze was so intense it almost had a physical presence.

She fought against reaching out to draw his arms around her. In the tower room, she had been enthralled by his touch. She knew how easily she could be lured back into such intimacy with him. And how much she wanted to be.

"China?" he asked when she remained silent.

"Excuse me," she replied. "I was thinking."

"So I noticed."

Hoping her face was not fiery red, she hurried to say, "I believe the others are delayed."

He laughed as he walked with cautious steps toward her. "We were the only ones smoked like sausages, and yet we are the only ones who made it to dinner on time."

"Maybe our adventure left us hungry."

He lifted a curl off her shoulder and ran his finger along the sensitive skin behind her ear. "You have no idea how hungry, darling."

She wanted to say that she understood exactly what he meant because she felt the same. That would be rash, because it would be an invitation to more soul-searing kisses. Even saying nothing, she was more aware of her skin—and his—than she had ever been of anyone else's.

He cupped her chin and tilted it up so she could gaze into his eyes. "Do you regret what we enjoyed in the tower?"

"No!" She smiled when he did at her impassioned answer.

"I am glad to hear that. I . . ." He coughed hard and deep.

"Do you want something to drink?"

He waved her question aside, but kept coughing.

Exasperated, she grabbed his arm and steered him toward a chair. "Sit." She motioned to a footman. "Bring Lord Braddock something cold to drink."

"As long as," Alexander added as the footman nodded, "you bring something for Miss Nethercott, too. She might like everyone to believe she is well, but I can hear how scratchy her voice is. Can't you?"

The footman glanced at her and gulped, as if he feared betraying her by answering. "Yes, m'lord, I can 'ear that." He gulped again.

As soon as the door closed behind the sprinting footman, Alexander said, "You disconcerted your servants."

"Me? He was unsettled by you."

"It is obvious, even to an outsider, how much your servants care about the Nethercott family. Too much to trap one of you in a tower room and set a smoky fire beneath it."

She wrapped her arms around herself. "Please don't say things like that."

"I was complimenting your household staff." He sighed. "To own the truth, I was showing my relief that you should be safe in the house. I doubt you can go anywhere without at least one servant's eyes upon you. As well, you can be certain that they will report anything out of the ordinary without delay."

Drawing out another of the tall chairs, she sat facing him. "The most out-of-the-ordinary thing was what you said in the tower room."

"I said a lot of things there." He ran his fingers against her cheek. "You need to be more specific."

"You said some things that made it sound as if you believed you were fighting the French again."

"What are you talking about?"

"You spoke of the French—"

"You must have been mistaken. Why would I speak of *them* when I was concentrating on getting you to safety?"

"I doubt you knew I was there."

"Nonsense."

"If it is nonsense, then why did you call me Rexleigh?"

He jerked his fingers back and looked away. She waited for him to reply, but he said nothing. It took all her strength not to demand that he explain what he was thinking, not to shut her out when they had been so close.

The footman returned with two glasses of lemonade. She took them, thanked him, and nodded toward the door so the footman would know that she wished to speak with Alexander without other ears present. Only when the door closed behind him again did she ask, "Who is Rexleigh?"

He did not answer quickly. When he did, he said, "I think you misunderstood what I said, China."

"You used the name more than once." She set a glass in front of him, but he did not pick it up.

"I think you misunderstood what I said, China," he repeated in a tone that suggested he did not want to speak about it further.

China started to answer, but was halted by the sound of footsteps from the hallway. She was pleased to see Sian escorting their guests—and Lady Viola's dog—into the dining room. Thank heavens for her sister! Sian was recalling her duties as hostess and performing them so well that their guests would not miss China's company.

"Lord Braddock!" Lady Viola rushed across the room, again with her dog in tow, to where he was slowly coming to his feet. "How are you faring? I tremble at the thought of what you endured this afternoon."

"Along with China," he said quietly.

The lady, dressed in a glorious cloud of white gauze and silk that matched her beauty, did not look at China. "All of England will be grateful that one of her greatest heroes did not die in a careless fire." She did not seem to notice how Alexander winced at her pronouncement, spoken so loudly every servant in the dining room and beyond could hear it. Continuing to prattle about how brave he was, she inched forward until she stood between him and China.

Several oaths filled China's head when Lady Viola's dog sat on her right slipper, but she was unsure whether she wanted to aim them at Lady Viola or her spoiled pet or Alexander. Knowing she must keep those thoughts to herself lest she embarrass everyone in the room, she went to where Lord Turnbull seemed quite intent on something Miss Upton was saying. So intent that he acted as if he had neither seen how his betrothed threw herself at Alexander nor heeded how she lauded him. Perhaps he was accustomed to how she flirted with other men, and accepted it.

"Forgive us for being late." Lord Turnbull was dressed as elegantly as his fiancée, his black coat worn over buff breeches. The buckles on his shoes glistened like mirrors. "I was so fascinated with the stories your sister was telling about some of the items we passed in the hallway that I daresay we lost track of the time."

"I am pleased you are enjoying yourself." China made sure her smile included Miss Upton, who was dressed simply in a pink gown that seemed to dust color on her otherwise pale cheeks. Her curls, China noticed for the first time, were the exact shade of her cousin's, but refused to be restrained in a perfect halo around her face as Lady Viola's did.

"It is a beautiful house, filled with incredible art." Miss Upton's voice was an intriguing contralto. "There was one painting, a painting of the moors, that took my breath away, for it was skillfully done."

"Tomorrow," China said, "if you want to point it out to me, I may be able to tell you more about the artist."

The viscount laughed. "We already have learned much about the artist, for it is Miss Sian's work."

China smiled at her sister. There was a happy glow around her that China had not seen in more than a year, and she understood why Sian had agreed to have guests at Nethercott Castle. Not to show off her work, but to share it so it might give others joy.

"On the morrow," China said, "I will show you my favorite piece done by my sister. It is a small charcoal sketch of the staircase, which is the only remnant of what was once Rosedale Abbey. She captured the lovely mystery of its age with the vines crawling up the old stones."

"I am eager to see it. I—" Miss Upton clamped her lips closed as her cousin approached with both arms wrapped around one of Alexander's. The dog trotted obediently behind them.

China exchanged a glance with her sister, whose shoulders rose and fell with a silent sigh. China shared Sian's regret that Miss Upton's brief conversation had come to an abrupt end when her cousin rejoined them. Miss Upton's comments were interesting and not solely about herself.

China learned quickly that Lady Viola monopolized everyone's attention. She flirted with Lord Turnbull and Alexander, assuming both men would focus their eyes on her. Handing the dog's leash to her cousin, she slipped one arm through the viscount's and the other through Alexander's as she led them to examine the herald crests in the windows. Miss Upton followed without uttering a word, even when the dog gave a low whine.

"She is quite the coquette, isn't she?" Sian asked.

Hearing a hint of admiration in her sister's voice, China frowned. "Why do you make that sound good?"

"Because I have never seen anyone—man or woman—who can bring every topic back to oneself so facilely and so relentlessly." Sian smiled. "She even shifted the discussion about every portrait or piece of art that Miss Upton paused to examine back to herself or that silly, spoiled dog."

"The table looks perfect," China said, wanting to change the subject from Lady Viola. "Thank you for tending to it."

"I arranged the seating as you asked, as well as the details you always forget." She laughed. "I know such things do not interest you."

"Which is why I was always grateful when you handled the arrangements for Father's guests." She glanced around the large room. "It is odd to recall that the last time we entertained here it was for his birthday."

Sian's smile fell away. "Don't think that way, China. Think of this evening and how much fun we can have trying to prevent Lady Viola from talking endlessly about herself."

"I would prefer to spend the evening otherwise."

"With Lord Braddock?" She grinned. "How is he? And you! How are you feeling?"

"Feeling that I will be glad when the evening is over." She gave her sister a hug. "And Alexander seems to be back to his normal self. He knows now where and when he is."

Sian gave her a puzzled look, but China pretended not to see it. She had never guarded her words from her sister, and she did not like doing so now. Yet what could she say? Explain how Alexander had acted oddly in the tower room? She would not cast aspersions on him until she could be certain herself what had happened.

Pushing the thoughts aside, she gathered the guests and herded them to the table. They found their chairs. China wondered if she was the only one who noticed Lady Viola's brief pout upon discovering she was not seated next to Alexander.

When the first course was served, Lady Viola insisted on a bowl for her dog. "My precious Princess is starving. The events of the day have left her distressed, and a nice bowl of soup will ease her stomach."

The footman said, "M'lady, if you would hand me the dog's leash, I will take it to the kitchen and—"

"My precious Princess does *not* eat in the kitchen." The lady's indignation alternated with her cooing apologies to the dog for the insult. The dog hopped on its hind feet, then nipped at the servers' ankles as they tried not to spill the hot soup.

"Hewson," China said, "please bring a bowl for the dog."

"And a napkin," Lady Viola ordered. "Princess likes one tied around her neck while she is eating so she does not dirty her fur."

Maybe the lady believed that, but China doubted anyone else did when the dog squirmed and growled while the footman worked to wrap the cloth around it. She was relieved when the process was finished without Hewson being bit.

After Lady Viola was satisfied that her dog would be served each course, she said, "Tell us the amazing story of your sister Jade and the ghost she saw."

"There is not much to tell." China dipped her spoon into her soup. "Jade first saw the phantom after the first anniversary of our father's death. Events unfolded from there."

"Oh, there must be more to the story. Your father was interested in peculiar subjects. What other strange creatures do you anticipate discovering in the wake of his death?"

"None." *But you and your spoiled dog*, she wanted to add. She refrained as she sampled the mushroom soup.

Lady Viola's lips pursed. "I don't believe that!"

China's head snapped up.

"Viola, my sweet," Lord Turnbull said, "this topic might be better discussed when our hostess is not on edge from what she experienced this afternoon."

Again China stiffened. The viscount's faint smirk intimated that he was speaking of more than the fire.

But why? Did he know how Alexander had held her in the tower room? Again she looked down at her soup. *Someone* had lowered the door and latched it. Whoever that was could have seen her in Alexander's arms. But could it have been Lord Turnbull? Yes, he and Alexander shared a deep antipathy, but she had always deemed the viscount a decent, albeit annoying man.

"Experiences?" Alexander asked in the same emotionless voice he had used before with the viscount. "I know of our hostess's experience with the fire. Has something else occurred of which I was unaware?"

"I mean the fire and the smoke, of course." His faint smile became a scowl. "If there were experiences beyond that, I am ignorant of them, Braddock."

"Gentlemen," she hurried to say, "do tell me how you find the soup. Cook is proud of her mushroom creations."

Lord Turnbull muttered an answer, while Alexander gave her a quick smile. Before there had been even a second of silence, Lady Viola dabbed the corners of her mouth with a napkin, then began her questions anew about ghosts and the late Lord Nethercott's studies. The lady did not seem deterred by her betrothed's subtle attempts to change the subject, or his more blatant comments about postponing the conversation until the morrow.

When they rose after what seemed like a jousting match rather than pleasant conversation, China felt only relief that her guests planned to retire early. She wished she could, too, but her nerves jangled with the dual assault of Alexander's touch and the horror of the smoke-filled room.

"But," Lady Viola said, pausing in the doorway as

she gathered her dog in her arms, "tomorrow evening we *must* talk about ghosts. Do you think your
late father sent them to prove he had been right in
his research?"

"We can speak about that then. Who knows what
we might learn from one another?" China wished
that Quintus would choose that moment to show
himself in full battle regalia. That sight would shock
even the verbose Lady Viola into silence.

As the others walked toward the staircase, she
turned to watch the footmen and the maidservants
clear the table. She had seen the worried glances they
sent in her direction when they thought she was not
aware of them. She wished she could tell them that
the hazard to the household would be past in less
than a fortnight. Some would believe her, for they
had been excited when it became known that Jade
had seen a ghost. Others would be as disbelieving
as Alexander.

"China?"

She spun about to see Alexander standing in the
doorway. Fatigue dimmed his eyes. Despite how
strong he acted, he had been confined to bed yesterday.

"Yes?"

"May I speak with you?"

"I believe you are."

He smiled, and she realized it was the first genuine
smile she had seen on his face all evening. "Are you
always so literal?"

"It makes it easier for one's words not to be
misunderstood."

"Then I shall be frank. Did you mean to be as

obvious as you were tonight with the table seating arrangements?"

"I did not think . . . That is . . . Sian—"

"I know you well enough now to be certain you instructed your sister where each of us should sit. You thought you would keep Turnbull and me as far apart as possible so we would not come to blows before dessert was served."

"I did not want you to feel uncomfortable this evening. Until a few hours ago, I had no idea why you were angry with the viscount."

"Until a few hours ago? What did you learn a few hours ago?" His eyes narrowed, making their intensity even more piercing.

"Only of your erstwhile expectations of marrying Lord Turnbull's sister."

He grimaced, then astonished her by smiling. "I should have guessed. I am sure as soon as your guests arrived, someone wasted no time in parading out the tale of my connection with the Turnbull family to entertain you."

She put her hand on his coat sleeve and looked into his eyes, but they revealed nothing. "Alexander, having your past resurrected here must make you ill at ease with the family of a woman who was once so important to you."

"Important?" He laughed, but a hint of sorrow stole the lightness from the sound. "You make love sound unemotional. You deserve to know the truth, China, rather than the elaborations that have circulated through the *ton*. When I offered marriage to Norah Turnbull, I adored her with a passion that was dangerously close to obsession. She did not feel the same, so she chose to wed Maurice Erwin. I assume that is the gist of what you were told."

"That is most of it."

"Your sources are well-informed."

"I doubt there is any house in England where the servants cannot ferret out every secret with the speed of a winter gale." She dampened her lips with the tip of her tongue, then asked, "Do you love her still?"

"I would rather discuss this beyond the ears of so many potential eavesdroppers." As he offered his arm, he glanced toward the table, where the servants were removing the last of the dishes.

"Are you sure? You are fatigued and not as steady as you were earlier."

"You need not fear I will fall on top of you." He gave her a rakish grin, adding quietly, "Unless it is on purpose."

"Now *that* comment is something *I* do not wish others to overhear," she whispered back, glad all the servants were by the table.

He drew her out into the hallway. "Can I hope it is because you want to keep what we have shared a tempting secret?"

"You can hope for whatever you please."

"You are being sassy tonight." He laughed. "Yet you scarcely spoke a word at dinner."

"I had nothing to say."

"Or any chance to say it. Poor Turnbull. His intended has never learned to keep her tongue behind her teeth. She appears to be as much in love with the sound of her own voice as with him."

"That is a horrible thing to say."

"Only if the truth is horrible."

Alexander continued to tease China as they walked out into the night. With light splashing through open doorways, there would be no suggestion of inappropriateness, especially with the terrace in full view of so many windows.

She walked across the uneven stones to gaze up at the ridge that marked the upsweep of the land toward the moors. The moon had emerged from above the cliffs. Its light, cool yet powerful, spread in a path across the pond beyond the garden before climbing up the front of the three wings of the house.

"Which one of your ancestors raised Nethercott Castle?" Alexander asked as he walked closer to where she stood.

"It happened after King Henry's men *razed* the abbey."

He leaned the walking stick against the half wall separating the terrace from the garden. "Tell me about who built this house."

"I have no idea how-many-times-great an uncle he was, but he bought the land from the crown and designed the house. He used the stones from what was left of the Rawcliffe Priory to have the house built."

"Even though he had parapets set on the walls, he must not have worried about defense, because there would be no way to protect this house against attack from higher ground. The land slopes up in every direction from where we are standing."

"Do you always think about war?"

He frowned. "I try not to think about it ever."

"But you make comments often about defense and battles."

"Perhaps it is as simple as that my mind has not yet completely returned to civilian life, even though the war is over."

"I would think you would be eager to forget."

"I am. Maybe," he said with a chuckle, "I should do as Turnbull has and find something to occupy me."

"What do you mean?"

"He has taken on the task of keeping his betrothed under control."

"A task nobody asked him to assume."

"Who else should keep her under control but her fiancé?"

She walked away, not wanting to quarrel.

Alexander moved to catch up with her far more quickly than she had expected, taking her arm for a moment. As his fingers brushed her skin she yearned to turn, throw her arms around him and find his mouth with hers.

Instead, she looked at him. "Yes?"

"Why are you stamping away like an old tough insulted by a young man's flirtatious smile?"

"Did you think you were flirting with me?"

He put his hand on the terrace wall. "What is bothering you, China? You are acting peculiar."

"You hardly know me."

"I know you are a strong-willed woman who has a sense of integrity." He gave her a heart-melting grin. "And a sensuality that thrills me as nothing has in far longer than I want to admit."

She lowered her eyes, overwhelmed by his words. He put his fingers under her chin and tipped it up. "China, you have saved my life twice. Don't you realize that creates a bond between us that allows us to forget the silly games that men and women play?"

"I don't know those games."

"That is no surprise. I must say it is a pleasure. Just as you are." He stepped closer and brushed his lips gently against hers. With a half-swallowed moan, he drew back. "If you did know how to play those games, you would be reminding me now that we are alone and that I should not take such liberties."

"Why should I tell you what you already know?"

"That, darling, is part of the game."

She could not ease the trembling that swept along her. "But I do not know how to play that game, or so you just said." Hearing her voice quaver, she fought to steady it. She needed to think of something other than his touch, his mouth, his firm chest so close to her. She latched onto the one aspect of the evening that had vexed her. "I suppose I could take lessons from an expert."

"Who?"

"Lady Viola."

He gave a mock groan. "The lady has learned the game too well, because she now is a challenge for Turnbull to control."

"Control! You said that before. Why should anyone want to control anyone else?"

"It is a man's place—"

She rolled her eyes. "Please do not lecture me about the differences between a man's place and a woman's. I saw too much of that in Town. Simply because I was six months short of my twenty-sixth birthday, it was unheard-of that I could oversee a household without a watch-dog. Had I been married or a bit older or a man, I would have been able to supervise that house all on my own."

"Are you done?"

His calm voice banished her outrage. It was unlike her to be so outspoken. "For the moment."

"Then if you would allow me to finish . . ."

"As long as you refrain from saying something incendiary."

"I have had enough fire for today."

The warm flush in her face vanished, consumed by a deathly cold. She had not meant to remind him of the near disaster. "Alexander—"

He put his fingers on her arm as he said, "Let me say what I need to, China, before you label me an unthinking cur."

She nodded. Speaking when his rough, warm skin was touching her seemed impossible.

"I was about to say," he went on, "that most men serving in the army follow a certain code of conduct. That standard becomes so deeply ingrained that it is difficult for most of us to shrug it aside when one's duty is complete."

"Are you speaking of Lord Turnbull?"

"Yes."

Even in the dim light, she could see his jaw tighten. She knew she should change the subject, but when she opened her mouth out spilled, "You never answered my question." She raised her gaze to meet his. "Do you still love Lord Turnbull's sister?"

"Maybe I did not want to answer it."

"Forgive me, Alexander." She shifted so she was not facing him. "I don't know what is wrong with me tonight. I am saying everything wrong. I should not ask you about what is clearly a painful subject."

"We both can be excused for being on edge tonight." He put his arm around her shoulders. "And the topic is not too painful." His other hand cupped her cheek, and she looked at him as he said, "Not any longer."

"I am glad."

"So am I." Drawing her toward the far edge of the light, he asked, "Why do I let you ask questions no one else would dare voice in my company?"

"Perhaps because you finally wish to answer them." She sat on a bench at the very fringes of the light.

Alexander's smile broadened. Her motion spoke clearly. She would not go into the darkness. Was it because she was unsure of what might happen? No, it was because she *was* sure of what would happen, and she was not ready to offer herself to a man she knew so little about.

She had no idea who he truly was, other than the great war hero, a mask the country forced him to wear. If he told her that he had fled to the nearly deserted moors to escape the endless public adulation, would she laugh? During the war, he had done as he had to. Nothing more, nothing less. Luck had kept him alive.

"I really am no good at the game between men and women," China said. "If I were, I would have devised some witty quips to ease you out of your dismals."

"I am not suffering from dismals, but exasperation."

"With me?" Her eyes widened.

"Not with you, but with myself for failing to discover who set that fire."

She quivered once, then stiffened her shoulders. She was not a woman who would need someone to control her. He admired her strength, which had not been obvious when he'd first seen her pretty face. The heart of a lioness hidden within a kitten.

"I found no answers either," she whispered. "I am sorry, Alexander."

"Sorry?"

"You could have been killed. I promised to keep you safe."

He shook his head. "No, China, I do not want to discuss ghosts and curses again."

"Whether you want to discuss it or not makes no difference. I pledged to protect you, and I almost failed. I am—"

He could not bear to hear her apologize again. He grasped her shoulders, pulled her to her feet and captured her mouth. She softened against him. A sensation more powerful than the agony pounding his skull erupted through him, hardening every muscle. Her delicious lips were sweet and warm, and the very thing he needed to forget what had driven him from home.

He drew her toward the grass, raising his mouth far enough so he could gaze at her face in the moonlight. Her lips were gently parted and swollen from his eager kiss. With a moan, he reclaimed them, as he ached to have all of her. Her arms curved up under his coat, and he yearned to rip off the linen and silk between his skin and her fingers. Edging his lips along her neck, he reached down to hook his own hand beneath her right knee.

Her soft gasp of amazement made him smile as he drew up her knee and slid his fingers down her leg. Reaching the hem of her skirt, he moved slowly as he slipped his knee between her legs. The ruffle on the bottom of her skirt teased his arm as his hand delved under it to stroke her leg through her thin stocking. Searching even higher, he heard her sharp gasp when his fingers found the bare skin above the garter at her knee. Her nails dug into his back as she arched closer to him, and he knew she was eager to share the pleasure awaiting them.

It was his turn to choke out a gasp when she shifted so her mouth was close to his ear. Her tongue, curving along its whorls, engraved his skin with a fiery need. She laughed softly at his reaction, and the pulse of her breath raced through him like a storm.

"You are a minx when you want to be," he whispered as he gazed down into her eyes. "So maybe you *do* know the game."

She opened her mouth to retort, but a low cry emerged when his fingers glided up her thigh. Her breasts caressed his chest as her head tilted back to offer up herself to him. It was the only invitation he needed . . . or wanted.

As his fingers slowly stroked her leg, he slanted his mouth over hers. Her tongue teased his, and her boldness thrilled him. She learned fast, and he had so much he wanted to teach her.

Suddenly she shivered beneath him, and he felt gooseflesh rise on her skin. Before he could suggest that they move inside to warm his bed, he was struck by a devastating cold.

"Alexander," she whispered, a hint of fear in her voice.

He looked up and saw that the moon had vanished. Not behind clouds, because the sky remained clear. It was as if someone had stepped between them and the moon.

Not someone. Something! It rose more than thirty

feet above the edge of the moors and cast a shadow even in the night. A light as garish as the sun at midday shone around the edges of the silhouette of a man—a giant!—while the blackness rose slowly up over the walls of Nethercott Castle.

Alexander jumped to his feet and, paying no attention to how his head whirled, reached down to take China's hand. He jerked her to her feet and was thankful she did not toss a dozen questions at him.

Heavy footfalls sounded like distant thunder. The giant was coming closer.

Chapter 11

"What is that?" China cried.

Alexander did not answer. He simply stared at the silhouette of a man outlined by the brilliant light behind it. No, not behind it, he realized, for it held a torch in one hand.

"Have you ever seen something like that before?" he asked, watching as it came closer. Its path was as unerringly straight as if the ground were flat.

"Do you think something like *that* could be on the moors, and nobody has ever mentioned it?" She leaned toward him, slipping her trembling hand into his.

"Get inside, China!" He shoved her toward the terrace. "Get inside now!"

"You too!"

He choked on his retort when the giant moved, revealing the moon once more. His hand groped for his side, but he was not armed. A nervous laugh tore out of his throat. Would a sword or even a pistol be enough to stop that shadowed colossus? Pushing China behind him, he backed away as it continued toward them.

Suddenly the other arm appeared out of the silhouette, rising impossibly high. Held in it was what appeared to be a sword. It swung toward them. He heard China's scream in the moment before the flat of the sword struck him, knocking him off his feet and against the terrace wall so hard his teeth rattled.

China crouched beside him, her face turning from him to the shadow and back. "Are you all right?"

"Yes." It was a lie, but it did not matter. She might believe she had sworn an oath to a ghost to protect him, but *he* needed no vow to protect her. "Go inside! I will—"

China gave a terrified cry as something pushed her away from him. He did not have a chance to see what. The huge weapon hit him again, swatting him back against the wall as if he were a fly.

A voice, so deep that it resonated in his head like thunder across a dale, ordered, "Leave here, son of Braddock, or you will wish you had."

He groaned as he tried to push himself to his feet. He got as far as his knees. China's arm slipped around his shoulders.

He pushed her away. "Go! The next blow could strike you."

"Look out!" she cried, pushing him to the ground beneath her.

Light vanished as the air seemed to be sucked out of his lungs. He struggled to draw in another breath, but it was impossible. The earth shook under him as the giant walked away.

Suddenly all was still. The moonlight washed down over them. He could breathe and felt her slight weight shift atop him. She was getting up.

Deuce take it! If he did not stop her, China might

go after the giant. She was obsessed with saving him from that curse.

He reached out and grasped her ankle before she could take more than a single step. "Don't go." Speaking the words took a surprising amount of strength. He was as weak as a newborn lamb.

"I wanted to see where it went, but I lost it in the shadows."

He slowly got to his feet. He needed her arm around him to stay upright. Glancing around, he saw only moonlight glittering on the ridge leading up to the moors. "What in the hell was that?"

"I don't know, but it may be connected to what Quintus warned me about."

"You heard it, too?"

She nodded. "But I don't understand any of this."

"Nor do I, except that I know you need to get inside before it comes back."

She shuddered against him. "Do you think it will?"

"I have no idea, but I don't want to face it again with anything less than a row of cannons. We need to get inside."

"But we need to see where it is going."

"Inside, China!" he ordered in a tone he had not used since he dressed down a sergeant for a mistake that could have left dozens dead.

She obeyed, helping him into the house. He watched as she closed the door and locked it. When she pulled the drapes over the nearest windows, he understood. He did not want to see that giant again either.

What *was* it? He half remembered fantastical stories from his childhood about monsters and ogres and dwarves roaming the moors, but had dismissed them even back then. What they had seen had not been a fairy tale. It had been real. Reeling to a table, he picked up a bell and rang it.

China put her hand on his arm. Her face was gray, and he suspected his was the same shade.

"Put that down," she said. "I will get Mrs. Mathers and—"

A scream tore apart the silence. Before it had even faded, another followed.

"Where?" he asked, too unfamiliar with the house to guess where the cries came from.

"Upstairs. The guest rooms." She rushed into the corridor before he could ask another question.

Alexander realized then that he had left his walking stick out on the terrace. His head spun, but he ran after her. His legs threatened to fail him again as he followed her upstairs. He locked his knees to keep himself from sprawling on the risers.

Another scream resonated through the house.

China did not falter. Neither did he as he followed her along the upper passage.

When Alexander reached Lady Viola's room, several steps behind China, the lady's shrieks had not lessened. She would shred her throat with such cries. Turnbull was struggling to avoid her flailing hands, while Miss Upton stood to one side, her hand to her cheek. Her eyes were focused on the window behind her cousin.

China crossed the floor, elbowed herself between Turnbull and his betrothed, then grasped the lady's face. Alexander watched, edging aside a half step to allow Miss Sian to come into the room.

"Enough!" ordered China.

Lady Viola wailed again.

"Enough!" she repeated. "Stop it *now*!"

The lady opened her mouth to shriek again, and China gently squeezed Lady Viola's cheeks. The sound came out in a squawk.

"Now see here—" Turnbull began.

"Calm yourself, Lord Turnbull," China said without looking at him, "and see to Miss Upton."

Alexander was amazed when the viscount rushed to do as she had ordered. Turnbull never had obeyed any direct command in the army, which had led to near disaster. Had China intimidated him as no officer had? Alexander dismissed that thought. That left only two possibilities: Turnbull was scared out of what few wits he possessed, or he *wanted* to do as she had told him.

As the viscount put his arm around Miss Upton, Alexander turned to see that China and Sian were urging Lady Viola to sit on the paisley-covered chaise longue. Her silly dog ran around them, yapping.

"Not by the window!" the lady screamed.

Calling to Turnbull to help him, Alexander moved the heavy mahogany chaise longue close to the hearth on the other side of the room. The Nethercott sisters steered a moaning Lady Viola to its soft cushions, and her dog ran to cower beneath it.

China dipped a handkerchief into the ewer by the dressing table. Placing it on the lady's forehead, she nodded when her sister sat next to Lady Viola and put a gentle hand on the cloth to keep it from slipping.

"How is she?" Alexander asked as China came over to him.

"Once she regains her composure, we might get

an answer to that. I saw nothing to suggest she is injured."

"He did not touch her," Miss Upton said meekly.

"He?" Alexander asked in the calm tone he had used when he wanted information from terrified soldiers.

"Someone peered into the window." Miss Upton raised her head, revealing her reddened cheek with a mark the size of her cousin's hand. "I saw no face, only a silhouette."

"A man?"

"If so, he was immense."

Offering Miss Upton a sympathetic smile, he said, "Go on. What happened then?"

"The window began to open, and something dark reached into the room."

"Toward Lady Viola?"

She shook her head. "Toward me, my lord. It withdrew when my cousin began to scream. She was so frightened that my efforts to quell her fears were futile." Her fingers went to her cheek, but she lowered them quickly. "Then, moments later, you arrived."

"Why would he have wanted *her*?" demanded Lady Viola from where she still reclined.

Alexander realized Lady Viola was as furious as she was frightened, offended that anyone—even some dark creature—would choose her cousin over her.

He had to admire China's restraint when she said, "You are asking questions that none of us have answers to."

With another emoted moan, Lady Viola turned her face away from them.

Miss Upton glanced at where Lady Viola groaned, her eyes closed. "I should see how she fares."

China took Miss Upton's hand. "*You* should sit. Let me get a cool cloth for your cheek."

"I should go to my cousin. She—"

"Is being tended to by my sister. It is your turn to sit and rest."

She guided Miss Upton to a chair before getting a damp cloth to put on Miss Upton's cheek. On the other side of the room, Lady Viola was groaning as if someone were trying to turn her inside out.

When Alexander gestured with his head toward the door, China followed him into the corridor. He swore under his breath when he saw she was hobbling. He waited for her to close the door behind her before asking how she was faring.

"I am fine," she said.

"You are limping."

"I twisted my ankle when I stumbled against the terrace steps." A flush of anger rose up her ashen cheeks. "What about you? That *thing* attacked you twice."

"I have been in a worse state," he replied grimly.

"I know. You need to sit down before you fall off your feet again."

He shook his head. "I want to check in the garden. If there is any clue to what that thing really was—"

"We will find out in the daylight."

"China!"

"Alexander," she fired back in the same exasperated tone. "Do not argue with me. This is *my* home, and you are *my* guest. I do not need you playing hero."

He recoiled as if she had struck him. Didn't she realize he was nobody's hero? He had no interest in being anyone's hero.

When he did not reply, she motioned for him to follow her along the hallway. Again and again, she was stopped by servants who wore identical expressions of fear. She calmed each one, but told everyone to stay inside until dawn. For a moment, he could imagine her standing on the parapets, calling orders to send knights riding over the drawbridge to defend the castle. A silly thought, because the castle had been a religious house during the medieval age, and there was no drawbridge. Yet China Nethercott was unquestionably a woman to be reckoned with.

Alexander was not surprised when she guided him into her father's book-room. It seemed to be her sanctuary, and he understood the need for one now.

"Would you like a glass of wine?" she asked.

"That is one of the best ideas I have heard in a long time."

"Sit, and I will get one for you." She put her hand on his arm, and every muscle in him reacted to her chaste touch. The hint of a flowery perfume wafted through him with every breath. He had savored its scent before that giant appeared, and he wanted to bask in it again.

He silenced his groan, knowing he was only tormenting himself. China was focused on finding out who had invaded her garden and terrorized her guests. She would not be thinking of anything else now.

She glanced toward him before quickly lowering her eyes, and he realized how mistaken he had been. The craving to be held, to be caressed, to be kissed until every other thought vanished had burned in her gaze.

"Why don't *you* sit?" he asked. "Let me get the wine."

He thought she would protest, but she nodded. He turned so she did not see his worried frown. She must be hurt more than she had intimated.

Moving past her, fighting the need to pull her into his arms, he went to the decanter of wine on a table near the window. He poured two glasses. He considered downing one in a single gulp, but decided not to cede to any yearning. He might not be able to deny satisfying all of them.

A muffled barking came from over their heads.

"Lady Viola's Princess," China said, her voice fatigued. "It is an old wives' tale that dogs resemble their owners." She gasped, putting her hand over her mouth. "Did I say that aloud?"

"Yes, but you were only voicing what *I* was thinking."

She smiled, then grew somber again. "I do hope they both calm down quickly. The whole house has been set on edge by her screams."

"She wanted to see a ghost." He held out a glass of wine to her. "She may have learned she must be careful what she asks for."

"That is unfair, Alexander. Whatever *that* was, it was no ghost."

"You sound sure of that."

"I am, because I have seen a ghost, and when Quintus Valerius materializes he looks as real as you or me. That thing was nothing but evil."

After taking a sip, Alexander lowered his glass and sighed. "I cannot argue with you about that. It wants me to leave Nethercott Castle."

"You cannot go!" She sat straight in the chair. "If it is part of the curse Quintus invoked—"

"Do not jump to conclusions."

"I saw that giant and I heard it, and I knew right away it was evil. I could *feel* it. Couldn't you?"

He turned away and propped one elbow on the hearth's mantel. As the excitement of the evening sifted away, every inch of his skull ached, and his eyes threatened to lose focus each time he blinked. He hoped he looked as if he were nonchalantly leaning rather than using the mantel to hold himself up as the dregs of his flagging strength drained away.

"I have learned," he said quietly, "that feelings have no place in ascertaining whether someone is an ally or an enemy. Feelings can lead one astray. Information is what one needs. Reliable information that can be confirmed."

"Which is why I am having the garden searched as soon as the sun is up."

He nodded, knowing that China would risk nobody going out of the house before then. "Does your father have a book in here about what we saw in the garden?"

"He never mentioned reading about anything like *that*." She shivered as she had as they cowered away from the giant. "It called you by name, Alexander. It has to be connected with Quintus and the curse."

Instead of answering, Alexander took another sip of the wine. He studied her profile as she stared out the window toward where the giant had appeared. She turned and caught him looking at her, and her blue-gray eyes filled with the need he wanted to satisfy.

Setting his glass on the mantel, he took her glass

and put it beside his. She slipped into his arms, her own curving up his back. When she tilted her head, he did not hesitate. His mouth found her open one. He deepened the kiss until she was gasping. Each pulse of her breath swirled in his mouth at the same moment her breasts stroked his chest.

He wanted her. Dear Lord, how he wanted her. He could not recall any other woman who had excited him with a simple touch. Hell, at the moment he could not recall any other woman. The only one he wanted was this one.

Now.

Moving her back one step, then another, her legs stroking his with each motion, he sat in the closest chair. He brought her down on his lap and cradled her in his arms. With a smile he plucked the pins from her hair and let the fiery silk fall around them. He ran his tongue up her neck to her ear.

She seemed to melt into him. Her hand drifted along his chest as he nibbled her ear. She quivered and clutched his waistcoat; then her fingers edged down his chest and wandered across his abdomen. He held his breath, not wanting anything to halt her in bringing his fantasies to life.

But his fantasies did not include footsteps coming to a stop in the book-room's doorway. Alexander did not attempt to silence his muttered curse as China pulled away and looked past him.

She hastily stood, brushing her hair over her shoulders. "Yes, Farley?"

The majordomo cleared his throat and tried to hide his discomfort behind a stern expression. It failed because his gaze kept shifting from China to Alexander and back like the pendulum of an overwound clock.

"Everyone has been informed of your request that nobody leave the house until sunrise." The butler's voice betrayed his disconcertment. "I thought you would want to know that straightaway."

"I did." She smiled weakly. "Thank you, Farley."

"Good night, Miss China." His eyes focused on Alexander, who had also come to his feet. "Good night, my lord."

"Thank you, Farley."

In the butler's wake, silence settled on the house. Even Lady Viola's spoiled pup was quiet. Then he heard China draw in a sharp breath. He was about to ask her what was amiss when something glinted in front of his eyes. He blinked several times, and his equilibrium almost failed him completely. He stumbled against a chair.

China put her arm under his shoulder again and around his back. "Come on," she murmured. "There is nothing else you can do tonight, so you should rest. We will need you to help us at dawn."

He knew she was right, so he let her assist him up the stairs to his room.

Opening the door, she whispered, "Rest well."

He stroked her face. "You do not need to go."

"Yes, I must."

"You could stay with me tonight."

Edging back, she gave him a saucy smile. "You need every bit of energy you have left just to walk to your bed and lie down."

"China Nethercott, you should be ashamed of yourself for belittling a man at his darkest hour."

Her smile faded as she met his eyes. "This is not your darkest hour."

She wished him a good night and walked away along the dusky corridor.

He whistled soundlessly. Could she have possibly guessed? And if she had guessed even an iota of the truth, why hadn't she thrown him out of her arms and out of her home?

China shivered as she drew the last of the draperies in her bedchamber. Usually she enjoyed the moonlight flowing across her bed, but not tonight.

She had not turned on the lamp, but there was no need. As she had expected since seeing the glimmer in the book-room, a ball of light expanded in the corner near the hearth. She waited for the ghost to assume his human form. As always, he wore a uniform and carried his weapons and shield. She was curious whether he had died with them, but was unsure how to ask such a question.

As soon as he was fully formed, she came around the bed. "Quintus! I had hoped you would appear tonight. Listen to what we saw." She gave a quick description of the massive silhouette and the searing light. "Do you know what it is?"

"It sounds like one of the ancients."

"More ancient than you?"

He gave her a cool smile. "Much older. One of those who lived when the world first formed. The first gods. What you saw is the evil part of the curse that awakes as the fifth of September draws nearer. It comes forth to keep the curse intact. When the mist releases me, other beings escape as well. I cannot control them, and they are more dangerous than you can imagine."

Her breath caught again before she choked out, "If anyone else had seen something like that on the moors recently, I would have heard of it."

"If that person had lived to tell of it."

She wrapped her arms around herself. "Quintus, don't! I have been frightened enough tonight. It threatened Alexander."

"What did it say?"

" 'Leave here, son of Braddock, or you will wish you did.' I will never forget those words."

"You must make certain that he does not encounter the ancient one again. You still live, so you have seen only a little of its power."

"Can you halt it?"

He shook his head and motioned toward the window. "Draw back the draperies on the window farthest to the left."

She wanted to ask why, but his face was set in somber lines that made it bear an uncanny resemblance to Alexander's. Going to the window, she pulled aside the draperies. She edged aside as Quintus came to stand beside her. The cold set her teeth to chattering, and gooseflesh rose again on her arms.

"There," he said, pointing out the window.

"It is too dark to see. I . . . " Her voice trailed off as she looked at the stream of moonlight flowing across one section of the garden. She stared at a smashed section of hedge. It must have been as broad as her outstretched arms from fingertip to fingertip, and longer than Alexander was tall.

"Do you see the footprint?" Quintus asked.

"Footprint?" She gasped.

"I warned you that my descendant could face danger before his fateful day. You saw proof of that tonight."

"But whatever it was went to Lady Viola's room after knocking him off his feet."

"Tonight may have been only for reconnoitering. It may have been seeking weaknesses in your house." The ghost shook so hard that the metal plates on his armor rattled. The light around him strengthened, and he began to merge into it. Before he vanished completely, he said, *"Omen sinistrum."*

The room darkened as the light faded. She was left alone with his words echoing in her mind.

Evil omen.

Chapter 12

The dark arcs under China's eyes threatened to creep down her cheeks. She turned away from the mirror. Sleeping had been impossible. She had spent half the night devising a way to persuade Alexander to heed the giant's warnings. If she spoke to him while he was next to her in bed, would he listen to her then?

That thought had kept her awake the other half of the night as her body was tormented with yearning. A heat had ached deep within her, making her feel empty and incomplete.

A knock sounded. Going to the door, China finished tying a pale gold ribbon in her hair.

She was both relieved and disappointed to see her sister: relieved that another problem had not sprung up, yet disappointed that it was not Alexander who had knocked. She gave her sister the best smile she could manage, a rather poor one.

"Are you ill?" Sian asked.

"No, just tired."

"I know." Sian dropped onto the chair at the desk and closed her eyes, rubbing her temples. "If I hear

Lady Viola whine or her silly dog yip once more, I swear I will strangle them both."

"I am sorry to have left you there last night."

"Do not fret about that. I know you wanted to make sure everyone in the house was safe." Sian opened one eye and smiled. "You missed an interesting situation, though. Lord Turnbull seemed more anxious about Miss Upton than his betrothed." She sighed. "I am sorry for agreeing to invite them here. I have no idea why I thought they might provide interesting conversation. Miss Upton is insightful when she is allowed to say more than two words, but Lady Viola and Lord Turnbull don't have enough sense between them to fill a bug's head."

China drew a chair away from one of the windows and sat beside her sister. "I doubt they will stay much longer. Lady Viola is distressed, and I cannot believe she wishes to endure much more excitement."

"Do not be so certain. She enjoyed the attention she received last night and said something about being too overmastered by the events to do anything today." Sian leaned forward as she lowered her voice. "What do you think they saw?"

"Whatever frightened them wrecked a swath of the garden."

"So I heard this morning." Anger sparked in Sian's eyes. "Some of those hedges were as old as the house."

"Their roots are deep, so they may survive. I am happy that no one in the house was hurt."

"I think this has something to do with the threats to Lord Braddock."

China was not surprised her sister had come to

that conclusion. Sian might be an artist, but she still possessed their father's cool rationality.

"I agree," she said.

"I suspect he does as well. Mrs. Mathers tells me that he wishes to move to a room in this wing. I believe he wants to be nearby in case there is an attack aimed at you."

"Why would Mrs. Mathers go to you about it?"

Color brightened Sian's cheeks. "Anyone can see that he is fascinated with you. I assume she did not wish to put you in a difficult position."

"So she decided to put you in one instead." She laughed. "Or not discover me in a compromising one."

"China!" Sian's shocked voice was followed by a quick laugh. "As long as you have your sense of humor, I know the situation is not as bad as I dreaded. What shall I tell Mrs. Mathers?"

"If it is all right with you, why don't we have him moved into Father's rooms?"

Sian nodded. "They have been empty too long and are right across from ours. That should reassure Lord Braddock that he will hear either of us scream." Her eyes twinkled as she added, "Maybe I should have Mrs. Mathers mention that sound travels both ways, in case he has designs on someone in this house. . . ."

Slapping her sister's arm playfully, China said, "You are needlessly worrying about your sleep being interrupted. All right. Tell Mrs. Mathers to move him into Father's rooms. It is a simple solution, because I am sure Alexander would not have taken no for an answer."

"He is a man who is not easily convinced to change his mind."

"Now you are beginning to understand, Sian."

"It is the only thing I have understood recently."

China nodded. "I feel the same, but I intend to get some answers. I am going to start with the curate at St. Mary's Church in Lastingham. Reverend Wilder knows as much about classical history and mythology as Father did."

"So you believe last night was somehow connected with the ghost?"

"I have no doubt."

Alexander put his walking stick on the carriage's small step and heaved himself upward. China hoped he would not topple onto his face. She was even more wobbly. She wondered if sleep had been as elusive for him last night. He had not said more than a few words during the drive from Nethercott Castle, other than to thank her for allowing him to move to another bedchamber. Neither of them mentioned the real reasons behind his request. Until she spoke with Reverend Wilder, she did not want to discuss what had happened last night. So while they drove toward Lastingham, she pointed out the farms they passed and talked about the weather.

When they stopped at the curate's house, his housekeeper said he was out and might be at the church. They drove to St. Mary's Church at the edge of the village, and she drew in the horse. The carriage creaked as Alexander stepped with care to the ground. China reached out to steady him as he swayed, but withdrew her hand when he scowled.

"As you can see, I have not ended up in the mud," he said, stepping back. "Nor will you, if you allow me the courtesy of handing you out."

As she put her fingers on his, he gave her arm a gentle tug, bringing her face close to his. "I do not need you coddling me."

"I am not coddling you. Why are you trying to start a quarrel about something so absurd?"

"With you, I know it is better to state my opinions bluntly."

"I daresay that does not seem to be a problem for you."

"Or you."

China laughed as he assisted her out of the carriage. She glanced around them. The tiny village was quiet on the gray afternoon. To her left was the public house, a long brown stone building with multiple doors. Voices came from inside, where some of the local men must be enjoying a pint. On the other side of the road, a slope rose quickly. Partway up a stone wall encircled the churchyard. St. Mary's Church sat at the peak of the slope. It must have once been an awe-inspiring sight, but even from the road she could see the missing and broken slates on the roof.

Lashing the horse's reins to a post, she said, "If you want my blunt opinion, I am happy we saw no sign of the highwayman today. On my last journey from Nethercott Castle, I discovered that being stopped twice in one day was more than enough."

"Twice?"

China scolded herself for referring to Quintus when she had not yet passed along to Alexander the new information she had learned last night. She hoped Reverend Wilder would help her understand what Quintus had told her.

"There have been so many sightings of the high-

wayman," she said, "that some people believe there
are two."

He gave her a skeptical glance. "But the description Turnbull's coachee gave me matched the one we
had the misfortune of meeting."

"We should go into the church and see if Reverend
Wilder is there." She hated not being completely
honest with him, but she had been frightened by
Quintus's fear. Giving in to panic now might be
deadly. She looked up at the church. It had narrow
windows in each section of the arc along the front,
and parapets marching along its curved roof. "He
may be on the main floor or below in the crypt."

"Crypt?" Alexander's eyes sparked with sudden
excitement. "There is a crypt under the church?"

"A saint—St. Cedd—is said to be buried there.
Come. I will show you." She motioned to the right
of the church. "The steps into the churchyard are
this way."

A half dozen steps led up to a gate that swung
into the churchyard. Sheep grazed among the grave
markers. They raised their heads as China led Alexander along the path. Each sheep went back to tearing grass from the ground.

"I am surprised the sheep are allowed into the
churchyard," Alexander said.

"They keep the grass low, and I doubt anyone
could keep them out." She glanced toward the
moors. "Sheep have ways of finding their way
everywhere."

"Your garden seems safe."

"Only because we continually chase the sheep
out."

"It must break your heart, what that trespasser did to the garden."

"It does." She felt tears rising, heated and heavy, in her eyes.

He paused on the uneven walk and faced her. Stroking her cheek gently, he said, "You do not have to be brave all the time."

"Why not? You are!"

"Don't!"

"Don't what?" When he touched her like this, she could imagine so many things she would like to do with him.

"Don't treat me as if I am the perfect hero with never a moment of doubt or any human trait other than incessant courage."

She searched his face, wishing he would explain why the mere mention of the word "hero" unsettled him so. His courage had been recognized by the Prince Regent. Why was he ashamed of it?

"Alexander—"

His finger against her lips silenced her; then his mouth covered hers as he tugged her into his arms. In the quiet of the churchyard, where the only sound was the occasional baaing from one of the sheep or a distant laugh from the tavern, she surrendered to the exhilaration of their kiss. Her fingers uncurled along his back, exploring anew the strong muscles that held her so tenderly.

Raising his head, he whispered, "If we continue this, I may forget we are on holy ground and make love with you right here."

Her breath caught as she imagined what else they could share. They must speak with Reverend Wilder, but she wished she and Alexander could slip away to some bower for several hours.

Opening a door in the north wall of the church, she managed to say in a somewhat normal tone, "Be careful. The steps are not even. Is your head spinning?"

"Of course it is. I just kissed you." He winked and grinned.

"Will you need help getting down the stairs?"

Suddenly, with a curse, he seized her around the waist and thrust her through the doorway. She hit the stone wall inside and choked back a gasp of pain. Before she could speak he leaped in beside her and reached to pull the door closed. Something struck the stone with a loud bang. Sharp fragments ricocheted around them. One hit the wall right beside her.

She gasped in pain when a shard sliced the back of her hand. "Someone is shooting at us!"

As he slammed the door shut, Alexander's voice held less emotion than she had ever heard in it. "Stay where you are, China."

She grasped his sleeve as he turned to go back out into the churchyard. "Have you lost your mind? Haven't you listened to anything I have told you? Someone wants to kill you."

"On the fifth of September."

"Unless the murderer has a chance to get the job done before that." Through her mind raged Quintus's warning: *The day of greatest danger to him is on the fifth of September, but every day until then is filled with peril.*

"I will not argue about this. Stay here."

"What if you are killed? That would leave me here

alone at the murderer's sparse mercy." She shook her head. "I will not allow you to do that."

"*You* will not allow?" He squared his shoulders, edging toward the door. He paused and looked at her bleeding hand. "China! You were hit."

He ignored her protests that it was a small wound and that she would be fine. Steering her ahead of him down the stairs, he sat her on the bottom step. He told her to wait while he went into the crypt to find a candle.

She tilted her hand to examine it, wincing as she flexed it. She then heard the door to the churchyard creak open. She paused, holding her breath as boots sounded on the stone landing. Jumping to her feet, she turned and saw an ebony silhouette at the top of the stairs—not of a giant, but of a normal-size man draped in a black cloak.

The highwayman!

She saw sunlight glisten off the pistol in his hand—pointed at her. He slowly lowered it, and she thought she heard him swear.

Holding out her left arm as if she could keep him from coming closer, she inched back from the steps. Cold struck her spine, and she heard, "No!"

She risked a glance over her shoulder and saw Quintus hovering a foot above the floor. His hand was clenched on his spear. A flash of light caught her eye, and she looked back at the stairs to see the highwayman rushing out the door.

Outside she heard raised voices. She hoped the men from the public house had captured the highwayman.

"Thank you," she whispered as she faced Quintus.

"Don't thank me! You should have fled from that

weapon that spews death with its iron balls." He was still scolding her when he vanished.

Candlelight came toward her as Alexander stepped out of the crypt. She ran to him, crying, "He was here!"

"He who?"

"The highwayman! At the top of the stairs." She gestured toward the door, then moaned as her lacerated hand burned with a fire as hot as the candle's flame.

Putting his arm around her shoulder, Alexander guided her from the steps. He glanced toward the stairwell, then sighed. He wanted to chase the highwayman, hoping to halt him once and for all. Instead he led her to a low bench in the crypt. Two sets of simple columns held up the arched roof. At the far end, the curved apse with a simple table was lit by a single small rectangular window. The air was stale, and a musty odor filled every breath. The stones beneath her feet were as cold as midwinter.

"I am sorry," China whispered as he sat beside her and loosened his cravat.

"What are *you* sorry for?" He began to wrap the fabric around her bleeding hand.

"I know how much you want to go after that highwayman and teach him some manners."

His smile was somehow gentle and angry at the same time. "More than you can imagine, China. It was bad enough to see the injuries to Turnbull's coachman, but to have him hurt you . . . I hope to have the opportunity to make him pay for it."

"Why would a highwayman shoot at us in a churchyard? I thought they robbed people along the roads."

"It would be a welcome change if just once you asked me a question I have an answer to."

"Ouch!" She drew back her hand and adjusted the knot he had tied in the fabric. It had pressed painfully into one of the cuts.

"Now it is my turn to say I am sorry. Wrapping wounds is not something I know much about."

"I would have guessed you had experience in the war."

He shook his head. "I left that task to others. The one time I was hit, I was senseless while they bound my wounds."

"I did not know you were wounded."

"The only ones who were not wounded were the carpet-knights who paraded through London with their uniforms perfectly clean." He kissed her uninjured hand and asked, "Can you walk to the carriage?"

"You want to leave?"

"Most certainly. You are hurt."

She put her hand on his arm and whispered, "Whoever is behind this is goading us and trying to make us do something stupid before September fifth." She hesitated, then added, "Quintus tells me that you are in danger every day until then."

He grimaced. "Why couldn't you be haunted by a ghost who has good tidings once in a while?"

"You believe there is a ghost?"

"*You* do, and I am coming to realize that you are always honest with me." His smile returned. "Sometimes too honest."

Joy exploded through her. Until that moment, she had not realized how she longed for him to believe her, that his skepticism remained a barrier between them. Now the barrier was crumbling. She leaned toward him, and his hand slid up her back to press her closer, but only for a moment. One thing had not changed: The passion between them must be tightly restrained, or it would burst from their control. He must have realized that, too, as he let his hand fall.

She glanced over her shoulder when she heard a noise from the staircase. Motioning for her to remain where she was, Alexander stood and edged toward the stairs. She held her breath, but his rigid shoulders fell as he abruptly laughed. She quickly joined him to discover a confused sheep trying to turn around on the landing.

He climbed up to push the sheep out. She followed him out into the churchyard, but lingered by the door as he went to speak with some men gathered nearby.

She saw the truth as he came back toward her with measured steps. "The highwayman is gone," she said.

"Apparently he made his escape up the hill. No one is willing to chase him across the moors where there are many places for a man to hide."

"At least he is gone."

"For now."

Chapter 13

China nodded when Alexander pointed toward the far side of the churchyard and said, "I want to check how the highwayman got away so quickly. There are brambles along the back, but there has to be a path through them."

"Do not be long." She glanced skyward. "Those clouds look as if they are about to release a flood any minute."

She watched him walk away, his shoulders tense with determination, before she turned to go in the other direction. She was almost to the churchyard gate when she saw Quintus materialize among the grave markers. He walked past several grazing sheep, which flinched, but kept grazing.

"Quintus! Did you see the man with a black cape out here?"

Quintus scowled. "No. Why didn't you heed me when I warned you that there would be other attempts before the fifth of September?" His eyes, so much like Alexander's, drilled into her. "Why did you bring him here, where he is in danger?"

She tried to submerge her frustration. It almost

strangled her not to spit out the words she longed to say. She was certainly trying her best, and he did not have to seem so dismayed that the only person who could see him was a young woman instead of a skilled warrior. How she would enjoy reminding him that this task had been forced upon her and that he needed her help after failing for more than fifteen hundred years!

She sighed, trying to calm herself. The only important issue was keeping Alexander alive.

"Answer my question," he ordered. "Why did you bring him here, where he could be in danger?"

"I brought him here because we had hoped to see the curate, who is well versed in mythology." Despite her efforts, her frustration broke forth. "My life was not nearly as dramatic until you put your descendant's life in my hands, and all I ask for is a little appreciation as I try my best to save his life, my life and your soul. A little courtesy, please." Her hand hurt. Her head hurt. She was worried about Alexander. She wanted him holding her.

"I apologize, China." His eyes begged her to accept what he was telling her, and she had to. How could she be annoyed at Quintus when the ghost was caught in a prison he had created for himself so many centuries ago?

"*Fata valentem ducunt, nolentem trahunt,*" Quintus intoned.

"Fate helps the willing and forces the reluctant," she translated.

She looked to where Alexander was kneeling by the bushes, peering at something beyond them.

"The fifth of September will be upon us soon," she said quietly. "And it is the truth that I am doing the best that I can. I would never endanger Alexander needlessly."

"I know." He hesitated. "Tell me about him."

"Alexander is a marquess. That is a title of great respect. He is considered a hero in England because of his deeds in the war. But there is more to him than just a warrior. He is kind and intelligent and curious about subjects like history."

"You have feelings for him!"

She could not halt the warmth climbing her face. "I have saved his life, and he saved my life today."

Quintus smiled slyly. "When you speak of him, your eyes glow like twin lanterns in the darkest night. I am beginning to understand why you were the one to whom I had to appear."

"I would try to save anyone's life." She raised her chin in defiance. "Even the highwayman's, if it came to that."

"So you will deny Alexander his vengeance on that *homo ignavus* for the injury you have suffered."

"Lazy man?" she asked, unsure if she understood his Latin words.

"No, it means coward."

She nodded. The highwayman was craven, sneaking about in the shadows, jumping out when his intended victims let their guard down, attacking easy targets and then fleeing.

"Is the highwayman the one who will try to kill Alexander on the fifth?" she asked.

"It is possible. He has shown he is my descendant's enemy. I . . ." He faded into light without finishing his sentence.

China scowled at the spot where he had been. For

a ghost who was so eager to put an end to the curse, he vanished at the worst possible times.

"Is your hand bothering you? Do you need help with the gate?" asked Alexander from behind her.

"I was waiting for you," she replied, then wished she had not tried to sound insouciant. Her light tone fell as heavily as a slate from the church roof.

He gave her an odd look. He held out a small piece of black cloth. "I would hazard a guess that our highwayman has a torn cloak."

"It looks like common black wool." She rubbed one corner of it between her fingers. "What is this gritty texture?"

"Gritty?" He frowned. "Someone recently used that word to describe material. Who was it?"

"I have no idea." She sighed as she looked at the small piece of cloth. "There is nothing here to help us identify him."

He smiled grimly. "But we cannot ignore any possibilities. If he seeks someone to repair his cloak or some thread to mend it on his own, we might be able to set a trap for him."

"We can spread the word, but he is as likely to hear it as anyone else. This is a different sort of battle than you fought. Then, you knew the enemy. The highwayman could be anyone. He could live in the village or be drinking ale in the public house right now."

"You have an insightful mind."

"You sound surprised."

He secured the black wool beneath his coat as his lips twitched into a smile. "Your father's interests were wide, and he instilled his love of learning in you."

"You can be very charming when you wish to be."
She wagged a finger at him.

He caught it, wrapping his much larger fingers
around it. The intensity returned to his gaze as he
raised her hand to his shoulder while his arm slid
around her waist. "You have no idea how charming
I could be," he whispered.

These warm embraces were no longer enough to
satisfy her need for him. She wanted to savor every
bit of him. She wished . . .

A man's shriek exploded across the quiet churchyard. The voices came from the public house.

"Get 'im and 'ang 'im!" someone called.

China tried to pull out of Alexander's arms. Before
she could turn even partway, he tightened his hold
on her.

"Don't look," he said.

"They are talking about hanging a man! Someone
needs to halt them."

"But not you."

"Alexander—"

"Heed me this once!"

His pale azure gaze caught her, and the sounds
from across the road faded. His fingers splayed
across her back.

" 'Tis not 'im!" she heard someone shout in disgust. "Let the poor man be."

Only then did Alexander release her so she could
rush to the stone wall at the far end of the churchyard. The sheep stared at her with dull indifference.
She looked at a group of men clumped around a
young man who could not be any older than Sian.
His hair was mussed, his cap on the ground at his
feet. His fists were raised to defend himself.

"Are you sure?" called another man.

" 'E is Petty's lad. 'E cannot be the 'ighwayman because 'e's a 'ead taller than the 'ighwayman."

China frowned. The men thought they had chanced upon the highwayman in the public house. They had been ready to erect a gallows.

She glanced back at the gate, then stepped over the low wall. As she stormed down the steep bank, she saw heads swivel toward her.

The young man took advantage of the distraction and fled, giving the mob no chance to change its mind and set him swinging by the neck.

By the open tavern door, a garishly dressed man called, "The next round is on me, chaps."

Cheers replaced the ugly rumbles of accusations, and she heard the men thanking Squire Haywood, who was handing the publican some coins. The men surged inside to enjoy another pint, leaving the squire alone. Shading his eyes with his hand, he looked in both directions.

China smiled, glad the squire had brought the situation to such a simple close. He tried hard to do his duties for the shire. From the first reports of the highwayman, he had worked to oversee the hunt for the thief and assign volunteers to search the moors.

"Good afternoon, Squire," she said as she crossed the narrow road. "I am glad to see that your cool good sense won the day."

He faced her and frowned as his gaze focused on her right hand. "Miss Nethercott!" he exclaimed with obvious dismay, his deep voice rumbling. "You are injured!"

"Yes, Squire, but I am fine."

He looked past her.

Half turning, she saw Alexander and motioned for him to join them. "Alexander, I do not believe you have been properly introduced to Squire Palmer Haywood. He was at Nethercott Castle the day of the fire, but it was so chaotic that propriety was shunted aside."

The two men shook hands; then the squire said, "I had heard, Braddock, that you had returned from the Continent, but I did not guess that you would be visiting Lastingham. I had thought such a hero would stay in Town and be feted by the *ton*."

She could not help noticing that Alexander's shoulders stiffened. The squire regarded him with genial interest, obviously expecting Alexander to offer a few stories of his experiences.

He said nothing, and an unpleasant silence settled around them.

China was relieved when the squire said, "I regret that I have made no progress in discovering who set the fire at Nethercott Castle." The magistrate took her uninjured hand and gazed at her.

"I am surprised you have had time to look," she said, drawing her hand slowly out of his. "I know that you have been busy chasing the highwayman."

"An onerous task," the squire said with a frown. "It was made more onerous by Lord Turnbull offering a generous bounty for the highwayman's capture and execution. Every man with empty pockets is hoping to fill them with the viscount's gold."

Alexander glanced at China. "Turnbull said nothing about a bounty to either Miss Nethercott or myself. It may be only a rumor."

"Whether it is true or false, the offer has galvanized the young men in the area."

"Which is sure to drive the highwayman into hiding—or lead to more horrific acts."

Squire Haywood's brows shot up. "How discerning of you, my lord."

"Nothing more than common sense. The man has two choices: hide until the excitement passes, or obtain some great prize that will tide him over until he can continue with his crimes."

"He might flee."

"He has had the chance to do that before," Alexander said with a cool laugh.

The squire nodded, his mouth in a straight line as he turned to include China in the discussion. "Did you hurt your hand in the fire at Nethercott Castle?"

"No. Lord Braddock and I were ambushed in the churchyard."

A ripple of fear rushed up her spine, and her knees seemed to lose their strength as she faced the truth of how easily she or Alexander could have been killed. She had pushed that thought out of her mind while in the church, but now the realization assaulted her doublefold. When she swayed, Alexander put his arm around her waist.

"Excuse us," he said as rain began to pelt them. "Miss Nethercott should not be standing out in a storm when she has endured so much today."

"It seems you hold your oath to the Order of the Bath to heart, my lord. You are pledged to protect maidens, widows and orphans." He smiled at China.

Unsure how to respond to such an odd comment, China bade the squire a good day before rushing with Alexander to the carriage.

Alexander handed her in and raised the top. He loosened the reins from the post and climbed in as the storm began in earnest. Picking up the reins, he turned the carriage around. She was glad to let him drive. Her mind was laced with pain and too many thoughts.

Closing her eyes, she said, "I am sorry we did not have a chance to speak with Reverend Wilder."

"We will another day." His voice was so strained that she opened her eyes. His face was as cold and emotionless as one of the carved stone heads on the church porch. "First I need to speak with Turnbull and find out if he was as stupid as rumor suggests."

"Not that it matters now. The offer of a bounty is out there, and people believe it to be true."

"Including the highwayman."

She nodded, even though her head ached at the simple motion. "We have already seen that the highwayman has become more audacious."

"And deadly. He missed us, but who will be his next target?"

"You."

"We cannot be sure of that. He attacked Turnbull's carriage, and now the bounty has thrown down the gauntlet in Turnbull's name. The highwayman is sure to want to show Turnbull how asinine that was."

"Lady Viola!" She gasped. "He could hurt her."

"It would be the best vengeance against the viscount. No Lady Viola means no hefty dowry for Turnbull to control and no massive inheritance when her father dies."

"We need to warn them."

He scowled at the road. "Whatever happens, you must persuade them to remain at Nethercott Castle. To leave now could put them right in the highwayman's path. You must be as persuasive, China, as if their lives depended on it, because they well may."

Chapter 14

When China led Alexander into Nethercott Castle, the house was in an uproar. She jumped aside as a maid ran past her. He put out a hand to steady her as two more servants raced in the same direction. He reached out his other hand to halt a footman speeding past, but the man dodged around him.

"What is going on?" China asked.

No one answered. From upstairs, the pounding of feet sounded as if they were trying to break through the ceiling. There followed a crash, shattering glass and a muffled cry.

"Wait here," Alexander ordered. "Let me find out what is setting your household on edge."

"No!"

He grasped her shoulders and spun her to face him. "China, if there has been another attack on your home and retainers, it could have been aimed at you."

"Or you."

"I will not argue—"

"Good! Because I do not want to either." She

twisted away and rushed toward the stairs, pausing in midstep when her sister called her name. "Sian! What is going on?"

"Lady Viola— Oh, my goodness!" Sian gasped as she looked at China's hand. "You are hurt! What happened?"

"It truly is not as bad as it looks."

"She is putting on a brave face," Alexander said as he steered China toward a bench. "It seems that every time she leaves the house lately she ends up bruised and battered."

China ignored his comment and quickly explained what had happened at the church. "Thank goodness for Squire Haywood's quick thinking. I must speak with Lord Turnbull about this rumored bounty."

Wrinkling her nose, Sian said, "You know the squire frets about everything." She smiled at Alexander. "His only redeeming quality is that he has always been madly infatuated with China. He vowed to do whatever necessary, change in any way she wished, if she would fall in love with him."

"Sian!" China knew her face must be bright red. "He never made any such vow."

"In *your* hearing. I overheard him ask Father if he could call on you, but he was too gracious to press his suit while we were in mourning. Not like . . ." Color flashed up her face as she lowered her eyes.

"Do not be embarrassed," Alexander said with a chuckle. "I have noticed Turnbull seems pleased with China's company."

"And every other woman's," China averred.

"Yes, I have noticed that, too. I wonder if Lady Viola has. She does not seem the type of woman to endure that with grace." He took a deep breath. "Nor do I expect Turnbull to accept with any sense of goodwill the dressing-down he deserves."

China pushed herself to her feet. "You do not need to speak to him, Alexander. I will. He might accept the comments more easily from me than from you. I shall . . ." She looked over her shoulder at the sound of Lady Viola's trilling voice. She hoped nobody heard her muffled groan. "What is she up to?"

"She is planning a party."

"For when?"

"The night after tomorrow."

China rubbed her aching head. "But the trip to York is long. Why doesn't she wait until she recovers from the journey?"

"Because she is holding the party here."

"Here?" she squeaked in astonishment. "At our house?"

"No. She has decided to hold an al fresco gathering at the Roman camp."

Alexander scowled. "Is she mad? That place is not fit for an assembly of any sort. More earthworks could come down, and someone could be injured."

"Apparently," Sian said, "she believes we have not had enough excitement, and she wants to provide some as a thank-you. A thank-you that adds to the work of our household! What sort of sense does that make? My efforts to try to talk her out of it have been for naught."

China did not answer. Sian, as always, was trying to be nice. Alexander offered to speak with the lady, but China doubted Lady Viola would heed any of them. However, Lord Turnbull might. She hoped she could be as diplomatic in dealing with the viscount as Alexander would be with the lady.

She slipped away, stopping several harried servants to ask where Lord Turnbull might be. One pointed her in a most unexpected direction.

When China walked into the book-room, she saw Lord Turnbull's legs stretched out from her father's favorite chair. He held a glass of brandy in one hand and a cheroot in the other. Thick, pungent smoke rose from it.

She was annoyed at the sight of someone smoking in the one room where her father had forbidden it. "Lord Turnbull, if you wish to enjoy your cigar, I must ask you to remove yourself to the terrace. My father's books are too valuable to be put in jeopardy from smoke or fire."

He ground out the cigar before coming to his feet. "I am sorry. I should have considered that." He gave her a smile and stepped around the chair. "I had hoped you would find your way here so we might have a chance to speak."

"I am pleased you feel comfortable enough to run tame through my house," she said coolly.

"This is a man's room, so I thought it a good place to relax while my fiancée is busy."

China saw no reason to explain that she and her sisters had used the room frequently their entire lives. "I was hoping to speak with you as well. I have heard a disquieting rumor, my lord, and I hope you will be able to ease my concerns."

Again acting as if he were the host, he selected a goblet and filled it with wine from the decanter on the table. "Madeira," he announced, holding out the glass to her, "brought all the way from the Portuguese islands for your pleasure. By way of York, I should add." When she took it, he added more brandy to his own glass and raised it toward her. "May it bring the same delight to your palate, Miss Nethercott, as you offer to the eyes."

In spite of herself, she felt a heated blush. Not because she was overwhelmed by his compliment, but because she was vexed that he had changed the subject. She sat and took a hasty sip of the wine. When she lowered the glass, she discovered his gaze on her and a slow smile slipping along his lips. She did not want Lord Turnbull flirting with her.

China kept her own face blank. "This rumor—"

"Is quite true."

"It is?"

"Yes, Lady Viola hopes you and your sister will attend our wedding in October."

He thought *that* was the rumor she wanted to discuss? She watched him from the corner of her lowered eyes. He was as tense as the squire had been in Lastingham.

"That is a kind offer," she said quietly. "I will convey the invitation to Sian." She put the glass on the table beside her and set her bandaged hand on her lap. It still burned fiercely. She wanted to finish this conversation and have the wound rebandaged. "But, Lord Turnbull, that is not the rumor I wish to discuss."

"No?" He sat and put his highly polished boots on the footstool again.

"Have you offered a generous bounty for the capture of the highwayman?"

"Yes. Inspired, don't you think?" He took a sip of his brandy. "The blackguard will be captured and sent to hang before he can harm someone else." He looked as pleased as a cat next to an empty dish.

"Did you consider the ramifications?" She repeated Alexander's concerns without revealing who had first voiced them. Mentioning that Alexander shared her opinion could infuriate the viscount, and he would heed nothing she said. "An innocent man was nearly hanged in Lastingham. You cannot fathom the hysteria this reward is creating."

He leaned toward her, wearing a smile he should have offered only to Lady Viola. "I have a broad and lively imagination, my dear Miss Nethercott."

"How fortunate for you." She would not allow him to infuriate her. "But I do believe you should meet with Squire Haywood posthaste, because he is the one having to deal with the consequences of your reward."

For a moment, the viscount frowned, ruining his nearly perfect good looks. His smile returned as he said, "I will have my beloved Lady Viola send him an invitation to join us at the old Roman camp."

"That is not a good idea."

"Where better to speak with the man than at a convivial gathering?"

"No, you should speak to him before then."

He took a sip and looked very reflective. "My dear Miss Nethercott, you should not judge until you see the results."

"I have seen them. Please retract the offer of a reward."

"As you wish. I can see that this situation disturbs you, and that was never my intention."

"Thank you." She stood and motioned for him to remain where he was. "Enjoy your afternoon, my lord."

He gave her his too-charming smile again and drawled, "There is another matter I would like to talk over with you. It is of some importance."

"Yes?"

"What has Braddock said about our experiences in the war?"

"Very little."

"Is that so?" He took another sip and stood. "So he seldom speaks of our time on the Continent?"

"Yes."

"I see." He tipped his glass, finishing it with a single gulp. He did not offer her more wine as he refilled his glass and carried it back to the chair. "Do you think it is possible he would do me a great favor and not speak to Lady Viola about our time in the military?"

"I cannot make any promises for him."

"But you can speak to him and ask him to indulge me." He emptied the glass again. "He might heed the request if it came from you, because he is indebted to you for saving his life."

"I see." She began to count on her fingers. "First I do you a favor by asking Alexander. Next he does me a favor by doing you a favor. Is that correct?"

"Yes, a perfect arrangement."

"Save that you would still owe *me* a favor."

Setting himself on his feet, he frowned. "What favor do you wish, when I have already agreed to withdraw my offer of a bounty for the capture of the highwayman?"

"Which you did before we began these negotiations." She smiled to ease the sting of her words. "As for what I would like in return, try to persuade your fiancée to halt her plans for a party at the old Roman camp. I do not want to be a poor hostess and forbid it."

"You may be asking the impossible. She is happier planning it than I have seen her in a long time."

"Please try, as I will with your request for Alexander's reticence."

"Assuring that he says nothing is your job, Miss Nethercott," he replied as she walked to the door. "I am quite confident that you will find a very special way to ask."

"I will pretend I did not hear that unseemly suggestion, my lord. This time." She faced him. "If you were to make another, I shall not be as forgiving. Good afternoon, Lord Turnbull."

She smiled wearily as she climbed the stairs to her bedchamber. She hoped Alexander had the same good luck in persuading Lady Viola to cancel her gathering.

Alexander had made frustratingly little progress. Lady Viola prattled during the evening meal about plans fit for the patricians of Rome. Comments that the weather was too cold, or that the area was too rough, or that the camp was too far from Nethercott Castle, or that the highwayman could make trouble were shrugged aside. She would not budge from her belief that she should arrange such an extravaganza to show her gratitude to the Nethercott sisters.

By the time the meal was over China's ears had been battered, and she was frustrated by the lady's refusal to acknowledge good sense. China knew she could insist that Lady Viola halt her plans, but she wanted to avoid having the uneasy situation explode.

She had enough otherwise to concern her without suffering through Lady Viola's outrage at being denied.

When Alexander suggested that Miss Upton might be able to help them, China agreed. He offered to speak with her, and China slipped out of the dining room. She heard Lord Turnbull offer to take his betrothed for a stroll in the garden.

China started toward the north tower room, then recalled that it still needed to be cleaned after the fire. Instead, she went to the door that led up the battlements, where she could be alone to think.

She smiled when she saw a ball of light gathering into itself a short distance along the crenelated walk.

"*Ave*, China," Quintus called as soon as he appeared amidst the eye-searing brightness.

"*Ave*, Quintus." She smiled as she walked toward him. "I had hoped you would return tonight."

"Why are you out here alone when you should be guarding my descendant?"

She gestured toward the French windows opening onto the terrace below. "If you peek through those doors, you will see him beseeching Miss Upton to help him change her cousin's mind about holding a gathering at the old Roman camp."

"*My* camp?" He frowned at her, and she recognized the expression from Alexander's face when he did not want to be ungentlemanly. "There were many who died at the camp over the centuries. Some have gone on, but others linger. It would be wise not to disturb them when they are resting."

"I agree, but Lady Viola insists on having her way. Would you speak to the others at the camp?"

"We do not speak. We just sense one another."

His fingers on his shield tightened until his knuckles blanched, and she thought she saw them shake. Was he frightened or angry?

"You must halt this," Quintus ordered. "It is drawing too close to the fateful day, and he must not go out."

"After the fire in the house, I am not sure where he is safe."

"Keep him away from others who may wish evil upon him."

"It has come looking for us here at Nethercott Castle."

"True, but traveling now could be more dangerous."

She clenched her hands by her sides, trying to silence her frustration. It burst out of her. "I am obviously terrible at this! Why was I chosen?"

Quintus shook his head. "When I emerged from the mist, I simply knew that you would be the one to help him, because you would never betray him."

"All right," she conceded with a sigh. "But I could use your help now to keep him safe. Isn't there something else you can tell me?"

"About what?" Alexander asked as he came out on the walkway.

With her hand on one of the crenelations, she turned. "How did you know where I was?"

"One of the footmen saw you come up this way. He was standing at the base of the stairs worried someone might try to do you harm."

She glanced over her shoulder to see that Quintus was still there. "I am not the one he should be worried about."

The lengthening shadows from the setting sun

played across his face as he smiled. "That is an argument you must have with your household. I have had enough brangles tonight to last a lifetime."

"Will Miss Upton help?"

"No. I suspect she picks her battles with care, and this is one she does not wish to engage in. She knows it is futile."

Resting her elbows on the parapet, China glanced at Quintus before saying, "Battles? You never speak of when you were in the army."

"It is not something a gentleman discusses with a lady."

"Your reputation and the honors draped over you since your return show you should be proud of your service to the king."

"I appreciate your faith in me, but you are mistaken. I am simply among the lucky ones who survived the din and horror of the battlefield." He leaned against another crenelation. "I would prefer not to speak of it."

"Lord Turnbull will be pleased to hear that."

"Why would he care?" His smile returned, doubly cold. "No doubt Turnbull is concerned that I will call into question some of his heroic stories. He is quite fond of repeating the tales of his adventures to anyone willing to listen, and even to those who are not."

"Whether or not the tales are true."

He laughed. "You have taken the measure of the viscount quickly."

"We have met on far too many occasions."

"Have you?"

"Before he asked Lady Viola to marry him, he intended to ask me."

"Now *that* is an interesting fact you could have

mentioned earlier. I can understand why Lady Viola is resolved to outshine you in your own home. But why are you asking me questions about the war and Turnbull?"

"I spoke with him earlier in my father's book-room."

"Turnbull in a room filled with books? Not his usual haunt."

Quietly she said, "Lord Turnbull hopes you will refrain from speaking of the war to Lady Viola."

"I wondered how long it would take him before his nerve broke again," he said with a rumble of laughter.

"Again?"

"He was not the bravest man on the Continent."

She looked along the battlements and realized that Quintus had vanished. She wondered how much of the conversation he had heard. "Quintus is gone."

He pushed away from the crenelation. "China, why do you have to inject that silly ghost into every conversation? You are letting that phantom obsess you."

Closing the space between them, she curved one hand behind his nape. "I am obsessed with making sure we stay alive past the fifth of September."

His arm edged around her waist. "I like that part of your obsession because it keeps you close to me."

"Now you are trying to be as charming as Lord Turnbull."

He grimaced and kissed the tip of her nose. "That is insulting." Shrugging off his coat and setting it around her shoulders, he said, "You are shivering, China."

She held up her hand so the wind wove around her fingers. "Yes, the wind is chilly," she said, putting her head on his shoulder when his arm settled again around her waist. "When I was a child, I would sneak up here and delight in the crispness of the wind. Up on that wall I could be alone."

He tilted her face up toward his. "You keep showing me your havens."

"There are times when I do not want to hear any voice but the wind's."

"Is now one of those times?"

"No." She pushed a stubborn strand of hair away from his eyes, but the wind blew it back. Smiling, she added, "I am glad you are here, Alexander."

Combing his fingers up through her hair, he loosened it to fall on the shoulders of his coat. He captured her lips with the fervor she had seen in his eyes.

Her fingers slipped into his hair, and she delighted in its dark silkiness. When his mouth moved to caress her ear, he laughed with the low huskiness that scintillated within her. As his lips found hers again, his fingers swept along her sides to brush her breasts. She moaned his name, hoping he understood how much she wanted him.

Raising his mouth, he whispered, "You have too many chaperones, darling."

"A whole houseful of them." She traced the hard line of his jaw that was rough with a day's growth of whiskers. Could he feel her rapid heartbeat throbbing through her like a water pump?

"You have sworn a vow to watch over me day and night."

"I have."

He cupped her face in his broad hands. "Then promise me that you will spend tonight with me."

Her heart dancing with joy, she brushed her lips against his. "Yes. But first I have some household matters to tend to. If I skip them, all my chaperones will notice. It should not take more than an hour."

"An hour?" He gave an emoted groan. "An eternity when I am waiting for you."

She jutted her chin toward him in her most stubborn pose. "You will not be the only one suffering through the wait. Do not forget that."

"I cannot forget a single thing about you, darling." He pressed his mouth against her neck, its heat resonating to her toes.

It took all her strength to pull back. "If you do not let me meet with Mrs. Mathers now and complete my duties tonight, it shall be far longer than an hour."

Taking her by the shoulders, he spun her about so she faced the door. He gave her a gentle slap on the backside and ordered, "Then get going."

She laughed as she walked toward the door. Putting her foot on the topmost step, she looked back. "Alexander, are you staying up here?"

"Don't worry. I will be waiting for you, darling. I just want to think a bit myself."

"If there is anything I can do to help . . ."

His roguish smile returned. "I will let you know in an hour."

Chapter 15

"China, may I speak to you for a moment?"

Turning, China smiled at her sister, even though she had never felt less like smiling. The hour for her day's-end duties had stretched into two and now a third, and she still had a few more tasks before she could join Alexander.

Join. The very thought of the two of them moving together as one sent an unquenchable need through her. She hoped Sian would not guess why she was discomposed. The splendid, sensuous thoughts vanished from her mind when she saw dismay on her sister's face.

Taking Sian's hands, she asked, "What is amiss?"

"It is Lady Viola." Sian spit out the woman's name with a fury she was struggling to restrain.

"What has she done now?"

"She invited Sir Henry to her silly party, but not his sister. How could she insult the Cranlers like that?"

China smiled wryly. "I can believe anything of her at this point. Do not fret about it. I will send Sir Henry a note asking him to bring his sister. I am sure *he* will attend. I think he is quite taken with you, Sian."

"I think so as well." Her sister looked glum. "Sir Henry is a dear man and a good friend to this family, but . . ."

"You have another man in your heart."

Sian's head snapped up, her eyes wide with astonishment. "How did you know?"

"Because when we first arrived home from London, every other word out of your mouth was about Constantine Lassiter."

Sian stared down at her toes as if she were Miss Upton. "I stopped speaking of him when people became confused, thinking his title of Lord Lastingham had something to do with the village."

"Was that the only reason?" China put her finger under her sister's chin and tipped it back so she could see Sian's tear-filled eyes.

"He told me he would write, but I have not received a single letter. I can only assume he has forgotten me."

"No one could ever forget you, Sian. You are so warmhearted that I am sure Lord Lastingham has had other reasons not to contact you."

"Do you truly think so?"

"I truly hope so." She would not lie to her sister. The earl had acted sweet on Sian, but that might have been an attraction only for the Season. She did not want to break her sister's tender heart, but neither did she want to offer false hopes.

Sian gave her a quick hug. "Thank you, China."

Promising again that she would write to Sir Henry first thing on the morrow, China gave her sister a kiss on the cheek before continuing along the hall.

It was almost another hour before China was able to climb the stairs to the wing where the family's bedchambers were situated. As she walked along the hallway she did not see light beneath Alexander's door.

China sighed. He must have tired of waiting for her. Pausing in front of his door, she reached for the knob. She lowered her hand. She had not allowed herself to think beyond the moment when they would be together. Had he? Was he having second thoughts as he might have expected her to? She did not have any. She could think only of him and the pleasure that would be theirs. Being the sensible Nethercott sister had grown to be a burden. Tonight, with him, she planned to shunt that role aside for a few glorious hours. Waking him was what she now wanted with every inch of her being, but if he had intended for her to come in, he would have kept a lamp lit. He would not sit and wait for her in the dark, would he?

Before she could answer her own question, she heard a sound.

A low moan.

"Quintus?" she whispered.

She looked in both directions along the passage, but there was no ghost glowing in the dark.

Hearing the sound again, she gasped. It was coming from beyond Alexander's door.

This time she did not hesitate. She opened the door. Stepping into the thick shadows, she left the door open behind her. "Alexander? Are you all right?"

He did not answer.

She took another step, sliding her foot along the

rug. The room was swallowed by shadow. She flinched when she heard another groan from the other side of the room.

From the bed.

It was the sound of deep despair and sickness. Her stomach cramped. Had someone attacked Alexander while she had been flitting about the house finishing up the day's work?

"Alexander?" she whispered.

Again she got no answer. She stumbled forward and stubbed her toe on a chair. Tears flooded her eyes. She blinked them away as her fingers reached for the edge of a nearby table.

Why hadn't Alexander acknowledged her yet? Even if he were ill, he should have heard her call his name. More groans came from the far side of the chamber. She inched toward the bed, whispering both his name and Quintus's. She could not tell which lump on the bed was a coverlet and which was Alexander.

She shook the mattress. "Alexander? Alexander, what is wrong? Are you all right?"

Suddenly Alexander exploded up from the far side of the bed. He seized her arms.

"What are you doing?" she cried.

He did not answer as he dragged her around the bed to where he was standing. He jerked her up against his naked chest, and she gasped as her fingers rose to that warm skin. She tilted her mouth for his kiss. She cried out in shock when, with a curse, he pulled her to the floor. She started to protest his rough treatment, but he knelt beside her and pressed his hand over her mouth. Fear twisted through her. This was not the gentle man who had held her so sweetly on the battlements and vowed to excite her with eager caresses.

She peeled his fingers away from her mouth. "What is wrong, Alexander?"

"Silence!" he snarled.

He slanted over her, rising so he could see over the bed. Tension made his chest taut against her. When she moved so she could look, too, he growled another oath as he pressed her to the floor.

"I told you to be silent!" His hushed voice was filled with savage fury.

"But—"

"Will you be silent before you alert them, Rexleigh?"

Rexleigh!

"Alert whom?" she whispered.

"Be silent!" His fingers curled into a fist.

Before he could raise it, she gasped. "Remember where you are, Alexander! I am not Rexleigh. I am China!"

"Be—"

She grasped his head and pressed her mouth to his. Leaning back on the floor, she brought him to lie over her. Her fingers curled around his shoulders and then down his naked back. He started to pull away; then his arm slipped beneath her, holding her closer. His hand cradled her head as he deepened the kiss until she was the one who moaned softly into his mouth.

At the sound, he drew back and stared down at her. Even in the darkness, she could see astonishment sweep across his face. "China? What are you doing here?"

Embarrassment swept through her, icy cold and

dousing the heat of her longing. *He* had invited her to his room, and now he acted surprised. Was this one of the silly games men and women played?

"Let me up!" she ordered.

"China, what in the hell are you doing here?" When she struggled to sit, he kept her against the floor. "Stay where you are! When the cannons begin to fire, you must—"

"Cannons? What cannons?" Sliding from beneath him, she rose to her knees and grasped his shoulders. "Alexander, there are not any cannons. You are in Nethercott Castle! Do you hear me?"

"The French are aiming to knock our heads off our shoulders." He pulled her hands off him so fast that her nails scraped his skin. "They are about to fire at us!"

China stared at his shadowed face. He was caught in a nightmare. Not even her kiss had woken him completely. She yanked her hands out of his. Framing his face, she whispered, "Look at me. Who do you see?"

"China, this is no time for games."

"You are right. It is no time for games, so tell me who you see."

He glanced over the top of the bed, then back at her. "I see you."

"Who am I?"

"China, I—"

More sternly, she repeated, "Who am I?"

"China Nethercott."

"Where am I?"

"On the battlefield at—"

"No! I am not on a battlefield. *Where* am I?"

This time he did not answer quickly; nor did he

try to peer across the bed as if gauging the range of French artillery.

"Where am I, Alexander?" she demanded. "Where am I really?"

"Nethercott Castle?"

She was amazed when he made it a question, but she kept her voice even as she replied, "Yes, I am in Nethercott Castle. So are you."

"I am?"

His question—so unsure and so unlike him—pierced her. Putting her arms around him, she sat and drew his head down over her heart. She held him, saying nothing while he shivered with fear. She did not want to imagine what haunted this strong, brave man.

Raising her head, she glanced around the room beyond the bed. Where was Quintus now? She could use his help. He, too, had been a warrior, so he might understand why Alexander acted this way—not just tonight, but that first night when she had found him on the floor with the bedcovers twined around him, having no idea how or when he had gotten out of bed.

She almost called out the ghost's name, but that would distress Alexander further.

When Alexander sat up, he looked away. She did not need to see his face to know he was ashamed that she had witnessed this.

"It is nothing," she whispered, putting her hand on his shoulder. His skin was deliciously warm beneath her fingertips, but she pushed thoughts of making love from her mind.

"Nothing?" He laughed humorlessly.

"It was only a dream."

"Only a dream?" He shook his head, but did not

look at her. "That is what my mother said, too, at the beginning."

"Your mother? She knows you have these nightmares about the war?"

"No, but she knew about my father's. Or so she thought."

"I don't understand."

"Insanity."

Alexander clamped his mouth closed when he heard footsteps creak along the hall. Standing, he grabbed a dressing gown from the foot of the bed and tied it around himself. He held out his hand to her, but she hesitated. Pain hammered him as if a cannon blast had hit him directly.

"Now you know," he said quietly as lamplight spread into the room.

"Know what?"

"That I am no hero."

She opened her mouth, then looked past him to the people peeking into the room. She placed her hand on his and came to her feet as if she had not heard their shock at discovering her in his private chamber. She glanced at the mussed bed and knew what the servants assumed.

"Oh, good," China said as she released his hand and walked toward the door. "Mrs. Mathers, will you send someone to check the chimney? I want to make sure no more bats come into the house."

"Bats?" squeaked one of the maids in the doorway. "I hate bats!"

Several other women echoed her sentiment. The men were silent, but Alexander noticed that about half edged aside. He guessed they were just as uneager to encounter a bat.

Mrs. Mathers rushed into the room, motioning to a footman to light the lamps. "I will have it checked, Miss China."

"Thank you." China's voice quavered. When she turned to him, he noticed she was limping. He groaned when he recalled how hard he had pulled China, believing her to be Rexleigh, down onto the muddy field of his nightmare. "And thank you, Alexander, for protecting me from my own foolishness when I burst in here. It was the closest door, and I made a complete fool of myself."

"Fortunately I was only half-asleep." He hated lying, but the idea of ruining her was far worse. He wanted to release another groan as he recalled why she had come into his room. She had kept her promise. He was the one who had had doubts when she did not arrive once the hour had passed.

"I will have the chimneys checked in the morning," Mrs. Mathers said. She shooed the servants out of the room. "Off to bed with you, and be quiet so you do not wake Miss Sian. We will be very busy with that extra work on the morrow." The housekeeper turned to face China. "Is there anything else I can do for you?"

He held his breath, waiting for China's answer. Her smile did not waver as she said, "Thank you, Mrs. Mathers, but that is all."

"As you wish." The housekeeper walked toward the door, then paused by the table. She picked up a piece of black fabric. "I thought this had been thrown out."

Alexander crossed the room in a pair of long strides and snatched the material from the housekeeper. "Why would you throw this out?"

"Because of the smoky smell. We disposed of all the gritty items we found in the hallway after the fire." Her nose wrinkled.

"Gritty!" He let his smile become predatory. "Mrs. Mathers, you described some charred fabric discovered in the wake of the fire as 'gritty.' I knew I had heard that word recently." He gave the housekeeper a warmer smile. "Thank you."

"Do you want me to toss that out?"

"No." He rolled the cloth into a ball in his fist. "I will take care of it."

The housekeeper nodded as he wished her a good night's sleep.

China stepped past him and looked around the edge of the door. She did not close it as she faced him. "Farley is waiting just out of earshot."

"You do have too many chaperones."

His attempt to make her smile failed. She walked to him and whispered, "Do you think the highwayman tried to kill us here in Nethercott Castle?"

"It would seem that way." His jaw clenched as he stared down at the rough fabric as she tilted his hand to get a better look at it. "Or someone wishes us to believe that."

"He did shoot Lord Turnbull's coachman."

"We cannot be sure if he did so on purpose or if the ball went awry in an attempt to frighten them." He drew his hand away from hers. Even that light touch threatened to destroy what control he had left. "He did not scare you."

"He did frighten me." Her eyes, their color deepening, rose toward his. "Just as you did tonight." She clutched onto his sleeve. "Alexander, you have evaded telling me the truth for too long. What is going on? Who is Rexleigh?''

''Nothing is going on.''

''But you said your mother—''

''Enough!''

When she stared in disbelief at his harsh tone, he flinched, wishing he had guarded his words. In the moment when he had feared for her life, he had blurted out the secret that he had hidden from everyone. But he was not angry with China, only himself.

She went to the door, pausing to look back at him. Hurt vied with anger on her face, but she held her head high. ''Good night, Alexander.''

''China . . .''

She waited for him to go on, but he was unsure of what to say. The secret gnawed at his soul. The curse, his mother had called it. And now China talked of curses, too. If he had half the sense of Lady Viola's dog, he would pack and leave at first light.

He stared at her. So delicate, yet so strong. So gentle, yet so formidable. So lovely and so desirable. She was the woman he had once dreamed he would find, but he had changed so much since discovering that madness stained the roots of his family tree.

''Answer one question,'' she said, her voice as precise as when she spoke to Lord Turnbull.

''I will try.'' He hated that he could not bare his soul, confess his feelings, explain the truth about what had opened a chasm between them. He just could not.

''Who is Rexleigh?''

He walked back to the bed, fisting his hand on the footboard. ''He is the friend I ordered to die so I could be lauded as a hero.''

Chapter 16

China got no sleep that night. More than once, she considered getting up and crossing the hall to Alexander's room. She played out several different scenarios in her mind. She would hold him while he poured out his heart to her. She would lean her head against his shoulder as he answered the questions he had avoided. She would lie in his arms while they soared away from sorrow.

But she remained in her bed, staring at the wooden canopy until the first gray light of dawn slowly seeped across the floor. As much as she wished one of those fantasies could come true, did he feel the same?

After he spoke the unbelievable words about Rexleigh, the pain on his face had deepened. She had just stared at him, too shocked to speak. She had tried to break the taut silence, but she stumbled over her words before they faded away. The questions she longed to ask went unspoken, and when he had told her good night, she wondered if he truly meant good-bye. So she remained in her room until morning, listening for his footsteps walking away from her father's bedchamber and away from her.

While helping China get dressed, Bernice was subdued. Her maid's normally deft hands were clumsy, and China took pity on her, sending her to take clothes to the laundry. Brushing her hair into place, China did not look in the mirror. There must be dark half circles beneath her eyes, and her lips trembled whenever she did not keep them pursed.

The breakfast-parlor, a cozy room with a wall of windows facing south, was empty when China entered. Food steamed in covered dishes on the sideboard, but the aromas did not tempt her. Her stomach was in knots, and she doubted she could eat, but she had hoped Sian would be there. She needed to talk to her sister and get her advice.

When a servant set a pot of chocolate on the table, she learned her sister had already eaten and left to spend the morning sketching. China sighed. Sian must be even more exasperated with Lady Viola than she had guessed. Otherwise her sister would not have left the house when they had guests.

Going to the window, she looked at the sunlight dancing on the dew, transforming the garden into a treasure trove of sparkling gems. She shared Sian's yearning to escape.

A hand cupped her elbow, and her skin came alive.

"Good morning," Alexander said.

Yesterday she would have leaned into him. Now she was unsure what to do. "Good morning to you." Facing him, she moved to put more space between them. The ravages of a sleepless night weighed heav-

ily on him, too. She longed to smooth the lines from
his forehead that had not been there yesterday.
"Please help yourself to breakfast."

"Will you sit with me while I eat?"

She was unsure if he asked in hopes that she
would agree or if he wanted to offer her a chance
to escape.

"There is much we need to speak of," he added.

"Thank you. I will be happy to . . . to have breakfast with you." She had been about to say that she
would join him, but that sounded too intimate to her
ears. When had common words taken on double
meanings?

Going to the sideboard, China took a small spoonful
of scrambled eggs and one muffin. She was not hungry, and she could not imagine eating more than a
single bite. Sitting, she noticed that Alexander's plate
was almost empty as well. He drew out the chair next
to hers while she poured two cups of chocolate. She
set the pot down and waited for him to speak.

"I am sorry," he said. "I know last night was not
what you expected."

"No." Her laugh was unsteady. "Nor you."

"True." His rigid expression eased slightly. "I regret hurting you. I saw you limping."

"My leg had gone numb while kneeling and was
filled with pins and needles. Nothing more."

She waited for him to go on, but he looked down
into his cup of hot chocolate. Putting her hand on
his arm, she was shocked when he recoiled.

Tears burned, and her voice shook as she whispered, "Now I must say I am sorry, Alexander. I did
not think that a commonplace touch would bother
you. I shall not—"

"Don't say that you will never touch me again." He stroked her cheek. "I know that the Nethercotts keep their vows, and that is one I cannot let you make." He glanced toward the door that led to the kitchen stairs. "We need to find a place where there are fewer ears. Somewhere beyond these walls."

She thought of Quintus's request that she keep Alexander within the house. She dismissed it as quickly she had on the wall, for two attacks had come within Nethercott Castle.

"I think I know a site on the moors that you would enjoy," she said.

"Will you give me a clue as to what it is?"

"No, but I can promise you that Lady Viola will be furious we did not ask her to join us."

For the first time since he had entered the breakfast-parlor, he grinned. "I like the site already."

She smiled too as she reached for the butter to spread on her muffin. Perhaps everything was not over between them yet.

The wind blew, scudding the clouds as if it could no longer wait to send them over the sea. The undulating moors were a dull shade. The few bushes in bloom were already donning their autumn drabness.

China drew her cape more tightly around her, but the wind lashed it about her ankles as Alexander handed her out of the carriage. When she told the footman to wait inside, he nodded gratefully. On the box, the coachee hunkered down into his cloak.

"What a wonderful day!" Alexander said as he gave up trying to keep his hat on his head. Reopening the door, he tossed the hat in on the seat. The wind toyed with his hair and burnished his skin, bringing back the color it must have had before his accident.

"You have a strange idea of what constitutes good weather."

"Do I?" He put his arm around her shoulders and drew her against his side. "If the weather was fair and mild, I would not have the excuse to do this."

"Do you need an excuse?"

"I thought I might today."

She pressed her hand to her bonnet before the wind could peel it off. "Can we pretend that nothing happened last night?"

"Nothing I had hoped for did happen."

Aware that the coachman and the footman might catch their words that were carried on the wind, she motioned toward a stile on the right side of the road. It was simple, consisting of a short bench slipped between the railing of the fence to make it easy to climb from one side to the other. She paused because she knew she could no longer put off asking the question that had plagued her all night.

"Tell me about Rexleigh, Alexander."

"Why ruin this pleasant day?"

"The pleasantness is only an illusion if you do not explain what you said last night about ordering him to die."

He put one foot on the stile and gazed across the windswept moors. "In a fit of patriotic fervor I decided to buy a commission," he said so low that she could barely hear him over the wind. "As well, I saw it as a way to prove my worth separate from my family, to remove myself from the whispers of my father's madness. Rexleigh insisted on going with me. He had served as my valet, and as my father's before that. Even though he was almost two decades my senior, he saw my military career as no reason to stop serving me. I tried to convince him otherwise, but he refused to heed me."

"So he went with you."

"Yes, through the horrendous months on the Peninsula and then on to the final battle at Waterloo. Rexleigh did not return from that battle."

"What happened?" She set her hand on his knee. When he put his gloved fingers over hers, she whispered, "Please tell me, Alexander. It is too great a burden for you to bear alone."

"If I tell you, then you will be burdened with the truth as well."

"Not knowing is worse."

"Do not be so certain of that." Folding his fingers around hers, he said, "I was certain that Napoleon would be defeated at Waterloo, and the battle would be my final opportunity for greatness. The idea of my legacy consumed me." His mouth twisted, and he sighed. "So I gave my men their posts. I ordered Rexleigh to hold his position, not to move even if retreat was called. No heroic retreats. He must hold his hard-won ground.

"When the order came to reform the lines as the French swarmed over us, I was so eager to be in the thick of the battle that I forgot to rescind my order to Rexleigh. He tried to hold his position, and he did . . . for a time. But the filthy frogs overran him while he stood there alone." Again he stared across the moors, but she guessed he was seeing the battleground on that fateful day. "I was shot before I did anything heroic, and the next thing I knew the battle had moved on, leaving me far behind the lines. I lost consciousness and awoke when the battle was over. Only then, when the madness had dissipated, did I try to find Rexleigh. I found him dead along with the corpses of the many enemies he had killed while trying to follow my stupid order. I betrayed him. I thought more about my reputation than I did of my men. Dropping into the mud beside him, I tried to tell him how sorry I was, but it was too late." He released her hand. "When I woke in a hospital tent, I was being hailed as a hero. I tried to tell them that Rexleigh had held the position, not me. No one heeded me. He was the hero. I was not."

She gazed up into his haunted eyes. "And you have never had the chance to tell him how sorry you are for what happened."

"Yes."

"Which is why you must bear the praise, because only then can you tell others that Rexleigh was a hero. You owe it to him to have his story be heard."

He tilted her mouth toward his. "Deuce take it! You are vexing when you are right."

"So you have mentioned before."

Giving her a swift, fiery kiss, he picked her up and set her on the stile. Leaning toward him, she brushed her mouth to his again. She longed to slip into his embrace as he led her to rapture, but she was aware of the chaperones in the carriage only a few yards away. He winked and put his hands to her waist to steady her as she climbed over the rail.

As he followed, China scanned the rolling hills. Other than sheep and the few trees that clung to a shallow brook at the bottom of the slope, they and her servants were the only living things for miles.

She wondered why she had not thought to bring Alexander up onto the moors before now.

He jumped down beside her. "Where to now?"

"We are here." She pointed to a low flat surface at one side of the field. It was paved with uneven stones and flowed in a nearly straight line toward the horizon. "Won't Lady Viola be peeved that I did not invite her to join us to look at this *Roman* road?"

His eyes widened as he walked along the path of stones. "Was it truly built by Romans?"

"That is what my father believed."

"Amazing."

Unexpected tears flooded her eyes. How many times had she heard her father utter that word when he discovered something that fascinated him? She stepped onto the uneven surface that was about six inches higher than the ground, quickly swiping at her eyes. "There is a legend, however, that a giant named Wade built this road. . . ." China paused as she heard hoofbeats.

She shaded her eyes, for the daylight was strong even with clouds above the moor. A rider was traveling fast along the road. Too fast for a man of his bulk. His black cloak bounced out behind him like wings.

Alexander grasped her arm and stepped in front of her. "Stay here. I left a pistol with your coachee."

"Alexander, that is not the highwayman. It is Reverend Wilder."

"The curate of the Lastingham church? What is he doing here?"

"Looking for us, I would wager."

The man dismounted by the carriage and walked to the stile. Calling a greeting, he heaved himself

over the fence. He was in his middle years and almost as round as he was tall, but the gray-haired
curate moved with the grace of a young, lithe man.
Years of exploring the moors and riding to tend to
his parishioners had kept him agile.

China quickly introduced the two men, then asked,
"Did you chase us from Nethercott Castle?"

"My housekeeper told me that you had called,"
Reverend Wilder said in his booming voice that overmastered even the wind gusts. "When I heard that
you wanted to talk to me about some of the old stories, I could not resist returning your call. Your
majordomo told me where you were headed."

Alexander smiled. "She was just about to tell me
about a giant and this road."

"Ah, you mean Wade." The curate gazed along
the road and led the way as they walked. "There are
many legends about the giant Wade and his wife to
explain various sites on the moors. The local children
enjoy them."

As if it were of little importance, Alexander asked,
"Are there any stories about giants walking across
the moors at night?"

"Most giants lived like humans, working during
the day and sleeping at night." He continued with
Alexander along the ancient road. "Have you heard
a different sort of tale? I collect stories of the moors
and hope to put them into a book one day."

China started to follow, then paused when the
light grew so strong she glanced skyward to see if
the clouds had broken to let the sunshine through.
She realized that the light came from behind her,
not above.

Turning, she saw Quintus. *"Ave."*

"*Ave*, China." He looked past her. "Are you sure it is wise to bring my descendant out here?"

"I would trust the curate with my life." Not wanting to explain what Alexander had told her by the stile, she added, "Alexander has been eager to see some of the old sites on the moors. Did you use this road?"

"I never went farther north than the camp." His aquiline nose wrinkled. "Barbarians wandered freely here, and I wanted nothing to do with them. I was a civilized man, a citizen of the empire."

"But you must know whether the road was here during your lifetime."

"I have never been here before now, when I needed to speak to you."

She smiled sadly. How lonely he must have been as he waited for the next generation to grow, hoping someone could soon help break the curse.

"I am sorry, Quintus. I thought if you knew more about the road, I could share that information with Alexander. He would enjoy knowing."

"You care deeply for him, don't you?"

"He is a good man who has been very unhappy." She did not want the conversation to continue in that direction, so she asked, "Why did you come to speak with me?"

"You must halt that woman's plans for the party."

"I have tried."

"You need to try harder."

"Let me talk with her again this afternoon."

He threw back his head and stood straighter. "You *must* make her see it is not a good idea."

China frowned. "Do you know something you are not telling me? Is it dangerous for Alexander to attend?"

He sighed. "I fear more for him as the fifth of September approaches. You must find a way to insure that he will listen before it is too late." He clenched his hands on his shield, and his voice rose with desperation. "If he dies now, my direct line dies with him. I have waited almost two millennia for this curse to be broken, and this may be my last chance."

"If only he could see you . . ."

"You know that is impossible. *You* are the one I was meant to speak with. *You* are the only one who can make a difference. If you fail, the curse will hold me for the rest of eternity."

"I know." She did not add that knowing it weighed on her as heavily as Alexander's guilt did on him. She gazed across the moor to where Alexander and the curate were pointing to something. With their attention elsewhere, they had not noticed yet that she was talking to someone they could not see. "If there was something sensible about this curse, I might be able to persuade Alexander to listen to me."

"I am going to try as well." His eyes narrowed as he glanced from her to Alexander. "I must do something to persuade him to listen to you."

"What do you plan to do?"

"You will be the first to know, China," he said, beginning to fade back into the bright light.

"What do you mean? What . . ."

Quintus had vanished. His odd expression made her very uneasy. It had been . . . She searched for the right words. Cunning. Covetous. Both. What was he planning?

"Thank you, Reverend Wilder," Alexander was saying as the two men approached her. "This is fascinating. I think I will have to search my grandfather's library for books about this old road."

The curate chuckled. "Avail yourself of the late Lord Nethercott's book-room while you are Miss Nethercott's guest. He has more research material on the moors than anyone in England."

The two men shook hands, and the curate bade China a good day before climbing over the stile.

Alexander offered his arm to her, but she did not take it as she stared at the spot where Quintus had been. "What is wrong, China?"

"Quintus may do something outrageous to break the curse on your family." She hastened to explain, then added, "I know you cannot bring yourself to believe that I have really seen a ghost."

"I believe that *you* believe you have." He lifted her hand and placed it on his arm. "I still resist believing."

"What further proof do you need?"

"It is not the need for proof." Sorrow dimmed his eyes. "If I *do* believe that there is a ghost, then I must believe in the curse. To believe in that means that I must believe you, too, may be condemned to die simply because you are trying to keep me alive."

"But if you believe, we can work together to break the curse."

"I will try, China. I cannot promise anything, but I will try."

"Thank you. I don't know what else to say."

"Say that you will spend tonight with me."

Joy flooded her. "I will."

"And this time, nothing will keep me from holding you."

"Nothing," she repeated, silently adding, *I hope.*

Chapter 17

A hand shook Alexander's shoulder. He snarled a curse. After all their years together, hadn't Rexleigh learned that Alexander would wake when he was ready? There was no battle or march scheduled today. He muttered an even more vicious oath.

"Alexander, wake up!"

That was not Rexleigh's voice. His sergeant's had been as gravelly as scree.

"Alexander, wake up! I cannot find China!"

The half-world between sleep and consciousness evaporated abruptly. Opening his eyes, he saw Sian in front of his chair, fear blanching her face.

"What do you mean?" He looked at the shadows crossing the floor and knew that his nap after returning from the moors had lasted far longer than he had planned.

"I cannot find her! She is not in her room or anywhere else she normally would be at this hour."

He glanced at the window, where stars glittered. "What time is it?"

"Almost midnight."

"So late?" His stomach growled, reminding him

that he had missed supper. "Where would she normally be at this hour?" *And why hasn't she come to wake me with her delicious kisses?*

"Sometimes she likes to read in Father's bookroom. Sometimes she goes up on the parapets to look at the night sky. She sneaks up into the tower room, but she would not have gone there after the fire."

"And you checked all those places?" He pushed himself to his feet and realized that his legs were bare beneath his breeches and his shirt was half-unbuttoned. He disregarded his state of undress, one that would have sent frailer women into a swoon.

"I have. No one has seen her since before supper." She began to wring her hands. "I am afraid something horrible has happened to her."

Alexander gritted his teeth so hard his head ached. As if she stood in the room, he could hear China saying, *Quintus may do something outrageous to break the curse on your family.*

He had dismissed her distress in his excitement of the night he would share with her. From the moment she had pulled him from the collapsed wall, she had been anxious about his well-being and the welfare of everyone around her. Not once had she expected anyone to be concerned on her behalf.

Now . . .

As he redid his shirt, tucking its tails into his breeches, he asked, "Do you see my boots?"

She ran across the shadowed room and brought the boots he had left by the hearth. Sitting on a chair as he finished dressing, she listed again the places she had looked for her sister.

Her voice was unsteady as she whispered, "What if *he* took her?"

"He?"

"The highwayman. He was bold enough to shoot at you in Lastingham."

"Highwaymen are not known to break into houses to abduct young women."

"But this highwayman has acted oddly from the onset."

He had to agree with her. Sian displayed a common trait of her sister's: She was logical and clear-thinking, even in the midst of a possible disaster.

"There are a few other places she might be," he said, going to the rosewood box on the table by the bed.

He heard Sian gasp when he lifted out a pair of pistols. He tried to ignore the fact that they would be useless against a ghost. Did he believe there was a ghost? No, but he believed China had seen *something*.

"Wait here," he ordered. "Do not leave the house before daybreak. Even then, do not go anywhere alone." With a bitten-off curse, he added, "Keep Lady Viola from the Roman camp. Whatever else you do, make sure she does not go there."

"Is that where you are bound?" she asked as he flung his cloak around his shoulders,

He picked up the pistols and nodded.

"Why?"

"I will explain when I get back."

"If she is not there, where will you look?"

"Everywhere," he said grimly, having no idea where else to search.

As Alexander approached the clearing of the Roman camp, an ethereal light seemed to be in a nearby tree. He crept forward, his heart pounding before he looked up to see moonlight sifting through leafy branches. He cursed his fancifulness. Before battles he had heard men telling stories of horror until they were so frightened that they were unfit for duty the next day. Those men seldom left the battlefield alive. He had struggled to control his emotions, even after seeing Rexleigh among the dead on the field near Waterloo.

Then he had met China. She had shredded his defenses, even as she worked to protect him. With others he could not share his private pain, but she welcomed him to free it. Her slender shoulders seemed ready to take over his burden, and he was learning that releasing grief was the best way to rid himself of its crushing pain. But the grief remained. It always would, but with her help, it was becoming something he could live with.

He held up his lantern to send light around him. The earthworks looked like giant, stiff snakes through the clearing. Only in two spots were they not in perfect alignment. The closer one was where he suspected a gate once had allowed people into the camp. Beyond that was the place where the wall had collapsed on him. Where China had begun the task of protecting him.

He saw no one. She must be here. It was the only place he could think of where she would go to after dark. He silenced the voice that suggested she may have been missing far longer than Sian believed.

"China! Are you here? China!"

He got no answer. As he was about to call again, the lantern glittered off something on the ground. Dropping to his hands and knees, he set the lantern beside him and searched through the grass. He held up a button the color of the dress China had been wearing earlier, and smiled coldly when he saw a break in the wall directly in front of him. He put the pistols on the top of the earthworks, not wanting to chance the gun firing by mistake.

He picked up the lantern and wiggled through the hole. It quickly opened into a wider area several times the size of the space that had collapsed on him. His hand brushed roughly planed boards, and he realized someone had been using this cave. Rising to his knees, he held up the lantern. At the back of the cave, he saw China lying facedown, half-hidden by a cloak.

"China!" he called, his voice echoing oddly inside the earth.

She did not move.

He called her name again as he crawled to where she lay.

As if she sensed his approach, she slowly opened her eyes. "Alexander?" she asked in confusion. Even the shadows could not dampen the gemlike glow in her widening eyes as she sat and looked around.

He swept her to him, kissing her hair, her cheeks, her nose, her mouth. When her bonnet fell back, he lifted his lips away to ask, "Are you all right?"

Wincing, she untied her bonnet and set it on the ground beside her. "Where are we?"

"The Roman camp."

"How . . . ?" Her eyes widened. "I remember. There was a light. I thought it was Quintus, so I followed it out of Nethercott Castle. Then . . ." Again her voice trailed off.

"Then what?"

"I have no idea." She ran her fingers along her

forehead, and he guessed it ached. "I don't remember anything after that. If I had to guess I would say Quintus arranged this, but I have no idea how."

"What is this place?"

"A poacher's den, I suspect. It would be an easy place to hide game that was taken illegally. It does not look as if anyone has used it recently."

"The cart is waiting on the path. Do you think you can walk that far?"

Before she could answer, the ground shook. He pulled her to him, leaning over her as dirt fell from overhead. Something groaned. The boards! They were struggling to keep the roof up.

"Get out!" he ordered. "Now!"

More chunks of earth tumbled down as the opening of the cave vanished into a cloud of dust and debris. He coughed and heard her doing the same.

Then it was silent for a long moment before a single small stone rattled down onto others.

China pushed away from Alexander and crawled across the rubble on the floor of the cave. Behind her he held up the lantern. She saw her shadow climb the stones in front of her, revealing what she feared.

"The entrance is gone," she said.

He stretched his arm past her and pushed at several rocks. They seemed to be locked in place. "It is well sealed. We are imprisoned here."

She held up her hand. "Air is seeping between the stones. We will not suffocate."

"Are you always so calm?"

"I am when I know panicking will serve no purpose."

He chuckled. "If Lady Viola were here now, she would be screeching."

"Then you are lucky I am here." She sat back on her heels and rubbed her forehead again. Her whole skull ached dully.

After spreading out her cloak, he put his arm around her shoulders and guided her back to sit on it. "We may have a long wait."

"Sian will come looking for us."

"That may not be for some time. I told her not to leave Nethercott Castle under any circumstances."

"She *will* wait, but I would guess by midday she will be searching for us. Does she know where you were bound?"

"Yes, and she is certain to see the pistols I left outside."

She smiled and nestled against his strong shoulder. "Good. We should be out of here within twelve hours or so. Unless Quintus arranges for someone to come before then." She sat up and moved away. "I don't think we can count on that."

"Why not?" He turned down the lamp so the light would last longer. "Do you think *this* is his outrageous scheme?"

"Yes." She could not bring herself to look at him. "I think he brought us here so we could be alone and then sealed us in to ensure our privacy."

He bent to press his lips to the responsive skin right behind her ear. "Remind me to thank him . . . if I ever see him."

She put her hands on his chest and inched farther away. "He did not do this for us. He did it for himself. He is hoping for another chance to break the curse if I fail to keep you alive after September fifth."

"But if I die there is no next generation to . . ." His eyes widened with understanding, and he chuckled.

She stared at him, wondering if a rock had struck his head. "There is nothing funny about this."

"To the contrary! I find this amazingly funny." He drew a pin from her hair, then another. "Or should I say amusing? Because I can think of nothing else I would rather do right now than have us amuse each other."

"Alexander, we should not—"

His breath caressed her neck, its heat seeping all the way to her toes. "I would be a fool not to take advantage of this."

"Aren't you the same man who told me I was silly to allow my guests to take advantage of me?"

He pulled her into his arms, his thumb tipping her chin up so her mouth was directly below his. "I do not want to take advantage of you, darling. I want to make love with you."

"Here?"

"Anywhere."

She softened against him and put her hands on either side of his face to bring his lips to hers. She did not close her eyes, wanting to see the longing displayed in his. He had not made his desire for her a secret, and she savored that powerful blue fire.

Her hands stroked up his sleeves and the strong muscles beneath the wool. His arms closed around her as his tongue teased her mouth open. On the pulse of his heated breath was his barely restrained need.

His tongue slid within her mouth, warmed by her own eagerness. As she sifted her fingers into his thick hair, he slowly caressed her mouth, inviting her to be as brazen. It was an invitation she could not spurn. She wanted every bit of delight they could share. Tremors, even stronger than what had brought down the stones, erupted through her as his tongue stroked hers.

She loosened his cravat. He gave her a languid smile before he pressed his mouth once more to her neck. As he leaned her back on her cloak, she drew him with her. Her hands curved up under his coat, pulling his shirt up out of his breeches. She slipped her fingers beneath to savor his warm skin. His quick intake of breath thrilled her.

In his warm embrace, she quivered as he laved the skin along her neck. His hair on her skin lit an inferno deep within her, a roiling firestorm ready to absorb her into its power. With a fervor that was taking control of her, she stroked up his back.

His lips traced a fiery path along her modest neckline. When he drew it lower, his tongue etched heat into the curve of her breast. She moaned with need that demanded satiation. She fumbled to open his shirt, aching for his skin on hers.

When he lifted her hand away from him, she was about to protest until he pressed her palm to his mouth. She smiled, wondering how he could make such a simple motion seem so sensual.

She admired his firm chest as she pushed his shirt along his arms. "I never knew."

"Knew what?" he whispered.

"How beautiful a man's body could be." She ran her fingers across his muscles, but halted when she touched puckered skin along his right side. "I am sorry. I should not have—"

He caught her fingers and drew them back to the center of his chest. "There is nothing you need to apologize for, unless you insist we stop. The wound is long healed."

"I was unsure whether I should touch it."

"Touch all of me, darling."

He rolled her onto her back. Leaning over her, he captured her mouth. She gripped his naked shoulders and gave herself to the desire she no longer wanted to fight. She wanted him and the passion he brought forth.

He quickly undid the hooks on her gown, one of his hands moving down her back as the other stroked her through her chemise. Drawing the dress over her shoulders, he brought her up to sit. The dim light cast shadows across his face, but she saw his hunger when her gown drooped to reveal the lace at the top of her chemise. He hooked a single finger in it and freed her breasts to fall into his eager hands. Bending, he pressed his mouth to the valley between them as he pressed her breasts to him. Sparks of pleasure danced along her skin.

After she had kicked aside her dress, he pulled off his boots and drew her back beneath him, entwining his legs with hers. His hands glided down her sides, so heated she could believe that her smallclothes would scorch away beneath his touch.

Steering his mouth over hers, she reached for the buttons on his buckskin breeches. He gasped each time she loosened a button and moved her fingers to the next. Her own breathing matched his staccato rhythm, and she was rasping along with him when she pushed his breeches down over his firm thighs.

"Beautiful," she whispered as she admired his male lines.

"I agree." He pressed his mouth over her belly button. "You are wondrously beautiful, darling. Even more beautiful than in my fantasies of you."

Her touch, at first tentative, then bolder, discovered the many different textures of his body. The rough skin across his chest led to waves of muscles along his abdomen. Lower, she stroked the silken warmth over the steely shaft that shivered beneath her touch.

With a growl he swept away the rest of her clothes. The gentle lover vanished as his lips demanded her surrender. His hands skimmed along her leg, down to her knee, then slowly back up. When she writhed beneath him, his tongue trailed up her breast before drawing its tip into his mouth, laving it until it hardened.

His finger drove up into her, and she cried out his name. She opened her eyes to see his smile. Her fingers curled into the cloak beneath her as each stroke probed higher, stoking the fire within her until she was sure she would be devoured by its power. He whispered something against her ear, but she could not understand anything but her need. Then she splintered into an ineffable bliss.

Opening her eyes to see him lift himself over her, she held up her arms to bring him to her and into her. The flame within her swelled. She moved with him in the most intimate dance they could share. Sensation came to a crescendo, and she heard his gasp in the seconds before she was consumed by their ecstasy.

It was everything she had dared to dream of, and something she never would be complete without again.

* * *

When China murmured against his shoulder, Alexander kissed her tangled hair that coursed across his bare chest. He knew she was distressed because she believed his ghostly ancestor had devised the whole situation so they would become lovers. Not only lovers, but parents of the next generation. His fingers settled on her abdomen. She had told him as he withdrew from her body that Quintus's hopes were sure to be dashed because of the time in her monthly cycle. He had not voiced his thoughts of how often a woman's cycle proved unreliable.

He closed his eyes and breathed in the fresh scent of her hair. He had enjoyed her private aromas, so uniquely hers. He wanted to again, but she was asleep. And holding her while she slept was splendid.

He did not realize he too had fallen asleep until a feverish kiss woke him. His arms came up to gather her to him.

"Come here, darling, and pleasure me again." He gave her a rakish grin.

"I can think of something else you might enjoy."

"More than you?"

She smiled. "Maybe not more, but definitely as much."

"That is unlikely."

"Don't be so sure until you look at this opening in the wall." She leaned back as he sat.

He stared at the place where sunlight poured through. It was not the hole where he had crawled in, because it was much smaller, but another about two feet to the left of the original. "Where did that come from?"

"We must have missed it in the darkness." She tossed his clothes to him. "Get dressed so we can get out and return to Nethercott Castle."

He noticed she was already dressed, and he sighed. "Are you sure you want to leave so soon?"

"Sian must be frantic." She ran her thumb along his jaw as she whispered, "Once we calm her we can excite each other again."

"Too late." He drew her hand down along him, watching her eyes widen as he curved her fingers around the shaft he ached to move deep within her.

She moaned, and every muscle hardened even more. With a groan of his own, he lifted her over him. Her skirts rose as she straddled him. He tore away her undergarments as he thrust up into her. His hands cupped her breasts, fondling them through her thin gown, and her head arched back as she moved up and down on him. She quivered, tightening around him, before collapsing on him, and he exploded within her. He knew that nothing, not even escape from their earthen bower, was more perfect than being a part of her again.

Chapter 18

With a laugh, Alexander put on his coat. It was difficult dressing in a space where he could not stand up straight. With a chuckle of her own, China tied his cravat.

"I daresay it is not stylish enough for an evening at Almack's," she said. "I watched Father tie his on many occasions, but watching and doing are two very different things."

"It will do." He slid his hand down her back and over her bottom. Knowing that her smallclothes were shredded beneath her prim gown was so erotic he had to force his lungs to work. Each time he made love with her, he wanted her more. It was the most thrilling obsession he could imagine.

"Let's get out of here."

He tore out the stones on the right side of the opening, then yanked out more in front of her. Within minutes, the opening was large enough for her to crawl out. He shoved aside a few more rocks before pulling himself out into the early-morning sunshine.

As he stood, he stared at the spot a few feet along

the wall where the sunlight seemed to coalesce into a ball. Was it possible that something extraordinary was still happening in the abandoned camp?

Yes, came the answer in his head as his gaze focused on where China was brushing dirt off her gown. One of the hooks on the back had been missed, and he went over to close it. She smiled at him and whispered her thanks.

"We should hurry back to Nethercott Castle," he said, "if we wish to be there before Sian sends out searchers for us."

"Alexander, we should talk about what happened. . . ." A pretty blush warmed her face; then all color faded away as she looked at the ball of light that had not moved. "We have to go. Now."

"What is it?"

"Something is going on at Nethercott Castle. Quintus says we need to go now."

He put his arm around her waist. Hurrying with her toward the road that led toward Nethercott Castle, he did not look back. It no longer mattered whether or not he could see the ghost. They had more trouble.

China heard shouts and calls for help as she and Alexander drove through the gate of Nethercott Castle. With every breath, smoke burned in her lungs. She jumped down from the cart and ran after Alexander to the back of the house.

I warned you that there would be more attacks before the fifth of September. The curse does not want to end. Quintus's dire words from the camp rang through her head with every step, heightening her fear. But how could this be an attack on Alexander?

The smoke thickened. She whispered a prayer when she saw several outbuildings near the stable afire. The stone stable was filled with hay. Gathering up her skirt to an unseemly height, she ran toward the dozen men who passed buckets of water between the well house and the stable. She hoped the well house could replace the water as fast as the men were lifting the pails out.

"We think it started behind the barn," a man shouted to her. She strained to hear him over the ear-pounding crackle of the fire. "Those buildings are completely destroyed."

"The stablemen? The horses?"

"All out." His smile was grim, but his teeth shone brightly in his smoke-stained face.

"My sister?"

He bent to draw out another bucket of water. Pointing with his elbow toward the far end of the stable, he called, "Last I 'eard, she was down there tendin' to those who be 'urt."

China choked back a gasp and turned to find Sian. She bumped into Alexander. He caught her arms, steadying her.

"Help your sister," he said, his voice calm, even though his eyes sparked with anger as dangerous as the flames. "I will help here."

"Thank you."

He gave her a swift kiss that almost undid her. Leaping over the trough, he stepped in line with the men and joined in moving the buckets.

China tried to breathe shallowly as she ran through the smoke. She gave her sister a quick hug before tending to burns and cuts. Aware of Miss Upton working with them, she offered the quiet woman a smile. Miss Upton gave her a shy one in return, but neither spoke. China was unsure what she would have said.

It was not until late afternoon that China had a chance to survey the full extent of the damage. The stable had been saved, but all the smaller outbuildings were burned to the ground or so damaged they would have to be torn down.

When Alexander came to stand beside her, she slipped her hand into his. He laced his fingers through hers as they walked through the ashes blanketing the courtyard and the gardens.

"Quintus knew about the fire," she said when they reached the place where the hedges had been compressed by something none of them had been able to explain.

"Before it happened?" He sat, bringing her down on a bench next to him.

"No, because he has told me that he cannot see the future. Yet by the time he told me about it, the worst of the fire was over. Nobody was injured *after* we returned."

"You are suggesting that a ghost arranged a small landslide in order to keep us safe." He shook his head with an ironic smile. "Listen to me! I am talking nonsense."

"Maybe."

His expression became as serious as hers. "Will you ask him when you next see him?"

"Yes, but he has not reappeared here. I was certain he would come to make sure you were safe once the fire was doused, but he did not."

A commotion arose on the other side of the garden, and China looked up to see Lady Viola haranguing her servants, who were toting boxes and stacks of fabric. Miss Upton walked in her wake, clearly trying to avoid being the next one scolded.

"She would not heed my request to move tonight's festivities into Nethercott Castle," China said with a shudder. "She said the camp is safer than here, where we have endured two fires. When I suggested that might be the best reason to postpone the party, she told me she plans to hold it tonight, whether she is a guest of Nethercott Castle or not."

"She is thinking of leaving for Pickering at this hour?" His mouth tightened. "The highwayman would be happy to learn of such asinine plans."

"That is why I told her she must stay. It may be safer for her to hold her absurd gathering than to let them leave. If something were to happen to them on the road, I would never forgive myself. Maybe if we beseech Lord Turnbull again he might listen."

"I tried to convince both her and Turnbull, and neither would listen. She is too excited. He seems unwilling to cross her."

She edged closer to him as a shiver raced down her spine. "I certainly hope she feels the same way after tonight."

He watched while Lady Viola insisted another box could fit into the already overloaded carriage. "I have a bad feeling about all this, too."

China stepped out of the carriage and tried to smile. It was worthless to pretend with her sister. Sian's expression was as uneasy as China's thoughts.

"Why did she have to do this to thank us for our hospitality?" asked Sian as she smoothed her gown. In spite of Lady Viola's request, neither Nethercott sister wore Roman garb. Sian was dressed in her favorite light blue dress. Its slightly darker ribbons looked black in the light filtering through the trees. "She could have simply left at dawn and taken her swain with her."

"I trust you will refrain from saying such things in her hearing," China replied.

"It is my misfortune that I have good manners."

A laugh burst from China. Alexander must have heard because he chuckled as well when he came forward after tying his horse to the back of the carriage. He had not explained to China why he had insisted on riding, and she had not asked. She had learned that he seldom did anything without a good reason.

He bowed first over Sian's hand, then China's, which he did not release. As he drew it within his arm, he murmured, "Stay alert for any signs of the highwayman."

"Maybe you should return to Nethercott Castle," China said as softly.

"I doubt I shall be any safer there, in light of recent attacks. Even though I am now well, at least here I have two beautiful women watching every move I make." He offered his other arm to Sian, who put her hand on it. "What more could any man wish for?"

The clearing looked so different from that morning. Sheer fabric had been draped over trees to create a pavilion. Lamps hung from branches. Chinese lanterns seemed out of place in a Roman encampment, but Lady Viola clearly had no interest in historical accuracy. Low tables were topped with food in ornate silver bowls. Chaise longues upholstered in the same white as the draperies surrounded the tables.

China did not recognize any of the furniture. Lady Viola must have had it brought from York.

She rushed forward to greet them, her pug yapping wildly around her feet. Lady Viola almost stumbled over the dog, but pushed past it, then paused. Her mouth was in a perfect moue of disapproval. "Didn't you realize it was a costume party?" She looked down at her white silk gown that would have been the envy of any Roman lady.

"I am afraid," China said, "that after the excitement this morning with the fire, it must have slipped my mind."

"And I am afraid I do not have my ancestor's armor and shield," Alexander said so seriously that China struggled not to laugh.

"You always jest with me!" Lady Viola slapped his arm playfully. Stepping between him and China, she drew him away. "Do come and make me laugh some more."

Alexander looked over his shoulder and arched a villainous eyebrow. He stepped over the dog that was trying to nip at his boots while he strolled with Lady Viola around the earthworks and into the camp.

China could not halt her laugh from bursting forth. Sian gave her a frown, so China asked in a whisper, "What do you think she would do if she knew he was being honest?"

"I do not like this." Sian rubbed her hands together. "I have heard so many stories about haunted places on the moors, but until you spoke of Quintus, no one ever told a tale about this old camp." Wrapping her arms around herself, she sighed. "I wish this party were over."

"So do I."

A deeper laugh came from behind them. "When we have just arrived?"

China turned to see two familiar faces. The shorter man, Squire Haywood, looked uncomfortable—and a bit cold—in his toga beneath a bright purple cloak worthy of a Roman emperor. Beside him, smiling broadly, was the man who had spoken.

Sir Henry Cranler was a pleasant-looking man with manners suited for Town and the highest echelons of the *ton*. He was as tall as Alexander. His black hair was thinning at the temples, but his face suggested he was not much more than a youth. He was, in fact, a year older than China. When she greeted him, he bowed over her hand and released it quickly.

He then took Sian's hand and smiled. "I see, Miss Sian, that you have proven once again to be wiser than the rest of us." He did not release her fingers as he plucked at the toga he wore beneath a dark cape that fluttered in the freshening breeze. "If I had half an ounce of wit, I would have chosen as well not to come in costume."

"Odd how it is windy here," the squire said. "It was quite calm earlier."

"Fortunately for us," China replied. "If the wind had come up this morning, the fire could have spread to destroy the house also."

While Sian went with Sir Henry toward the tables, explaining about the near-tragedy at Nethercott Castle, Squire Haywood shook his head and said, "You have been suffering greatly in recent days, Miss Nethercott."

"It has been trying." She knew he could not guess

how challenging her life had become with ghosts and death threats. Only the splendor of being in Alexander's arms as he moved with her to the intimate tempo of love made any sense among the madness.

As if she had spoken the last word aloud, the squire lowered his voice to say, "I am not surprised the specter of insanity has reared its head again."

"Specter?" she asked, trying not to flinch.

"Of insanity." He nodded, then glanced at where Lady Viola had her arm looped through Alexander's while she flirted with both him and her fiancé.

"She is calculating, but I would not call her insane."

"She? I am not referring to Lady Viola, but to Lord Braddock." He spoke quietly, so she had to lean forward to catch his words. "You must have heard that both his father and grandfather had periods of madness and melancholy that rival our king's."

She remembered Alexander saying something about madness and his father. His sorrow echoed through her memory along with Quintus's warnings.

"I did not have the chance to speak to you before now," he continued. "Lord Braddock was always nearby, and I did not want to embarrass him when his family has been humiliated enough. You know that I care deeply for you . . . and your sister." He cleared his throat and hurried to add, "That is why I want to urge you to be very careful. You have suffered many accidents since his arrival at Nethercott Castle. Are you sure he did not have a hand in them?"

China raised her eyebrows at the suggestion that Alexander was mad enough to start fires that could have killed himself and others.

"Yes," she said finally, adding nothing more.

The squire sputtered, shocked at her calm answer. An uncomfortable silence rose between them before China bowed her head to him and went to where the others had gathered.

Miss Upton came over to her. "Are you all right, Miss Nethercott? You look flushed."

"I will be fine in a few moments." She noticed how the other woman shivered in her sleeveless garment. "You are cold! Let me get some of the fabric so you can wrap it around your shoulders."

"Do not do that! My cousin would not be pleased to have her design ruined."

"A single strip of cloth will not undo her work."

Miss Upton shook her head. "Please do not. I will be fine as soon as the breeze dies down again. Look! Lord Braddock is signaling to you. I think they are ready for the toast."

China guided Miss Upton toward the others. Miss Upton edged to one side when they reached the chaise longues. China bit her tongue, not wanting to draw unwanted attention to the other woman.

Lord Turnbull held up his glass of bloodred wine as Alexander handed China another. "What an amazing setting you have created for us, my dear," he said with a smile at Lady Viola, who preened in his praise. "Only you could look at a ruin and see the possibility of loveliness. I am sure it is a reflection of your own beauty and grace."

As he continued, China glanced at the others gathered around the table. Sir Henry smiled at Sian, who was enjoying whatever sally he had spoken. Next to them, Squire Haywood quickly looked away when China's gaze met his.

"Why are you looking daggers at the good squire?" Alexander whispered.

She saw no reason to dissemble. Under Lord Turnbull's rambling toast, she answered, "He suggested that you may have had a hand in the fires at Nethercott Castle."

"Did he?"

Her fingers tightened on her goblet. "I have no idea why he would accuse you. It is unlike him."

"Because he wants to do me damage in your eyes."

"What?" The word came out more loudly than she had intended, and the others looked in her direction. Acting as if the sound had been a cough, she pretended to expel several more.

Alexander waited until the attention was once more focused on the viscount before murmuring, "Sian mentioned that the squire is enamored with you, China." He stroked her back. "I can understand why."

She was about to reply when Lord Turnbull raised his glass and shouted, "To our hostess! To Lady Viola!" When a gust of wind swirled a drape around his head, he tore it away. "To Lady Viola!"

The words echoed oddly around the clearing. Heads swiveled as the toast seemed to be repeated again and again from every direction, tossed at them on the wind that blew one way, then another.

"How did you make *that* happen?" called Sir Henry, his hand on Sian's arm to keep her from being knocked over by the wind.

Suddenly a bright orb moved through the trees, and the wind gathered around it.

"Quintus!" cried China. "Alexander, we need to get out of here now."

Taking her goblet, he tossed it on the table with his. Glass shattered, but the sound was swallowed by the noise welling up amidst the trees.

"Run!" someone shouted as wind slashed at the trees, driving through their branches like a thousand spears. The trees shuddered, trying to hold on to the ground. Overhead, the stars were consumed by roiling clouds driven by the maddened wind.

Paper lanterns shredded or exploded in flame. Sparks swirled into the air in a furious rush. The fabric seemed to come alive. It tore off the trees and lashed wildly. Alexander almost tripped, but China reached down to tear the thin material away from around his legs.

"To the carriages!" shouted Lord Turnbull. He ran around the earthworks toward his carriage. He reached it and opened the door. The wind tore it from its hinges and smashed it into a tree. Climbing in, he pulled Miss Upton in beside him.

Where was Lady Viola?

China untangled fabric that was wrapped around her head. The lady huddled between the table and a chaise longue. The wind whirled around her, a cyclone tearing at her clothes and hair.

Running toward her, China looked at the light in the thrashing trees. "Quintus, stop it! She means no harm!"

The wind roared like a maniac's cry. Leaping through the wall of swirling leaves and debris, she winced as something hit her face. She grabbed Lady Viola by the arm, yanking her to her feet. She shoved the lady ahead of her through the twisting wind.

Screeching more madly, the wind drew them back into the maelstrom. Strong hands seized her arm. She raised her head, blinking through the burning wind, to see Alexander holding on to her.

"Don't let her go!" he shouted.

She could barely hear him, but nodded. As he dragged them away, she kept a tight hold on Lady Viola.

The wind abruptly died.

They tumbled to the ground, and Lady Viola's sobs were loud in the abrupt silence.

China pushed herself up, then collapsed. Every inch of her felt as if muscle had been torn from bone. Alexander slipped his arm beneath her and turned her against his shoulder. She breathed in his warm, living scent.

"Don't ever do that again," he said.

"Do what?"

"Risk your own life."

"I could not let Quintus hurt her."

He sat, bringing her up with him. "This has gone too far."

"Sian!" China called, jumping to her feet. Her head spun as the wind had, but she reeled toward the carriages. Where was Sian? Was she safe?

Seeing two people emerge from a carriage, China slowed and leaned against a sapling no taller than she was. The top had been sheared off. She stared as the man helped the woman out and pulled her into his arms, kissing her with undisguised passion.

Lord Turnbull and Miss *Lauraine* Upton? He buried his head in her hair, crying that he was unsure how he could have gone on living if she had been killed. He gazed into her eyes and said he needed her in his bed tonight.

China choked back a gasp.

"I love you, Sidney," Miss Upton said, making no effort to keep her voice low.

"If only *your* father had been the heir." He gave a heartfelt moan. "And mine had not been such a consummate gambler, with the worst luck in Britain."

As China whirled toward where the Nethercott carriage waited, she faltered. Behind her, close enough to hear the impassioned words of her betrothed and her cousin, Lady Viola stood. Shaking Alexander's hand off her arm, she walked forward.

"Princess is missing," she said as the two broke apart with identical guilty looks. "Lauraine, please find her while my dear fiancé helps me into the carriage."

"Right away," her cousin replied, staring at the ground, a pose that had allowed her to hide her love for Lord Turnbull.

China looked away when Sian called her name. Flinging her arms around her sister, she hugged Sian tightly, then stepped back. A bruise on Sian's left cheek was already swelling, and her skin was scraped. Fury surged through China. She had done all Quintus had asked, and he still had hurt her sister.

"I am fine," China said, trying not to clench her teeth on every word. "I see that Sir Henry and the squire are leaving. Go with them to Nethercott Castle and wait for us there."

"But, China—"

"Go with them *now*." The wind gusted again, whirling around them as if warning them not to return to the clearing. "Go while you still can. I will be there as soon as I speak with Quintus."

Sian's eyes widened in comprehension. With another swift hug, she ran to catch the carriage that was already turning in the narrow space to return to the road.

"You should go, too, Alexander," China said.

"I will leave when you do."

"Quintus is behind this."

"How?"

"I don't know, but he is." She looked through the trees where the familiar orb glowed. Walking in its direction, she was not surprised that the winds grew stronger as Quintus took his human form. "Do you see him?"

Alexander shook his head as he matched her paces. "Only flickers of light. They could be glowworms in the grass or distant lightning or stars peeking through the clouds."

"*I* see him. He is motioning for me to come and speak with him."

"Then we should do as he wants before everything in the wood is flattened." He growled under his breath, "Damn that woman."

"Lady Vi—"

"I would be careful of saying her name aloud, after what happened when Turnbull did." His terse chuckle was almost lost beneath the surging wind. "I have to say *that* scene by the carriage was a surprise."

"Not for Lady . . . Not for her. She must have known about her cousin and her fiancé."

"Maybe so, but that is their problem. Ours is that Quintus's rage created the powerful winds when Turnbull said her name."

China waved him to silence as Quintus stepped

from beneath the trees to stand on top of the wall not far from where she had first met Alexander. She said nothing until she was an arm's length from the ghost, at a spot where the cold enwrapping him could not reach her. Wind blew her hair back from her face and pressed her gown against her legs, but Quintus's cape did not move.

"Keep those trespassers away!" he growled.

She met his eyes steadily. "They are not trespassers here, Quintus. You are!"

"Careful," Alexander murmured.

Quintus's lips curled. "This is my home."

"Yes, but it is mine, too," she retorted, after repeating his words for Alexander, "and to the others, these abandoned earthworks offer the opportunity for something wonderful."

"They acted like the low creatures Nero invited to his table."

"How they acted is irrelevant. How *you* acted is what matters." She put her hands on her hips and glowered. "Quintus, why did you attack us? If the fire from the lanterns had spread, the whole wood could have burned, including the remains of the camp. Was that what you wanted?"

"I wanted them to leave."

"It has to be more than that."

Quintus's shoulders sagged slightly. "He spoke her name."

"Lady Viola's?" She steeled herself for another gust. It did not come, and he seemed to shrink within his armor. "Her name was Viola."

"Her?" Then it dawned on China. "The woman you betrayed?"

He nodded. "The woman who bore my son after

she had left me for another. When I heard another man speaking that name tonight, I was furious."

"I had no idea, Quintus." Tears welled in her eyes at the regret he had endured for more than a thousand years. "But, Quintus, you cannot allow your pent-up rage to betray you now." She glanced at Alexander, then back to the ghost. "Did you consider what would happen if your last heir died tonight?"

"*Ultimus haeres*," he whispered, his anger sifting away.

"Did you even consider that?" she pressed. "Or did you see the only chance to go to battle against the barbarians invading your camp? We are not barbarians, Quintus. We are the descendants of the Romans and all before and after them." She put her hand on Alexander's arm and realized his sleeve was in tatters. "He is your descendant. Your sole surviving descendant."

"I did not intend for the storm to be so strong." He tapped his spear against the ground. "When I summoned the old magic, I could not control it."

"Old magic? Whose?"

"The old gods like the one you saw in your garden, but there are even more ancient powers in this land from the people who were here long before us. We could sense it when we camped here. I dismissed the stories when I first heard them. Then one night, as I sat at the top of the path down the cliff, I heard it."

"What did you hear?"

"The whispers of spirits that walk these empty hills, the whispers of those who were here before Rome was built. We couldn't understand their words, but each dawn in the wake of the whispers, there would be changes in the camp." He shuddered, and the light surrounding him grew dim, as if anxiety drained his strength. "Sometimes it was broken weapons or missing supplies. But when the seasons changed, sickness swept through the camp or poison in the grain killed both men and beasts." He laughed without humor. "When I first came to England I did not believe in ghosts, but I do now."

Alexander leaned forward, impatient. "What are you talking about?"

She quickly told him, relieved that he believed she was actually talking to the ghost he could not see.

"More ghosts?" He shook his head. "That is the last thing we need."

Quintus said, "He is like the others. Unwilling to accept me unless he sees me."

China repeated the centurion's words to Alexander.

"Quintus is right," he replied. "Perhaps it *is* time to believe in what I cannot see. Where is he?"

"On top of the wall in front of us."

"Where the moonlight gleams?"

"Yes."

Alexander walked closer to the wall, motioning China to stay where she was. She watched and held her breath. His boots pounded the earth, and his hands clenched into fists. Even so, his voice was even when he said, "Hail to thee, Quintus Valerius, father of my fathers. Know this: I offer you respect as my ancestor, but if you try to harm this woman or her sister or any of her friends, you will be my sworn enemy, and you shall be doubly cursed."

Quintus angrily reached for his dagger, then looked at China and lowered his hand. "Guard him well until the last hour of the fifth of September is past."

"Quintus . . . " She did not bother to finish because he had vanished.

The wind died to a whisper.

"Is he gone?" Alexander asked.

"Yes."

"What did he say?"

She repeated the ghost's injunction. "Three more days, Alexander."

"Three more." He added nothing else as they turned to walk away. There was nothing else to say.

Chapter 19

Brandy had never tasted as good as it did when Alexander sipped it in Lord Nethercott's book-room. Looking out the window at the swirling rain, he murmured, "Deuce take it!"

He had stated over and over that a ghostly ancestor with a warning from beyond the grave was impossible. Tonight he had confronted a ghost he could not see. It was insane.

Wincing at his own thought, he took another drink. He frowned and put the glass on the windowsill. Dulling his wits with brandy was foolish. If the ghost was real, then the accursed curse was too. His fingers curled into a fist. He *knew* his family was jinxed. It was one of those things that everyone knew yet would not speak of to his face.

A motion through the rain caught his eye, and he peered out the window. The huge silhouette rising up from the moors was the same one he and China had seen in the garden. He tensed, but the giant moved away from the house.

Raised voices drifted from an upper floor. Women's voices.

Alexander ran to the door, then paused as he recognized Lady Viola's imperious tone. He could not discern her words, but the tone was clear. She was furious. He went back to the window, glad he was not the focus of her rage. He wanted to be sure that the shadowy giant did not change its course and come toward Nethercott Castle.

Footfalls punished the floor outside the book-room before he heard Turnbull snarl, "So this is where you are hiding, Braddock! I knew a rat would find a comfortable hole."

Drawing in a deep breath, Alexander let it sift out through his teeth as he turned to face the viscount. Turnbull's face was a blotchy red. Was the man furious or about to weep?

"I think you are mistaking my ways for your own, Turnbull." He was in no mood for Turnbull's outburst. "I am not planning to marry one woman while in love with her cousin."

The viscount's face became a deeper crimson. "Do not bring her into this."

"Her? Lady Viola or Miss Upton?" He picked up his glass and took a slow sip. "A word of advice, if I may, Turnbull. Next time their lives are in danger, make at least some effort to pretend you care about what happens to your fiancée. It is no wonder she is distressed."

Turnbull strode across the room and jabbed his finger into Alexander's chest. "You know damn well that is not the reason she is upset."

"I have no idea why she is upset. But I know what I saw." He shoved Turnbull's finger aside.

"Braddock, I should have known you are not to be trusted!"

"We have had enough dramatics tonight. Say what you must and leave."

"You agreed not to speak to my betrothed about what happened during the war."

"Yes." He laughed tersely. "And you agreed to dissuade your betrothed from holding a soirée at the Roman camp."

"I tried. You obviously did not."

He frowned as he realized what must have led to the shouts he had heard. "I have not spoken to Lady Viola about the war. She has asked me several times, but I always changed the subject. Neither of us has mentioned what you did."

"She knows."

"I did not speak of it." He fought his irritation that Turnbull sought to blame him. "China asked me to say nothing, and I was pleased to agree. It is not a topic that I enjoy discussing."

"But she knows! Who else could have told her?"

"You need to ask Lady Viola that." Taking another sip, he set the empty glass back on the sill. "Surely you did not think you could keep the truth hidden forever. Too many saw you turn and run in the opposite direction, Turnbull. Some must have already enjoyed telling the tale of the officer who tried to sell his commission in the midst of battle."

With a roar, Turnbull swung at him.

Alexander ducked, and Turnbull groaned as his fist hit a stack of books that toppled in every direction. Drawing back his arm, he aimed at Alexander again. Alexander had been waiting for this opportunity, and he was going to take advantage of it. He drove his fist into Turnbull's gut. Turnbull rocked back and hit another table, scattering more books.

He heard a shocked cry and saw China standing by the door. Then Turnbull's fist rammed into his cheek. Pain erupted through his skull, but he shot out another blow into Turnbull's chin. Another pile of books fell to the floor when the viscount reeled back into a table.

"Stop it!" China cried, rushing forward. She stepped between them and stretched out her arms to keep them apart.

For a moment, Alexander feared Turnbull would not be able to halt his fist. He did before it hit China, who scowled at both of them.

"I will not have fisticuffs in my home!" she said, rage seething through her words. "Especially not in my father's book-room."

"Forgive me, China," Alexander said. He glared at the viscount, who remained silent.

Finally Turnbull said, "We will finish this later, Braddock. I will not have everything ruined because you cannot keep your word." He turned on his heel and stormed out, kicking aside books in his path.

China gasped as she heard leather bindings crack. Rushing to gather up the books, she fought back tears. These books were a precious connection to her father, and she had hoped to keep them just as he had left them. Now they were torn and broken.

Behind her, Alexander said, "China . . ."

"Don't tell me you are sorry," she snapped, "when I could see you enjoyed pummeling Lord Turnbull. You have wanted to do that since his family turned their backs on you after his sister married someone else."

He recoiled as if she had struck him. "Is that what you think this is about?"

"Whether or not that is the cause of the fight, it is one of the reasons it kept going, I'm sure."

When he did not answer, she continued to pick up the books. She ran her hand over each cover, blinking back the tears she did not want to fall on the ripped pages. She set them on the chairs. On the morrow she would go through them and determine which ones she would send for repair.

Alexander's broad hands settled on her shoulders, and he turned her to face him. She saw remorse in his dim eyes and sad frown.

"You look just like Quintus when he talks about his Viola. Is it regret or shame?"

"Both." He stroked her shoulders tenderly. "Regret that I upset you tonight, and shame that I have not yet put aside my anger toward Turnbull."

She stepped away from him, knowing she would quickly forget everything but his touch if he kept caressing her, and she had too many questions that needed answers.

"Why were you fighting?" she asked.

"Turnbull accused me of telling his betrothed about his blemished military service."

"You promised not to!"

"And I did not." His gaze locked with hers. "You believe me, don't you?"

"Yes," she said without hesitation, "but Lord Turnbull clearly does not."

"No, and he refused to accept the truth. When he angered me further, I goaded him about his cowardice." He shook his head and walked back to the window. "I knew better, but tonight has unsettled us all."

"Alexander, you fool!"

He spun to face her, shock widening his eyes.

"Lord Turnbull believes you have betrayed him," she said as she crossed the room. "Quintus warned that you are in danger from someone who feels betrayed by you."

"Turnbull never liked me."

She took his hand and folded it between hers. "Can't you see, Alexander? Lord Turnbull has built a fragile house of cards. But it all falls apart if it becomes known that he created the legends of his great deeds."

He grimaced. "Once again you are right. I know what I must do."

"Apologize to Lord Turnbull."

"No. I have another idea."

The sobs could be heard through the thick door. China did not hesitate as she knocked.

Miss Upton opened it quickly. Her face was reddened with another slap. "Lady Viola is indisposed and does not wish to be disturbed."

"Would you ask her if she would speak with Lord Braddock? He has something important to tell her."

"Lord Braddock?" came Lady Viola's voice from the bed. "Do let him in. I could use the presence of a real hero to ease my fears now."

China saw Alexander wince at the adulation, but he smiled as he entered the room. Miss Upton gasped, then put her hand over her mouth as she looked from the mark on his cheek to the viscount, who was coming to his feet. He swayed, then straightened his shoulders.

China submerged her fury. Had he been present when Lady Viola struck her cousin? When her gaze flicked from Miss Upton's reddened face to him, Lord Turnbull hastily looked away. At that moment she knew he would allow Miss Upton to endure any ordeal at her cousin's hand as long as he could have what he wanted, including flirting with other women as he had with China. He was even viler than she had imagined.

"Have you found her, Lord Braddock?" Lady Viola asked. "Do tell me that she is in the hallway and you are planning to surprise me with a reunion."

When Alexander looked perplexed, China whispered, "I think she is asking about her dog."

He gave a slight nod, then continued to the bed. "I am sorry, my lady, but I have no tidings for you about Princess."

"The servants will look for her when they collect the boxes from the camp," China added.

Alexander's eyes narrowed. "You sent servants there?"

"I will after the sun comes up," she whispered before adding to Lady Viola, "No doubt they will find her enjoying the food we did not eat."

"My poor precious Princess." The lady hid her face in a lacy handkerchief. "The only one in my life who has never betrayed me with lies."

As if she had not heard her cousin, Miss Upton sat on the chaise longue and picked up some mending. She did not look up as she began to sew, but China noticed her hands trembling. With fury or shame? China knew she would never understand how the three could go on pretending that everything was just as it should be.

"Do not weep, Lady Viola," China said, putting

her hand on the lady's arm. "It is not as bad as you think."

"No?" She flung her other arm toward Lord Turnbull. "I have recently discovered that the man I am to wed has lied to me about his military service. How will I show my face in York? I will be ostracized in London. My life is over."

"Who told you about this?"

"My maid." A smile twisted her lips. "Your servants did not realize she understands English. She overheard them and then brought me the truth."

China did not want to call the maid a liar, but she knew the well-trained servants at Nethercott Castle would not gossip about Lord Turnbull's military record.

"Your maid is mistaken," Alexander said in an even tone. "Lady Viola, I can assure you that your betrothed deserves the title of hero as much as I do."

"Really?" Her eyes became round with excitement. "Oh, Lord Braddock, I had no idea!" Her mouth tightened again. "I shall have to scold Yvette for carrying such tales." Holding out her hand to her fiancé, she added, "She has wronged you."

As Lord Turnbull rushed forward to kiss Lady Viola's hand and profess his undying adoration, China edged toward the door. She breathed a sigh of relief when Alexander closed the door behind him. He held out his arms, and she slipped into them.

"What you said about Lord Turnbull was kind," she whispered against his coat.

"There was no kindness intended, I assure you."

She stepped back and looked up at him, expecting to see him frowning.

Instead he was smiling. "I did that for you, not them."

She curved her hand around his head and tilted his mouth down over hers. She did not want to think about the past. She wanted him. But in her mind whispered the words, *You might have him for only three more days. . . .*

Chapter 20

China waited in the solarium for Alexander, her foot tapping restlessly on the stones. The fifth of September had dawned like so many other days, but it was unlike any other. The cursed day that had plagued Alexander's family for so many generations was here once again.

Alexander told her at breakfast that he would join her in the solarium after speaking with Lord Turnbull. The viscount had made it clear that he wished to apologize to Alexander before returning to York. She had wanted to go with him, but knew the two men could not speak plainly with a woman in the room.

"I am alert and forewarned," Alexander had told her before giving her a swift kiss that promised more to come. "Once I have spoken with Turnbull, I will let you watch over me like a mother hen the rest of the day."

"I wish it were tomorrow."

"As do I, even though I do not want to lose a single moment I can have with you."

She had laughed as he went to meet the viscount,

but she was no longer smiling. Every minute passed
slowly, and she had to remind herself to breathe.
Again and again she glanced around the room, won-
dering if Quintus would come to the house today.
Last night, she had seen the giant's shadow stretch
across the moors as it had for the past three nights.
Perhaps Quintus was busy trying to placate that old
Roman god and keep it away from Nethercott Castle.
If so, she was grateful.

"Miss China?" asked a footman who peeked into
the room. "You have a guest. Squire Haywood."

"Show him in." She smoothed her light blue dress
across her lap, then grimaced when she saw the
dampness from her sweaty palms. For a moment, she
considered asking Palmer Haywood for his assistance, though she doubted he would believe the story
of a nearly two-thousand-year-old curse.

The squire was shown in. As he came toward her
chair, holding a basket over one arm, he grinned like
a proud child. When she heard a bark, she clapped
her hands with glee.

"Lady Viola's dog!" she cried. "Where did you
find her?"

"Cowering in my carriage. I did not discover her
until the morning following the debacle at the old
camp. I should have sent a message earlier to let you
know she had been found, but I have been distracted
with many things."

"The highwayman?"

He nodded. "He keeps me busy. When I heard
that Lady Viola was taking her leave today, I could
not wait any longer. Is Lord Braddock departing
today as well?"

She heard hope in his question. "No, he is staying

with us a bit longer." She needed to change the subject because she could not tell the truth of the curse. Taking the basket, she set it on the floor and opened the top. The dog bounded out, gave them a disgusted glance that was startlingly similar to Lady Viola's and ran out of the room toward the stairs. Moments later, they heard a happy squeal announcing that Lady Viola was having the reunion she had hoped for.

"Thank you so much," China said with a smile. "You have made Lady Viola very happy. She has been fretting about Princess."

"And you? Have I made you happy, too?" He grasped her hand again.

She tried to ease her fingers from his hand, but he did not release them, and she gave him an uneasy smile. "We should be thinking of Lady Viola now. She is the one who lost her dog."

"Her heart is full now. What of yours, China?"

"I am very happy for her," she said, feeling overcome by his questions.

His face hardened. "You know that is not what I mean. Lady Viola has her fiancé and her dog and a wedding that will be the premier event of York's season. Her heart and her life are full. What of yours?"

"My life is very full, too," she said as she pulled her hand from his grip. "Just as yours is. We both have friends and our duties, which we enjoy."

"I am not speaking of duties. I am speaking of love."

She clasped her hands in front of her. "That is not a subject I am comfortable speaking about."

"With me?"

"With anyone." She knew she might be foolish, but she put her hand on his arm. "Today is not a good day."

"You look tense."

She almost laughed. Tense was such an understatement. She felt stiff and as if she would shatter at any moment. Where was Alexander? He should have been done with Lord Turnbull by now.

"My guests are leaving today, so I must help them with all the details. That is why I must ask you to excuse me. I want to be certain that all their clothes have been brought from the laundry."

"China, a favor, if I may, before you get back to your tasks. Reverend Wilder mentioned a book he once borrowed from your father and suggested I ask you if I may borrow it."

"Certainly." She smiled, glad to change the topic to much simpler territory. "I ask only that you return it in good condition once you are finished with it. The same stipulation my father always insisted on. If you give me the title, I shall be glad to find it for you."

"You are so busy. If I may, I can get it myself. I know where your father's book-room is."

"Certainly," she said again. "I hope you enjoy the book."

"I will enjoy everything about it, I am sure." His chuckle sounded forced, but his eyes sparked with anticipation as he said, "Reverend Wilder is looking forward to hearing my opinions on the author's premise. No doubt we will disagree. We always do, but the debate is what we relish most." He took her hand and bowed over it.

She sat down again as he left the room, and her brow furrowed as she thought of him. Poor Palmer Haywood. He seemed as stressed by failing to capture the highwayman as she was about what could happen before midnight.

And what was keeping Alexander? He knew she was beside herself with worry. She would wait a bit longer and then go to discover what had delayed him.

"Is there something you are looking for, Miss China?"

"Can I get you something, Miss China?"

"Do you need me to find someone for you, Miss China?"

To each servant's question, China answered simply, "I am looking for Lord Braddock. Have you seen him?"

Every time the answer was the same. No.

"If you see him, tell him that I am looking for him," she always added.

As she left the tower room, China wiped smoky dust from her dress. A few dried ashes crunched under her shoes, even though Mrs. Mathers had done her best to clear away signs of the fire.

A light glowed brightly in front of her, and she bit her lower lip to keep from calling out Quintus's name in excitement. She could use his help to find Alexander.

"*Ave*, China," he said as soon as he materialized.

She did not bother with a greeting. "Alexander is missing!"

"Where did you last see him?" His hand tightened

on his spear. Nodding as she explained how she had planned to meet Alexander in the solarium more than an hour ago, he said, "Wait here."

"Quintus, no!" she cried, but the ghost was gone.

She fought the urgent need to search for Alexander. Pacing from the window to the stairs, she decided to give Quintus five minutes. She began counting off the seconds, and gasped when the light reappeared before she had reached the end of the first minute.

Quintus's face was drawn. "I think he is still alive."

"You *think*?"

"I could not touch him to find a pulse. He is not moving."

"Take me to him!"

He began to lope along the hallway. She ran after him, trying to keep up. A chilly breeze flowed back to her, but her heart was even colder with fear.

When he led her to the top of a staircase leading to a seldom-used section of the house, she cried out in horror at the sight of a crumpled form at the bottom. The cold burned her, but she pushed past Quintus to rush down the stairs.

Alexander was facedown. Scattered laundry was spread around him. By his right ear was a crimson line, and his hair was stiff with dried blood. She frantically searched his neck with her fingers and choked back a sob when she felt a steady pulse. The pile of clothes must have cushioned his fall, saving his life.

"He is alive, Quintus," she said, looking up at the centurion on the stairs. "This must have happened at least a half hour ago, because the blood is matted in his hair.'' She was certain whoever had attacked him was long gone. ''I need help to move him.''

''Check him for broken bones. I will bring help for you.''

''How?''

''Let me worry about that.'' He gazed down at Alexander with dismay. ''You keep him alive.''

Kneeling, China bent over Alexander, running her hands along his arms and legs and sides. He groaned when her fingers brushed his ribs on his right side, but he did not stir.

''Who did this to you?'' she asked, not expecting an answer.

''I don't know.'' His voice was barely a whisper.

''Alexander!'' She wanted to throw her arms around him but feared injuring him further.

''Quieter, China, please.''

She lowered her voice. ''Can you move?'' When he put his hands against the floor and tried to push himself up, she wanted to weep with elation. His groans of pain threatened to burst her bubble of happiness, but he was alive. There was still hope they both would survive until day's end.

Alexander winced with every step into the dining room. After chiding China for telling silly tales about ghosts, he had proven to be the greatest fool. He had avoided answering her questions about how he came to be in that area of the house. What would her reaction be if he told her that he had seen a curious light and given chase, hoping to see Quintus and perhaps ask him some questions?

It must have been nothing more than the sun

gleaming strangely, for he did not see the light again and got lost looking for it. When he paused at the top of the stairs, trying to discern where he was in the castle, he had been struck from behind. He recalled hearing a rustle behind him, and as he turned his head to look, a flash of pain came up against his skull. If he had caught any sight of his attacker, he could not recall it.

His head ached, and his ribs ached each time he breathed. He had been hurt worse in training exercises with his soldiers, but even so, he measured every motion with care.

When he looked around, he understood, as if for the first time, why someone raised in this house found it easy to believe in ghosts. The scent of history clung to the walls, an alluring aroma that teased him to peel back the layers and reveal what had occurred here in the past.

The high ceiling was plastered with friezes. Emblems of Queen Elizabeth's crest were interspersed with heraldry symbols for the Nethercott family. He saw the light of learning, books and rearing gryphons with their claws outstretched toward swans that seemed indifferent to the beasts hunting them. In the center of the ceiling, directly above the long oak table, was a quartered shield. Bells were set across from a dolphin above a crouching lion and the swan again. Bits of paint were still visible.

"The heraldic red is called gules," China said as she came into the room. "Black is properly termed as sable, green as vert, blue as azure, and purple as purpure." She smiled. "The last sounds to me as if an infant is trying to say 'purple.'"

Facing her, he savored the sight of her in her pink

gown. The magnificence of the room dimmed in comparison to her gentle beauty.

"I am doing much better," he said. "The headache is now just a low rumble."

"I did not ask," she said as she closed the distance between them.

"But you would have. Your expression said you were deciding between chiding me for not resting and being glad to see me." He ran his fingers along her cheek. "I have not thanked you for rescuing me yet again."

"There is no need, especially when I like the idea of you being in my debt. You will need to find some way to repay it."

"I can imagine some ways."

"I am sure you can." She smiled more broadly, and the light of desire flared in her eyes.

When she drew out a chair, he did not protest. He appreciated being able to sit.

"Are the farewells over?" he asked.

"Yes." She sat next to him. "I am glad that Lord Turnbull did not insist that they leave right after the debacle at the Roman camp. That way the squire was able to return the dog to Lady Viola."

"And Miss Upton may have wanted three more days' reprieve before she had to ride back to York with her cousin and Turnbull and that silly dog."

"I don't think that was it. Lady Viola treats her cousin with the same level of contempt as before. I think she has been aware all along that her fiancé is in love with her cousin, but she accepts it as the price of marrying a man who she believes has the reputation to open doors for her among the *ton*. Lord Turnbull's title is an ancient one, while her father's is new and suspect because of his background in trade." A mischievous smile tipped her lips. "And we all know what a hero Lord Turnbull was."

"You are suggesting that she is more intelligent than I have given her credit for."

"She knows what she needs, and she is not going to be waylaid from obtaining it, even when Lord Turnbull keeps her cousin as his beloved mistress in her own household." She smiled sadly. "At least until she can make other plans for her. I would not be astonished to hear that Miss Upton has been betrothed to someone who lives far from the viscount's estate. Maybe that is what Miss Upton has hoped for all along. As manipulative as the other two are, she may be using them, too, as a way to escape her cousin's household. I am not used to thinking the worst of people, but with them, it is difficult not to."

He waited for her to say something more. She ran a finger along the smooth top of the table. A bit of moisture had gathered there, and her finger made abstract patterns in the water.

Leaning toward her, he put his finger under her chin and brought her mouth under his. He stood, drawing her up and deepening the kiss until she quivered against him.

"It is almost over, China," he whispered after lifting his lips from hers. "It is midafternoon, and we are still alive."

"I am thrilled that we are, but I cannot stop thinking of Quintus and how the curse hangs over him."

"Why? You saved me once again. Isn't that supposed to break the curse?"

"It should, but something feels wrong to me."

"Don't look for trouble where there is none."

She smiled. "Good advice, even though I cannot rid myself of this uneasy feeling."

"Right now, *I* feel like kissing you."

With a laugh, she pressed her lips to his. Even as he savored holding her in the dining room and later in his bed, he sensed she could not release herself totally to their desire. He would be glad when the last toll of midnight struck.

China sat by the window of the book-room. The garden was reddened by the sunset. She was filled with joy that the attack had not come, but remained uneasy. Why hadn't Quintus come back to share in the excitement of the curse being lifted? He had not even returned to see how Alexander fared. She had expected that he would be appearing hourly during this fateful day.

"I thought you might be here." Sian drew a stool up next to China's chair. "I am surprised, because I doubted you would leave Alexander's side all day today."

"He is dressing for supper, and one of the footmen is with him. I told Alexander I would meet him here."

"I am surprised he would let *you* out of his sight." She drew her knees up and wrapped her arms around them. Leaning her chin on her knees, she said, "He loves you."

"He has never said so."

"Does he need to speak the words? Don't you know?" She pushed her hair back, revealing the small bandage on her cheek in the aftermath of the gale in the old camp. "He believes in a ghost he cannot see because you have told him it is there."

"*You* believe, too."

"And I love you, sister!" She smiled. "But he loves you as I have always dreamed a man would love me. Jade found love with the help of a ghost." Sian's expression turned pensive. "Do you think Father has decided he would prove to the world that his research is correct by sending matchmaking ghosts for you and Jade?"

"Making a match for me and Alexander is not Quintus's primary concern."

"It is making sure that Alexander is not the end of his line." Sian giggled. "I should not have said that."

China gave her sister a hug. "You can say anything to me anytime. That will never change, no matter what else changes in our lives." She donned her most impish smile. "Now that you have turned the conversation personal, I can ask you how Sir Henry's call went."

"He is calling again tomorrow."

"He seems very attentive, Sian. He has called each day since the windstorm at the Roman camp."

"He is pleasant company, but no more than that. I know he wishes I had stronger feelings for him, but it is difficult when my heart is already full." Sian's smile vanished. "Not that it matters to anyone but me."

China took her sister's hands. "Your attraction to the earl has been obvious since you met him in London. Your face softens whenever you mention him, and you try to hide your reaction when anyone else speaks his name. It is clear that you hope for any hint of news about him."

"That is why I have been trying to welcome Sir Henry warmly. I know it is silly to pine for a man who never wrote as he promised."

"Now you are trying to be logical, Sian, about

something that defies logic." When she saw a shadow cross the doorway, she smiled. "Come in, Alexander, and join us."

He did not answer.

She exchanged a worried glance with Sian, then came to her feet. Going to the door, she looked both ways along the corridor. It was empty.

"Did you see anyone, Sian?"

"No." Coming to feet, her sister asked in a tremulous voice, "Did you?"

"Just a shadow." She almost choked on her abrupt fear. "The giant that frightened Lady Viola and Miss Upton first appeared to be a shadow, too." She did not want to frighten her sister by mentioning that she had seen the giant the past two nights. "I need to check on Alexander."

"Go!"

China ran toward the closest stairs and sprinted up them. She thought she felt a cold spot in the upper hallway, but did not pause to investigate. Without pausing to knock, she threw open Alexander's door. It slammed into the wall.

He turned, one half of his face still covered with soap. He wiped it off as he hurried to her. "What did you see?" he asked as he enfolded her to him.

"I don't know. It might have been only a shadow, but . . . " She pressed her face to his shoulder. "I had to make sure you were safe. Don't think I am deranged!"

"I know you are not." His voice tightened. "I know what madness is."

Drawing back, she held on to his arms. "You mentioned your father once, and madness, and then the night of Lady Viola's party, Squire Haywood—"

"Provided the rest of the details?" Bitterness sliced through his words.

"Only innuendo. I did not want to listen to what I knew might be gossip."

He went back to where he had left his shaving equipment. Lathering his face again, he peered into the glass. He picked up his straight-edge, and she hoped he would not cut himself when his back muscles were rigid with the tension.

"Will you tell me the truth?" she asked, sitting on a chair close to him.

"The truth is that my father was mad, as his father was before him. I have heard that insanity comes to every man who claims the title of Lord Braddock. It has happened since the time the title was bestowed by Henry the Second on the first baron. My grandfather's long-lived madness drove my father and mother from the family estate because they feared for their unborn son."

"You."

"Yes. He hoped that, by his leaving Braddock Court, the infection of madness would not inflict either of us, but it was too late. They stayed at a friend's house in Commondale, north of here on the moors. They stayed less than a fortnight, and by the time they left North Yorkshire, my father's madness had begun to reveal itself."

"How?" she asked, wishing she could put her arms around him, but resisted as he drew the straight razor along his jaw.

He lowered the blade into a dish of water and cleaned off the soap and whiskers. "I did not know the truth for years. My parents hid it. I was a child, no more than six or seven, still being tutored in the house where we lived in London. In only one way was I different from my playmates. Each month, when the moon was full, I was sent to stay with my mother's aunt on the other side of the square. I never questioned it until I heard one of her maids mention how I seemed untainted, but that I might one day become like my father."

Wiping his hands on a towel, he patted his face dry. He reached for his cravat and began to tie it.

"Did you discover what she meant?" she asked, knowing she must hear the whole of the tale.

"Yes." His hands paused, and he released the cravat half tied. "That night, I skulked into my parents' house. I saw the truth. My father—a man who seldom raised his voice—was raving like a lunatic. He spoke of visions he could not push from his mind. The full moon brought them forth."

"Visions of what?"

"Monsters and shadows." His jaw worked; then he snarled, "And a giant striding down from the moors to capture and devour him."

She put her icy hands to her even colder face. "A giant? Like the one we saw?"

"It may be the same one he ranted about. It could be a harbinger that it is now my turn to lose my mind."

"But you are sane!"

"Am I? I believe in ghosts and curses."

"I believe that, too!"

"Which may only prove that you are also deranged. You have convinced me that an extraordinary windstorm is the work of a ghost, and I even went so far as to talk to a trick of light as if it truly were a phantom."

Coming to her feet, she put her hands on his smooth cheeks. "You are not insane, Alexander. If you were insane, what you experienced on the battlefield would not haunt you."

He sighed. "I wish I could believe that, but the madness seems to flow through my family from father to son in each generation."

"And each firstborn son's life is destroyed by the year of his thirtieth birthday." She blinked back tears. "It is not madness, Alexander. It is the curse Quintus put upon your family."

"It is one and the same now. I wonder who was supposed to help my father and left him to his demons." He stepped away from her. "China, you should leave. If I go mad, as my father did, you could be hurt."

"Do you honestly think I would leave you before midnight tonight?"

"I think you should." He sighed with a smile. "But you will stay here until the bitter end, won't you?"

"It does not need to be bitter." She draped her arm around his shoulders. "It could be very sweet." She raised her other arm over his shoulder and pressed into him, taking care not to lean into his bruised ribs. "I want to stay close to you, Lord Braddock."

He clasped his hands behind her waist and brushed her lips with a teasing kiss. She shivered with the powerful cravings that refused to be ignored as she walked with him to his bed. She drew out of his arms and went back and locked the door, before she returned to where he waited with a smile.

"Are you satisfied?" he asked, standing after removing his boots.

She smoothed hair back from his forehead. "Not yet, but I expect I shall be soon."

He slipped his arms beneath her knees and lifted her up against his chest. Placing her on the bed, he said, "I will do my best."

"I know you will."

"Tell me what you want," he whispered as he leaned over her.

"You to love me."

His broad hands framed her face as his mouth slanted across hers. Slowly, with a smile that told her of his pleasure, he explored her lips as if he had never tasted them before. His tongue traced their softness, teasing her. She laughed as he laved her ear with his eager breath.

He smiled. "I did not expect you to laugh at my best efforts."

"I am so happy to be with you."

When his fingers moved over her breast, her laugh became a soft gasp. He stretched out beside her, then drew her over him. He undid her gown so slowly that the anticipation of his touch was agonizing. She loosened his half-tied cravat and pressed her mouth to the pulse at the base of his neck.

Needing every bit of pleasure as he slipped her gown down to her hips, she kissed him. Her chemise quickly followed, and he drew her breast into his mouth, taunting its tip to harden as he moved his hands down over her hips. She could not remain still. Her body craved the motion she had shared with him.

She shifted to toss her clothes from the bed, then undid his shirt and pulled it off as well. Her lips explored his firm chest and muscular belly with an excitement that grew stronger each time she was with him. Smiling up at him, she brushed his dark hair back from his blue eyes, and the flames within them threatened to envelop her. She wanted to cede herself to that blazing passion while she drew aside his clothes until he was naked and glorious beneath her. He quivered with the uncontrollable craving, and she straddled him at the same moment she bent forward to kiss him.

She cried out in eager delight as he slid inside her. When he began to describe how warm she was around him, rapture soared through her. Sharing his pleasure made hers even more deliciously unbearable. She wanted release. She needed release. When his words dissolved into a low moan, a frenzy overpowered her. She became the need, his and hers, merged and melded, not knowing where he stopped and she began, utterly one.

Then she became the explosion of ecstasy, which was part of him, part of her, both of them together in that one perfect moment. Everything she wanted. Everything she needed. Everything that she had dreamed.

"Are you satisfied?" Alexander panted against her neck.

"Yes," China whispered, "for the moment."

He laughed and kissed her hard. "You are a demanding woman."

She smiled as she moved to rest her head on his shoulder. She closed her eyes and savored the pure happiness, knowing how fleeting it could be.

*   *   *

Hours later, China whispered, "It is past midnight. September fifth is over!"

"And we are still alive. We need to celebrate," he murmured, pulling her back to him. "Come and thrill me anew, darling."

That was a request she could gladly obey.

China brushed her hair in front of the mirror in Alexander's room. In its reflection, she could see him pulling on his boots. Neither of them had said anything about what would happen now that the fatal day had passed without incident. She did not want to ruin this moment, as she imagined that every morning would begin as this one had: waking in his arms, his flesh warm against her, his fingers curving along her breast. They had not hurried out of bed, and she would have to apologize to Cook for being late for breakfast.

"I will be back before sunset," Alexander said as he stood and came to press his lips to her neck.

"Back? Where are you going?"

"First I must call on Rexleigh's family in Rosedale Abbey."

She stroked his face. "They will want to know about his bravery."

"I know." He cleared his throat, and she knew he was battling grief. "Later I am meeting Reverend Wilder. He offered to show me a few of the old stone monuments near Rosedale Abbey. At the Roman road, I told him I would meet him today." He gave her a wry grin. "Assuming we would still be in one piece and breathing."

"Be careful."

"I thought any attack would come by the fifth of

the month." He glanced around. "Has Quintus shown up again with another warning?"

"No. We should not see him again now that the curse is broken. But there are other dangers on the moors. The highwayman has not yet been caught."

"Do not fret. I shall be cautious, and I will be back before supper is served." He picked up a sketchbook that Sian had loaned him. "I hope you will be interested in seeing what I have drawn from my study of the monument."

"I will be interested in whatever you have to show me."

His eyes twinkled as he tapped her nose. "I like how you think, darling." He gave her a sweet, lingering kiss before walking to the door.

She smiled, glad to see his lighter steps. It was not only that the fifth of September was past. He had relinquished the rest of his unseen burden by sharing the story of his father's madness. Through the night, she had held him close and listened to his breathing as he slept. The nightmares she had feared never occurred. Maybe trusting her with the truth, as he had with his pain of losing Rexleigh, had eased his heart.

China spent the morning working on accounts and other matters of the household that she had neglected of late. If anyone noticed that she hummed cheerfully while she added up the rows of figures or that her steps were as buoyant as a country reel, nobody spoke of it. They simply smiled in response to her smile.

As she walked into the book-room, she saw the unmistakable glow that heralded Quintus's arrival, and her smile widened. What an unexpected pleasure! She had hoped Quintus would return to bid her farewell before journeying to the next world that awaited him.

"*Ave*, Quintus," she said, her happy voice making his name into a melody. "Isn't it a wonderful day?"

He looked around the room. "Where is he?"

"Alexander is out on the moors looking at the ancient monuments."

"On the moors? Alone?" His voice rose on every word, and the air in the room started to stir.

"Calm yourself," she ordered. "There is nothing to be distressed about. He went with Reverend Wilder, and they are forewarned about the highwayman. They went to view some ancient crosses and cairns."

"In the old places where the old magic lingers, waiting to be awakened by anyone foolish enough to bestir it?" He waved his hands, and the pages of open books flapped in the sudden rush of wind. "How could you allow him to go? Didn't I warn you that the danger to him could come at any time?"

"Yes, but what does that matter now?"

"Because the day of the attack has not yet dawned."

She grasped a book that was sliding off a table, blown by the rising wind. "What do you mean? Yesterday was the fifth of September. He was attacked! He could have been killed, but he was not. The curse is broken."

"You are mistaken. If the curse had been broken, I would not be here now. The fifth of September is still almost a fortnight from now."

"No . . ." She gasped and held the book to her swiftly beating heart. "Oh, my! The difference between the Julian and the Gregorian calendars."

"What are you talking about?" The wind began to calm as he stared, puzzled.

"The calendar changed in 1752," she explained as she put the book down.

"How does one change a calendar? Days continue to fall in the usual progression."

"But the calendar set up by Julius Caesar no longer matched the seasons."

"So my September fifth—"

China quickly counted on her fingers. "Is our September seventeenth!" She rushed to the door, calling for a horse to be saddled. "Come with me. We must find Alexander and warn him before it is too late."

Chapter 21

"It is rumored to have been placed here only a few hundred years ago, but I disagree," Reverend Wilder said as he knelt by a standing stone that was almost four feet tall. "Some of these stones were set in place to mark burial sites."

Alexander bent to examine one of the smaller stones. It was almost lost in the low growth. "Amazing. This ancient monument is not on any map."

"There are many hidden places on the moors."

"I noticed that these stones are set in a circular pattern."

"I believe that was intentional." Reverend Wilder smiled and stood. "It is a shame that we have lost the truth. The people to whom these places were sacred believed in a magic and gods older than legend."

"Old magic . . ."

When the curate looked startled, Alexander smiled. "Just something I was discussing with Miss Nethercott. There have been whispers of ancient magic and strange happenings at the Roman camp."

"I am sure the whispers exaggerate what Squire Haywood has come to believe must have been a passing thunderstorm," the curate said, brushing his hands against his worn breeches. "The weather has been freakish all summer. However, Squire Haywood has been acting odd himself. He seems to be taking the situation with the highwayman too personally, especially since you and Miss Nethercott were ambushed. He has spoken about you while in his cups." He cleared his throat. "I apologize. I should not be carrying tales."

"You are not telling me anything I do not already know."

He shuffled his feet in the broken stones. "It is Miss Nethercott. He has been bragging for the past year to anyone who would listen that once she was out of mourning he would make her his wife."

Alexander smiled. "I had heard that as well. That she continues to be the epitome of kindness and friendship to him reveals how gentle her heart is."

"I thought you would understand," the curate said. "You seem quite taken with her as well."

"She is an impressive woman."

"She . . ." He peered south across the low scrub.

Alexander heard the hoofbeats that resounded up the curve of the moorlands. He scowled when he recognized the neck-or-nothing rider. What was sending China at such a perilous speed over the uneven ground?

She pulled on the horse's reins as she reached them. "Thank heavens I found you, Alexander! Good afternoon, Reverend Wilder," she added as she slid from the saddle. Not giving him a chance to reply, she said, "Alexander, you must return to Nethercott Castle immediately."

"Why? Is something wrong?"

She glanced at the curate, who was trying to pretend he had not heard her frantic tone. Alexander took her arm and led her a few yards past the standing stone.

"What is wrong?" he asked.

"The calendar! Quintus uses the Julian one, while we use the Gregorian calendar. It is almost a fortnight before the day when the curse must be broken."

He muttered an oath. "I never considered that."

"You must return posthaste. You cannot stay out here and endanger yourself. Quintus said you could be in danger every day until then." She grasped his arm with both hands. "Alexander, I will not let you risk yourself."

"And I will not risk you."

Releasing him, she held out her hand. He slipped his hand into it. When he noticed how it trembled, he knew she was more frightened than she wished him to know. She was right to be scared. They had been shot at and struck and endured fires and more. Now it could happen all over again . . . and worse.

China sat up in bed and stared at the light near the door. Quintus! She put out her hand to wake Alexander, then wondered why. She glanced out the window at the waning moon. The hour was past midnight. Today, the curse could be broken. He needed to rest to face what might be ahead of him. Even if nothing happened, the waiting was dreadful.

And why wake him when he could not see or hear Quintus? She drew on her dressing gown and tiptoed across the floor. The light had gone through the door and now shone underneath it.

With a glance at Alexander, she opened the door

and slipped out. She closed it behind her and followed the faint light toward the stairs.

Again she hesitated. Should she get Alexander before giving chase to a ghost in the middle of the night?

"Do not be silly," she chided herself, as she had so often since first encountering the centurion. *She* was not the focus of the curse. As she hurried to catch up with the orb, she told herself that whatever Quintus had to tell her must be important. Otherwise he would not lead her out of the house to a private place to talk.

Her steps faltered again when she reached the smashed hedges in the garden. Where had Quintus gone? She scanned the darkness. Where was his orb?

"Quintus?" she whispered, then repeated it more loudly. "Quintus, you brought me out here. What did you want to show me?"

There was no answer. It was not like the centurion to appear, even as a faint light, and then say nothing. Was there something wrong with him? Could something hurt a ghost?

A shadow rose up behind her, higher than the ruined shrubs, higher than her head, higher than the upper windows in Nethercott Castle, until it seemed to blot out the moon. She wanted to scream. She wanted to run. She was paralyzed as she stared at the giant. Was this the doom that awaited Alexander?

She spun about to run. She went only two steps before another shadow rose from the ground. She tried to stop, but the dew on the grass sent her feet out from under her. She fell. Her head struck something. Hard. An explosion of pain. She seemed to be falling again. She fell . . . and fell . . . and fell. The light vanished. Shadows grew thicker as the pain devoured her. With her last conscious breath, she screamed Alexander's name, hoping he would hear it and be warned.

Alexander opened his eyes and smiled. Bright sunshine filtered through the bed curtains and played across the coverlet. The past days had been wondrous. Not once had nightmares assaulted him. Instead, he had dreamed of the pleasures he had found with China. But even those dreams were not as luscious as what they shared while awake.

He listened for her soft breathing. She must have turned away from him in her sleep, because he could not hear it. He smiled again. Once he drew her into his arms, her breath would come fast and frayed, warming his skin and beguiling him.

Not once had she asked him what he planned after the day of doom, as they had come to call it. He thought of the women who had been eager to gain his title and his prestige in exchange for anything he wished. He had not been tempted by them, too lost in his grief and his failings. China had not cared about his title or the adulation offered him. She had sought only to protect him—both from whoever wished him dead and from his own wretchedness.

But now it was time for him to speak plainly.

"China, I think we should . . . " He rolled to face her side of the bed and paused.

It was empty.

Where was she? She never would have left him alone this morning. Every day of the past twelve, she had insisted that she would stay with him all day today.

Alexander pushed aside the covers. China's dressing gown was gone. Dressing, he rushed toward the door as he tied his cravat. A bone-gnawing cold halted him.

"Quintus?" he called. "Are you here? Did you take China somewhere safe?"

From the corner of his eye, he thought he saw a flicker of light, but he could not be certain. It might be nothing more than sunshine. He went and threw back the heavy draperies and gasped. In the garden below, more hedges were battered. Flimsy wisps of cloth fluttered across them. They had come from the Roman camp, and he must go there.

"Damn," he growled, shoving himself away from the window. He went to retrieve his pistols, even though he knew how useless they would be against a ghost or an ancient god or whatever awaited him there. As he turned to the door, he said, "Quintus, I hope you are around. I think I am going to need your help."

The woods were silent as Alexander rode to the edge of the Roman camp. The odd quiet threatened to unnerve him, but he concentrated on finding China. There were thousands of feet of earthworks. She could be hidden anywhere.

Swinging down from his horse, he lashed the reins around a broken sapling. He put one hand under his coat and touched the butt of his pistol. It was ready for him to pull back the hammer and fire. He drew in a deep breath and walked toward the earthworks.

"Quintus! Where are you?" he shouted.

"Who is Quintus?" asked a deep voice only a few feet to his left beneath the vanguard trees.

Slowly Alexander faced the speaker. Instead of his bright colors, the squire was dressed in unrelieved black.

"Squire Haywood, what are you doing here?"

"Waiting for you." He raised a dueling pistol and, walking forward, jabbed its long barrel into Alexander's chest. The gun quivered, but at this range even the worst marksman could not miss.

"What do you want, Haywood?" he asked.

"Isn't it obvious? I want vengeance."

"Vengeance?"

"For stealing the woman I love. I don't know what you have done to her mind. She has been acting strange ever since she dug you out of these walls."

Alexander said nothing. The wrong word could persuade the squire to fire the gun. Where was China? He did not shift his gaze from Haywood.

"She would not have chosen *you* over me," the squire continued. "We have known each other since we were children. I knew from the first time I saw her that I would have her for my own." His eyes glittered as they slitted to take aim on him. "You are a great hero! You could have any woman you want. That blonde who is betrothed to Turnbull was eager for your attentions." The squire's face crumbled into pain. "I have loved one woman my whole life— China Nethercott—and she will be mine. I will not let you steal her from me!"

"I did not steal her," Alexander argued as realization tore away the hatred he had let gnaw at him since Norah Turnbull decided to marry another man. "A woman has no more choice in deciding when and to whom she will give her heart than a man does. What the heart wants, it will demand."

"My heart demands that China will be mine."

"Even if it makes her miserable?"

The squire's face reddened. "I shall make her happy. She will love me as she has loved no other, including you."

"And if she does not?"

"It will not matter to you. You will never have my sweet China. All you will have is one of the old stones that fascinate you for your grave marker. Buried within these walls, you will never be found."

Alexander cursed under his breath. Being reasonable would not work with a man irrational with jealousy. "All right," he said with regret, because he had hoped he would never have to aim again at a living man. "If you wish to duel to settle what you see as an insult to your honor, then I agree."

The squire laughed. "I do not intend to duel. I intend to kill you right here and now. There have been too many other times I have missed my chance to do so, and too many times you have put my beloved China in danger."

"Me?"

"I should have ended this when I stopped you and my beloved China as she was first taking you to Nethercott Castle."

"You are the highwayman?" asked China as she climbed over the earth wall and slid down to stand beside Alexander. She watched the squire's eyes widen as he looked at her dressing gown that was stained with dirt. She guessed Alexander was shocked, too, but an explanation would have to wait. "I have always admired you as a man who does the right thing. Why have you been frightening half the shire?"

Squire Haywood made a soft sobbing sound. He backed away a pair of steps, even though she knew he still could easily kill Alexander. "Because I love you, China. That is why I stole a kiss from you that day."

She stepped forward a single step and stretched her hand behind her back to motion to Alexander to remain where he was. Anything he said or did now could bring the death that Quintus feared.

"Be honest with me, China," the squire begged.

"Of course."

He looked past her at Alexander, and fury filled his eyes. "Do you love that man?"

"Yes."

"Does he love you?" When she did not answer as quickly, he pressed, "Has he *ever* told you that he loves you?"

"I have now. I love you, China," Alexander said behind her.

She closed her eyes, wishing he had remained silent. Why did he have to speak the words that were guaranteed to enrage the squire? Her heart beat with joy, but it soon could be filled with grief as she mourned Alexander's death at the hand of a man she had known her entire life.

"Silence, Braddock!" snarled the squire. "Or I will kill you, even though she is watching."

Hope fluttered weakly through her. Squire Haywood wanted to spare her the sight of Alexander's death. While she kept him talking, he would not fire. She was not sure how long she could convince him to wait, but every minute brought a new possibility of saving Alexander's life.

"Tell me why you decided to play the role of a

highwayman. You are the respected face of the law in our shire. Why would you don a mask and frighten people? You do not need their money or their fear."

"But I wanted you." His lips were so tight he almost spit out each word. "I was promised a title after the war, but the Regent has been too busy conferring medals on men like Braddock, who did nothing but follow orders and survive a battle. That respect was denied me, so I decided to expose them as the weakhearted cowards they really are."

"I still do not understand," she said when he paused for a breath. She needed to keep him talking until he released his anger. Maybe then he would lower the pistol. "What does that have to do with me?"

Again he gave a low sob. "Because with the peers too frightened to come out of their fine homes, and the rest chasing false trails of the highwayman, I was waiting for the moment when I could sweep you away. Everyone would have believed you had been taken by a real highwayman. There would have been so many rumors that no one would have known what was true and what was not. While they sorted it out, I would have taken you to Scotland and made you my bride."

"But you tried to kill me! You shot at me at the Lastingham church."

"I did not realize it was you! When I saw Braddock kissing someone in the churchyard, I had no idea that China Nethercott would be such a hoyden. I was heartbroken when I saw your wounded hand." His mouth became a straight line. "I never intended to hurt you. I saw Braddock go up into the tower at Nethercott Castle, but I had no idea you were there too."

"When you started the fire." Her stomach cramped with disgust. She never could have guessed her gentle friend, who had cared enough to bring Lady Viola's dog back to Nethercott Castle, would be capable of such a heinous crime.

"I saw how upset you were." His voice was almost pleading, as if he were begging for her forgiveness. "That is why I made sure you did not witness my attempt to rid our lives of that cur once and for all. I thought he was dead by the time he tumbled down to the last step."

She struggled to remain outwardly calm, but she feared she was going to be ill. The squire was admitting that he had struck Alexander in the head and pushed him down the stairs. Appealing to his sense of fairness and justice would be futile, she realized. She needed to try something else.

Swallowing the bile churning in her throat, she forced her voice to be calm. "What do you want in exchange for Alexander's life?"

"Don't negotiate with him!" Alexander whispered sharply.

She motioned him to silence as she met the squire's eyes. "What do you want in exchange for his life?"

"A kiss. Not on the hand this time." He grabbed for her.

She jumped aside, but he caught her, spinning her toward him. When she tried to pull away, he struck her across the face. Pain detonated in her head. She heard Alexander shouting as if from a great distance. She clung to her senses as she fell to the ground. Blood was salty in her mouth, and her face was on fire. She clawed at the ground, fighting to stand.

The squire grabbed her arm and pulled her to her

feet. He twisted her to face Alexander. She knew from the lack of color in Alexander's face that the gun was pointed at her.

Furious, she jabbed her elbow back. The squire grunted and wrapped his arm around her neck. He tightened his hold. She tried to drive her elbow into him again. She could barely move. Her strength vanished as she fought to breathe.

"Let her go and leave her alone and you can kill me, Haywood," Alexander said.

"No!" she cried, but the sound was swallowed by a thunderous yell that echoed across the top of the cliff and through the trees.

"Gloriae cupidous!" came the shout again.

It was Quintus, calling for glory in battle for himself and his allies. Light flashed through the clearing, and thunder seemed to roar around them.

The squire flinched at the noise. His arm jerked away from her. He choked out something as he looked around in terror at another clap of thunder. Spinning to flee, he tripped and fell hard to the stone-strewn ground. He did not move as blood oozed through the hair tangled across his brow.

China knelt beside him, putting her fingers to his neck. His pulse was faint, but she could feel it. Reaching across him, she pulled the pistol from his senseless fingers and stepped away while Alexander rolled him onto his side. Alexander wrapped his cravat about the bloody spot on the squire's forehead. He bound the limp arms using some rope the squire had with him. She did not want to think what he had intended to do with it.

"That should hold him," Alexander said, then sniffed his fingers. "The rope smells of tar."

"His family works in ship repair. They use a great deal of tar."

"So he would know it creates a smothering smoke when it burns." He stood and wiped his hands, then pulled her into his arms. The kiss was swift, but it told her everything she needed to know. He was safe, and he loved her.

Together, they turned to where Quintus was emerging from the light. When Alexander gasped, she asked him what was wrong.

"I can see him!" he said. "*Ave*, Quintus Valerius."

Raising his hand in a salute, he replied, "*Ave*, Alexander Braddock, son of my sons."

"Why can he see you now?" she asked Quintus.

"Because I was able to save his life with your help, China, and break the curse. Now I wish to offer him a warning."

She looked from the ghost to Alexander, seeing the resemblance in their stances and their expressive blue eyes. And the stubborn streak that had destroyed one of them and threatened the other.

"What warning do you wish to offer me?" Alexander asked.

"Do not take love for granted. I did that, and the woman who was the mother of my son turned from me. I wavered in listening to my heart, and she went to another. Fury overwhelmed me. I hated her and myself."

She slipped her hand into Alexander's as he said, "I understand that all too well."

"If you succumbed to the madness of jealousy and hatred, as each of us has before you," Quintus said sadly, "then the curse would never be broken. You seem to have learned what I did not, for you controlled your rage rather than let it consume you." He glanced at where the squire was trussed on the ground. "But that man felt betrayed. I have learned that there is nothing so painful as being betrayed by love. When I challenged my Viola's new lover to a battle to the death, I lost my life, but I had already lost everything that truly mattered by betraying her trust in me. In my last living moments, madness overtook me, and I wanted her to suffer as I had. It was with my last breath that I spoke the curse that has since afflicted me and my son and his son and his son and his son through time. I did not want you to make the same mistake, Alexander, with another Viola."

"You worried needlessly," Alexander said.

Quintus remained somber. "Like me, too many of my descendants have lost the women they loved and let acrimony eat at them until they were destroyed in body and mind and soul."

"I love China," Alexander said, squeezing her hand.

"Which is how she helped save you. If you had not opened your heart to her, you would have remained in your miserable condition, hating yourself and denying those who believed you were worthy. Eventually your own hatred would have driven you mad."

"Did you drive my father mad?" he asked.

"No, for he never saw me. I tried to contact him, but it was impossible, just as it was for me to talk to you while the curse held me captive." Quintus glanced toward the moors rising in the distance. "But we both saw the giant."

"The same one we encountered?" asked China. She

shivered and edged closer to Alexander. "And the one I saw in the garden last night?"

"I am sorry," the ghost said, "that I had to knock you senseless again, but I could not let him see you. A god who is no longer worshiped becomes angry and vengeful. If I had not stolen you away, you would have died." He shuddered. "Or wished you had. And all chances of saving Alexander would have died with you."

"Do you know who it was?"

"It was Mithras, the god of the Roman warrior," he said. "He carries a sword and a torch of true light."

"I know about that sword all too well." Alexander frowned. "The sight of that ancient god roaming the moors was more than my father could endure, so the memory of it came back with each full moon to haunt him. Shall I go mad for having seen Mithras?"

"No, for you are a warrior."

Alexander put his arm around China. "What about her?"

"She is a warrior at heart. She has fought many battles. She will be fine as long as you love her. When I am gone Mithras will go with me, for I am the last Roman warrior here." Quintus began to fade into the light. "*Aeternum vale.*"

"Farewell forever to you, too," she whispered as the ghost disappeared. His orb of light remained for a heartbeat longer; then it was gone. "*Requiescat in pace.* Rest in peace, Quintus Valerius." She glanced toward the squire when she heard a groan, but he was still unconscious. They would need to bring him to another magistrate to be tried. Tears filled her eyes.

Alexander gently turned her to face him. "Thank

you," he whispered. "I never had a chance to thank Rexleigh for saving my life, but I can thank you."

"I am sure he knows." She pointed to something glittering among the leaves. "Who knows who else lingers here to watch over us?"

"Whoever it is can witness me saying how grateful I am that you persuaded me that life, in spite of its bumps, is worth living in the present. With you, I can let the past be in the past. I want to be with you in the here and now."

"Where I want to be with you too."

"There is a very good chance of that, because I think a husband should remain by his wife's side. Do you agree?"

Happiness flooded her. "Are you asking me to marry you?"

"Yes. If there was one lesson I learned from Quintus, it is to treasure what one holds in one's heart. Let me hold you in my heart forever."

"Forever," she whispered as she went into his embrace.

About the Author

Jocelyn Kelley has always had a weakness for strong heroines and dashing heroes. For as long as she can remember, she's been telling stories of great adventure. She lives in Massachusetts with her husband and three children. Visit her Web site and blog at www.jocelynkelley.com.

Also from
Jocelyn Kelley

LOST IN SHADOW
Nethercott Tales: #1

Her dear father died before convincing
people of the existence of ghosts, so Jade
Nethercott and her sisters set out to prove him
right. Meanwhile, a ghost named Renshaw
reveals to Jade his murderer's identity—Lord
Bannatyne, notorious rake—so that she might
protect Renshaw's fiancee. A nervous Jade
finagles a meeting with Bannatyne, but he
proves to be anything but rakish when he risks
arrest rather than ruin Jade's reputation.
Now she must decide whether to heed the
ghost's warning—or follow her heart...